DRAWN TO DISCIPLINE

'I think we have an eager pupil here,' said Liss. 'So, girl, shall we get on with it?'

Judith nodded and handed her the cane.

'OK. Basically it's all about accuracy: you can build up your force later. Now, it's best always to start in the middle –' she leaned forwards and drew a blood-red nail across the fullest part of the boy's globes '– then work outwards, both above and below. If it's to be a high count, you can come back to the middle, which will take plenty of overlapping strokes without the skin breaking. You're unlikely to do that with this cane, anyway, but who knows what lethal weapon you might graduate to when you get a real taste for it.'

DRAWN TO DISCIPLINE

Tara Black

This book is a work of fiction.
In real life, make sure you practise safe sex.

First published in 2001 by
Nexus
Thames Wharf Studios
Rainville Road
London W6 9HA

Typeset by TW Typesetting, Plymouth, Devon

Printed and bound by
Cox & Wyman Ltd, Reading, Berks

ISBN 0 352 33626 9

Contents

PART I

1

Fucking Men

The first glimmerings of returning consciousness were suffused with pain. Judith lay not daring to open her eyes, aware only of the fierce throbbing in her temples and the coarse sandpaper that was apparently lodged in her throat. An exploratory movement of her left arm revealed the presence of a body next to her in the bed and, with a lurch of her insides she knew where she was. Oh, shit. Shit, shit, shit! Forcing her gummed eyelids apart, she sat up, but in doing so unbalanced a full ashtray on the edge of the table, the contents of which cascaded over her neck. Instantly she retched and leaped from the bed, stomach heaving, out into the hallway. Jee-sus, where the fuck was it? Then she saw the half-open door at the bend of the stairs and, heedless that she was bare from the waist down, dived through it. Reaching the lavatory bowl, Judith wrapped her arms round the cold porcelain, indifferent to its state of cleanliness. She had more pressing concerns. Then for five minutes what could come up came up and, when it was all over, she slumped back against the side of the bath, gasping.

She hauled herself to her feet and doused her face from the cold tap, then took a glass from the shelf and rinsed out her mouth. Feeling marginally less hellish, she sat on the closed lid and drank several mouthfuls of water. Back in the bedroom, Judith found her knickers under the bed, crotch stiff from last night's desire. She grimaced and stuffed them into the pocket of her denim jacket. No way were they going back on, but nor was she going to leave a trophy. As the knickers demonstrated, it had started so well. She had been really turned on snogging in the hallway towards the end, when most of the party-goers had either left or passed out downstairs. Then it all went wrong. First he couldn't get a proper hard-on, and when he did he couldn't seem to get it comfortably inside her, even though she was well lubricated. And then he took what seemed like hours to come, with all his weight crushing her down. If she hadn't been so pissed herself she would have pushed him off her and fled. But that was the demon drink for you. The state she had been in, she wouldn't have made it to the door. Legless. Absolutely bloody legless. Appropriate term, she thought. I may as well have been actually without them for all I was capable of leaving the building.

Judith stood for a moment, looking at the still unconscious body in the bed. Never again, she told herself firmly. That had to be the worst fuck of my short life. The worst. She found her jeans and pulled them on over her nakedness, zipping up with care over the pubic mound. The trainers were not such a simple exercise, since bending down to lace them brought a rush of blood to the head. A wave of nausea made her sit on an upright chair and close her eyes for a full minute. It passed and, laces tied, she put on the jacket and went quietly down the stairs, going by the living room and kitchen without a sideways glance.

Outside she breathed in the fresh air with immense relief. 'Fucking *men*.' Judith expressed her disgust to the empty street then headed for home.

An hour later Judith was soaking in a hot bath, deep in thought. The residual hangover had sharpened the critical edge of her self-examination and the early results of it were less than encouraging. Here she was, nineteen years old and at the end of the first year of university. With no family resources to back her up she was already heavily in debt with a student loan. It was going to be essential to find a job now that the term had ended. At least she hadn't failed her exams; but then she hadn't exactly done brilliantly either. In fact, she had just scraped a place in Honours English for the autumn and could easily be chucked out if she didn't work her butt off. But how could she settle down to that when her social life was such a mess? OK, she said to herself, let's not gloss over this. The phrase is: *sex* life. Your sex life is up the spout, girl.

Judith sighed and ran some more hot water. Coming from a small town, where she attended a single-sex school, she had never had a boyfriend as such and sexual encounters had consisted of clumsy fumbles under the influence of illicit booze. Scrub the illegal bit and that's exactly what it had been last night. She gave a bitter little laugh: so much for the free-and-easy promiscuity of student life that was going to solve all her relationship problems. A girlfriend once told her that she was too 'forthright' and that put boys off; her attitude was 'unfeminine' and that was why she only got propositioned by a potential lover when alcohol was flowing. In other words, thought Judith grimly, I only get taken on by guys when they're so plastered that they can't fuck me properly.

She pulled out the plug and stood up in the bath, reaching for a towel. Putting it round her shoulders, she padded through into her bedroom where an old-fashioned gas fire was burning. Though it was June and not at all cold, Judith was feeling weak from the excesses of the previous night. She knelt down before the heat and dried herself slowly. Then she stood up and turned this way and that in front of her wall mirror. You can't really blame your appearance for any of this, girl, she told herself soberly. The mirror showed her a pretty face with dark hair layered to the head, black eyebrows, straight nose and quite full lips. As for the rest, well, no tits and a big bum was the derogatory way she usually thought of her body shape. But Judith was not actually unhappy with what she saw. While a larger bosom wouldn't have gone amiss, she liked the sensual curves of her arse and dressed to show it off, enjoying the way that the gaze of passers-by was often drawn to that part of her anatomy.

All the scrutiny of her nude body was reviving the randiness she had felt at the party before it careered downhill. Warm and dry, Judith knelt back on the floor with her legs apart and began to stroke the inner lips between them. Feeling the juices start to flow, she ran a slippery fingertip around the bud of her clitoris, revelling in the sharp sensations of arousal this action generated. She closed her eyes and rocked back a little, settling into a rhythmic pattern of movements as she felt the climax building. Then, at its height, when wordless cries were forced from her throat, there came unbidden to her mind a vivid image of the rear view of a bending woman, between whose small firm globes were clearly displayed the brown pucker of her anus and the pink slash of her vulva amidst a fuzz of blonde hair.

A little later, Judith washed between her legs and dried herself. Back at her dressing-table, she put on a clean pair of white pants, then a T-shirt and a fresh pair of jeans. That was the third time this week that her flatmate's rear end had featured at the very peak of a masturbatory sequence. And what a rear end it was – as flagrant as a fucking baboon in heat! Judith remembered well how she had charged into what she believed was an empty bathroom to find Catherine bending over the tub washing some knickers. That was three weeks ago, yet the image continued to pop into her mind whether she was sexually excited or not. She had

6

apologised but Cat told her to carry on and take the towel she had come in for, making no move to change her position. In fact, she'd said to stick *her* towel into the wash too, all the time scrubbing away so that her buttocks made little movements around the sexual parts that were right in Judith's face as she stooped to collect the dirty articles. OK, so they weren't at all prudish in the small flat and both frequently wandered around dressed only in a top that covered neither their behinds nor the pubic bushes in front. But on that occasion Catherine's nether openings could not have been more blatantly on view had she been posing for a porn magazine. And it *was* a pose, Judith was sure. She had been meant to drink in the sight, though for exactly what purpose she still could not fathom.

Had the girl been, like, *offering* herself? Surely not. OK, she had no steady boyfriend, nor does she seem to do one-night stands. In fact, there appeared to be no men on the horizon at all in her life; but then nor were there women either. And she had never made a move before in *this* direction, despite plenty of opportunities. Judith sighed: she wouldn't really mind if Catherine did. The idea of lesbian sex didn't bother her like she knew it bothered some girls. It had just never figured in her own life and she didn't know what she would feel if a lady who really swung that way came on to her, really went out to seduce her. The idea made Judith shiver, half-aroused, half-frightened. Given the way her assertiveness seemed to discourage the opposite sex, she had in the past cultivated a femme look with short tight skirts and low-cut blouses. *Then* to have even thought about a sexual interest in other women might have made a bad situation worse. In fact, she had only cut her hair short a year ago, assuming that university would liberate her from all that pretence. Ha bloody ha! As if.

'Enough.' She said it aloud, suddenly resolved to stop introspecting and do something. Now where was that

7

application form? She spotted the buff-coloured sheets under a pile of books on her desk and took them through to the kitchen. Their tiny flat had only two bedrooms, in each of which was crammed a three-quarter bed, a working surface and built-in cupboards. There was no sitting room but the kitchen was large enough to contain a cooking and eating area in one half and an L-shaped seating arrangement in the other. Judith sat down at the table and spread the papers out. Under the heading *OCEANUS INC. (Eumenides)* was the text: *The Catalogue Department of The Nemesis Archive has a vacancy for the post of assistant. Initially for a period of three months, the successful candidate may be offered an extension to her contract.* Below this was a job description which Judith studied carefully.

The woman appointed to this position will work under the supervision of the director of the collection, Miss Samantha James. She will be taught the necessary cataloguing skills, after which she will be expected to exercise them independently. The women's writings which constitute the books and manuscripts to be handled, deal with the vexed questions of emancipation and subjugation and contain highly sensitive material that must on no account be revealed to a wider public. Thus discretion, together with a preparedness to put aside prejudice, is essential. We believe that the work could be most stimulating for a certain kind of open-minded young feminist, while those of a doctrinaire persuasion are certain to find it uncongenial. Applicants should note that Miss James has high standards of punctuality and neatness which are strictly enforced.

Phew! She sounds like she belongs in my old school. Judith thought back to the English mistress who had coached her into getting the examination results that

8

had brought her here. Miss Johns – Stella, as Judith had called her privately in the final year – had a great enthusiasm for literature which inspired many a girl, but she was a stickler on details of uniform and proper behaviour in class. Her form room was set apart from most of the others, across a small courtyard, and there were occasional stories of unofficial punishments being meted out to persistent offenders after school hours. Judith remembered one that did the rounds about a thick leather strap with two tails that was locked in the cupboard under her desk. Amongst some of the older girls there was giggling speculation about knickers coming down for it, but the idea of corporal punishment produced in Judith an uncomfortable combination of interest and embarrassment and she always shied away from the subject. It was as if, she thought once, she was afraid of revealing a special fascination for the idea that went beyond her schoolmates' more general preoccupation with sex. Anyway, she knew no girl who admitted to getting a dose of the rumoured instrument, and it was probably all myth.

For now, there were these forms to be dealt with. If she could get on with Stella Johns, strap or no strap, she would surely be able to work with the 'strict' Samantha James. Judith felt quite hopeful that she was in with a chance. First of all, the job had not been advertised; talk of it had circulated by word of mouth through women's circles at the university. So said her friend Marsha, bar manager of The Phoenix, who was in the thick of such things, being an ex-student and stalwart campaigner for equal rights. She'd passed on a telephone number to Judith, telling her to go for it since orthodox feminists were put off by the director's personality and by persistent gossip that The Nemesis, shamefully for a women's collection, housed a lot of obscene and degrading material.

A phone call had resulted in an envelope arriving through the post with a single sheet of paper in it. At the top it said: 'Please write a brief statement of your reactions as a woman to *Story of O* or any similar text.' A little intimidated by the final phrase – what similar texts were there? – Judith had in the end said that it was O's business and that if women's freedom meant anything, then it had to include the freedom to offer yourself into slavery. She of course supplemented that statement by saying she herself couldn't conceive of doing such a thing, but then, in a burst of candour, said the whole thing managed somehow to be erotic and disquieting at the same time. She had sent the paragraph back to the return address and had received the forms she was now filling in.

The first three sheets wanted information on all the things you would expect: educational background, academic interests, hobbies, career intentions and so on. These completed, there was a last sheet that Judith had not noticed before which was headed with a single request. *Since many core documents in the collection contain passages of a sexual nature, it will help us judge your suitability to handle them if you write below as frankly as you see fit about your own sexual interests and practices.* Judith thought for a few moments then pulled over a lined pad and began to write about her sex life. Memories of its many disfunctional episodes, culminating with painful vividness in last night's débâcle, seemed all of a sudden to demand to be set down with as much honesty as she could muster. After attempting to recount and analyse the nature of her difficulties with men, she recorded with some misgivings the frequency with which she masturbated and even that an image of female genitals had entered into these sessions. She ended by saying that she felt herself to be quite strongly sexual but with little idea as to how those impulses might find more satisfying channels of expression.

Judith sat back and looked over her hasty scribble. She made two small corrections of grammar and began to copy it out on the buff sheet in a careful, precise script. Then she read it once more, heart beating faster at words which revealed to a woman she had yet to meet, more about her most intimate doings than any friend had been told. She gathered the pages together, folded them into the return envelope provided and sealed it carefully. Then Judith took her jacket from the back of a chair and headed out to the post office to be in time for the last collection. As the item left her fingers and dropped into the box, she had a moment of panic. However, it was now too late to retract her statement and she made herself think positively. This is a well-paid job that's going to be at the very least interesting, and very likely more than that. So it's no good starting off by hiding things. Then she turned and walked back home with a lighter step.

The following Wednesday a letter arrived which summoned Judith to attend for interview the next Monday morning at nine o'clock *sharp*. Ooh, better not be late. If Samantha James is anything like Stella Johns, then . . . But then what? Judith smiled and shook her head at the image of her old teacher wielding the fabled piece of leather that had come into it. Silly schoolgirl fancies, she decided. This is a proper job I'm going for that requires a sober and responsible adult to do it. However, getting as far as an interview definitely calls for a celebration, and I know where I'm going.

At eight o'clock that evening Judith sat at a corner table in the saloon of The Phoenix. With her was her friend Marsha who had taken her usual hour's break from running the bar before it started to get busy.

'Hey, Jude, that's great news, honey,' Marsha said in her American drawl.

Judith had told her about the interview that had resulted from the information she'd sent back together with the statements about *O* and about her own sex life.

11

'It all fits with the stories. You can see why a lot of the sisters wanna keep well clear. But what about you? Are you feeling nervous about how it will go?'

'Should I be?' asked Judith. 'I mean, the way people talk, you would think the lady was some kind of dominatrix.'

'Well,' said Marsha, grinning, 'I did hear that she used to keep a sex slave and that she was drummed out of her previous job over it. But I've done a little business with Miss James and I found her straight-talking and straight-dealing. By the way, it *is* Miss. If you "Ms" her you'll likely be out on your ear. As she sees it, the very thought that she could be married is a total insult.'

'I'll go along with that,' said Judith, laughing. 'But sex slaves? You've got to be joking. And I thought I was being silly when she reminded me of a mistress at school who may have handed out unofficial spankings.'

'There's no joke here, honey. This lady is into discipline of the whips and bodies variety and I *understand* –' she emphasised the word mysteriously '–that there's plenty in the collection on the same subject. And she needs someone – with luck you, Judith – to catalogue it. What I'm trying to say is you don't have to *do* it: there is a post here for a trainee librarian, not necessarily a sexual submissive. But you will have to read about that stuff. I mean, does that bother you?' She stopped her flow and stared directly at Judith, who felt herself colouring. Marsha was a woman in her thirties with bold features and a crew cut, and her sharp blue eyes gave the impression that there was nowhere to hide from their probe for a straight answer.

So Judith found herself spilling the beans about her uneasiness with the subject of corporal punishment; how she'd backed away from it at school and how it hadn't really arisen since. 'What it amounts to,' she finished, feeling that she had become clearer about the thing, 'is that I have a fascination with it that I've always

12

suppressed. What I'm afraid of here I don't know, but it's got to be a good thing if the job makes me face up to it.'

'Well said, sister.' Marsha banged on the table several times in applause. 'Confront your inner demons before they confront you, that's my motto. Let me get you another beer before I go back to work.'

Much later the sliding doors to the club were open and Judith leaned just inside the area, drinking from a bottle and feeling the bass vibrations in the floor and the wall at her back. Since the summer term had finished last week there was not the usual pulsating mass of sweating bodies and her attempts to spot a half-decent guy were so far unsuccessful. So she posed in her lemon bra and hot pants, watching and waiting. Then there was a commotion at the entrance of the lounge bar itself, where she had been sitting with Marsha earlier.

'If that's how you feel, just fuck off, then.'

'That's exactly what I'm going to do!' The sharp, raised voices were quite clear above the boom of the music. Then a blonde woman in a frilly pink dress banged out of the swing doors and a man walked over to the bar, where Marsha was poised to deal with any trouble. He spoke a few words to her, shrugging, and she nodded and gave him a drink. When he turned, leaning on the bar, first impressions were borne out. Hold it right there, thought Judith, and let me get an eyeful. She just had time to take in the sardonic expression, the muscles and the slim hips when her gaze was noticed and he stood up straight and walked directly towards her.

'Do I pass muster for a dance?' he asked when he reached her.

Judith ran her eyes up and down him. 'Body does. And is this the stage of the night when you change bimbos?'

13

He looked at her sceptically. 'Your gear says you're up for dancing, hence my question. You'll have to explain how bimbos come into it.'

'I thought I saw one come in with you but then she went out. Hence *my* question.'

He threw his head back and laughed. 'May I have the pleasure, miss?' he asked with a little bow.

'Indeed, kind sir, you may, but the pleasure is mine,' said Judith, laughing too, as she put her arm through his and they moved towards the dance floor.

Much later still they were climbing the stairs to his room. Judith was not at all sure what she was doing there since they had not kissed, though they had executed one very slow number locked together, where her attention – and she was sure his – had been focussed on his erection pressing into her thigh. He had asked her back for a nightcap to the small hotel in the next street and she told herself it didn't have to be a big deal. Anyway, after the most recent disaster, she had gone out to pull a guy and wipe out the memory. And this one had three things going for him already: he had dark good looks, he was a great dancer and he had scarcely drunk a thing. Nor had she, and that was setting some kind of record for her recent encounters. All the talk they had exchanged was a form of mild sparring in which his tone never wavered from an ironic banter that kept a clear distance between them. Well, so be it, thought Judith: I didn't come out tonight to find the love of my life.

Inside, he produced a bottle of Glen Grant and poured out two drams. She nodded at the offered jug of water and he added a little to each shot of whisky. They clinked glasses, sipped and savoured the taste for a moment, then, as if of a single mind, downed the remainder in one. They sat down on the small sofa with refills on a low table in front of them. Then he leaned

14

forward and pressed his lips into her cleavage. With a glance up at her, he said: 'May I?' and reached his hand round to the fastening at the back. When Judith nodded again he undid the bra and dropped it on to the floor. Then he swung round on to his knees before her and started to work on the small uncovered breasts with his mouth, holding her hips with his hands. After the first shock at the unexpected escalation of intimacy, Judith gave herself up to what was happening. Her companion took the nipples one after the other right into his mouth, sucking and licking and biting in a concentration of energy. As she became more aroused he bit harder and harder until she was gasping with the extremity of the sensations.

Then he stopped and said: 'Stand up.' It was more of an order than a request and Judith obeyed without thinking. Still kneeling in front of her, he pulled down the front zip of Judith's shorts and pushed his mouth into her pubic bush, nipping the flesh of her mound with his teeth. He put his hands inside the knickers and shucked them down over her hips to the floor. As she stepped out of the garment, he turned her about and began to palpate her buttocks with his hands. The massaging movements grew increasingly vigorous until Judith felt the biting begin again. Again he stopped all at once and stood up. They faced each other and she made a move to kiss him but he put a hand across her mouth. Then his shirt and trousers came off in almost one movement and the underpants directly after. Now they were both naked, having already discarded their footwear at the door.

He lay on his back on the bed and pulled her so that she straddled him. Judith needed no encouragement. After all that stimulation of breasts and buttocks she was aching to be penetrated and she lowered the slick lips of her vulva over the glistening tip of his stiff penis. He thrust up with his hips and put his hands round her,

15

kneading the dimples of her arse. They moved together, each one's eyes fixed on the other's. Judith tried to spin it out but it was no use. Then he slapped her once on each rear cheek and all the pent-up frustrations of recent weeks came together with the exquisite stimulation her body was getting, and the waves of her orgasm broke over her. She closed her eyes and threw back her head and was for a time lost to the world.

Afterwards Judith lay with her back to him, curled inside the curve of his body. In a while his hand took hold of her behind and at once there was an answering prickle in her loins. He stroked and squeezed without speaking, then got up on to his knees on the bed. She followed his movements and went on all fours, sticking her bum in the air. With growing excitement she felt her anus being probed while his hardness pushed back inside her vagina. Then there was a finger in there too, finding her clitoris below his cock and Judith thrust against him as her new climax built up. At the moment the spasms overtook her, he slapped her as before, but just once. They subsided on the crumpled sheet and she slept.

Early on Thursday afternoon, Judith sat at the kitchen table, drinking coffee from a fresh pot. Catherine, her flatmate, was due back any time and she would want to sit and chat about what had happened in the week she had been away. She was a student too, but in nursing, and beginning next week she would be juggling shifts at the local hospital with summer work serving tables at a big hotel on the outskirts of town. Not much of a wage for that job but Cat's pretty face and blonde curls should bring in the tips just as they had done before.

While she waited, Judith thought back for the tenth time to the events of the night before. She had surfaced at 5.30 a.m. with Thomas sound asleep beside her. Thomas. That was the name he had given her when they

16

met, but it felt odd to call someone she knew only as a body by a standard human name. The body had been all, while the mind had been cloaked in a flippant and ironic fencing match. But what a body! It danced, massaged, bit and fucked almost to perfection and she had come like she had given up expecting a man ever to make her do. No complaints there, none at all. However, there was the kissing, or rather the absence of it. It was as if, mouth-to-mouth, the exchange of breath and the mingling of tongues would be getting too close for comfort to a contact of spirits or minds. That thought alone, in the early light, had made Judith gather her things quietly and dress in the bathroom before slipping out of the room and out of the silent hotel. She just didn't want to deal with what was effectively an unknown person waking up on his own territory.

And then there was the slapping. It hadn't been too hard and only served to fuel her sensuality even further. But it had been so *deliberate*. It wasn't the kind of thing you would do in the heat of the moment like you might sink your fingers into a lover's bum. But of course, it struck her suddenly, all that biting of her nipples was the same. He wasn't about to come *then*, that was early on, and he must have judged very carefully how far he could go. Judith gave a shiver at the idea of all this calculation, but then the flat door opened and she was pleased to hear a voice call out: 'Hi, it's me, Judith, are you home?'

'Hi, Cat. I've just made some coffee. Come and sit down.'

Catherine dropped her bag on the kitchen floor and held out her arms. Judith took one look at the open face and the warm smile and hugged her flatmate rather more tightly than usual.

2

Miss James

It was seven o'clock precisely on Monday morning and Judith was trying to keep panic at bay. What was she going to wear for the interview? She went through to the kitchen in her T-shirt and poured a glass of orange juice from the fridge. If she were going for the usual sort of clerical job, like the one she had last summer in an office, there were a couple of dark, sober dresses hanging there in the cupboard. But this was no ordinary position and it could give the wrong impression to wear the conventional outfit. And, given that the Director of The Nemesis Archive by repute had little time for men, it might be a bad idea to wear a dress or skirt at all. But, worse than all that, what about the person inside the clothes? How on Earth was *she* going to pass an inspection by the formidable Samantha James?

'Hey, you all right?'

Judith looked up from the table with a start.

Catherine stood in the doorway in a little pair of silk shorts, hair tousled from sleep. 'I heard you pacing about and thought you might need someone to hold your hand till it's time to go.' Catherine came over and her arm went round Judith's shoulders, squeezing.

Through her thin cotton top Judith felt the warmth of her body fresh from bed, the softness of a breast pressing against her.

'I'm sorry, Cat, I've disturbed you. I just can't decide what to put on.' Judith felt suddenly close to tears.

The other woman hugged her again. 'Girl, you are so tight,' she said and stood up with an air of purpose. 'We are going to do something about this. Now you go and run a bath, while I go and select your costume.' Catherine's voice was firm. 'No arguments,' she said. 'I know a bit about Miss James, so leave the choice to me. And make that water really hot, cos there's something we're going to do before you get into it.'

Judith did as she was told, setting doubts aside in her gratitude that someone had taken control of the situation. When she came back from the bathroom, there was laid out on the chair a black satin thong, black stretch trousers and a white blouse with a small frill down the front. On the floor stood a pair of black boots with a thick but lowish heel.

'You see,' said Catherine, looking at them too, 'stylish but sensible.'

Judith picked up the trousers. 'Cat, these are a really close fit here, and here –' she put her hands on her bare hips and thighs '– do you think I should?'

Catherine laughed. 'Look, what do we know about dear Samantha? One, she has an eye for the ladies and, two, she has an interest in rear ends, the correction of. So when you're a girl with a nice arse like yours, don't hide it. You're on to a winner here, Jude.'

'By that logic, I could make certain of the job by handing her a cane and bending over the desk.'

Catherine laughed again. 'One step at a time, my dear. Who knows what you'll be doing before the summer's out?' As Judith reddened, taken aback at the way Catherine seemed tuned in to the disciplinary side of things, her flatmate went on. 'Right, now we've organised the gear; we need to take some of this tension out of your body. Come with me.' She led the way into her room where two L-shaped arms were clamped, one

19

each side, to the footboard of Catherine's bed. From the ends of these, about two feet above the mattress, hung broad bands of soft leather.

'Jee-sus,' said Judith as it clicked what the equipment was all about. 'This is a bit, er, gynaecological, isn't it?'

'Ha! Got it in one. But a girl in that position is ready for more than just an examination. Up you get, now. No arguments.' Judith got on her back and manoeuvred first one foot then other through the bands and Catherine helped her wriggle down until her calves were held and her legs were well parted and raised up. Then she eased a pillow under the base of Judith's spine.

'There,' said Catherine, sounding delighted. 'I use this myself when I need a really good session. You can get at both your openings without straining to keep your legs up. But you, girl, are going to get a helping hand 'cos you're too wound up to be left to your own devices.' She produced a purple vibrator and spread some lubricating jelly over the end of it with her fingers. 'Now just relax, Jude. I'm not making a pass at you; this is purely a medical procedure. Trust me – I'm nearly a nurse, after all.'

This is a bit far down the line for a *pass*, thought Judith, for a moment uncomfortably close to a fit of the giggles. But it went by; Catherine was so guileless, she had to be taken at face value. So she lay back as instructed while the plastic was inserted. She felt a slippery finger in her behind, then two, after which the buzzing started and the sensations escalated. Again and again Catherine brought her to the edge of climax, only to ease back, but then the vibrations reached a new level and Judith shrieked out her orgasm at the top of her voice. The instrument was withdrawn and Catherine's hand caressed her through the abating spasms until she lay still, drenched in sweat.

After several seconds of silence Catherine helped her pull her legs out from the loops. 'Bath,' she said quietly, and Judith followed her meekly and climbed in. More hot water was added to the tub that was fragrant with oil. 'Ten minutes, then you get dressed,' said Catherine. 'I'm going to make coffee.'

Judith lifted a foam-covered arm out of the water and pulled Catherine towards her. She ran a wet hand over her flatmate's bare back and kissed her on the cheek. 'Thank you,' she said and subsided back into the steaming heat.

At 8.55 a.m. Judith entered the new lobby that had been added on to a side entrance of the old building and, watched by a security camera, pressed the button beside the brass plate that read in bold capitals: THE NEMESIS ARCHIVE.

'Who is it?' asked a voice through the intercom.

She replied: 'It's Judith Wilson. I'm here to be interviewed for the assistant's job.'

'Come through as soon as the door opens. We are on the second floor.'

A steel panel slid smoothly back then there was the clunk of a solenoid-operated bolt. Judith pushed the swing door open and stepped in. Directly ahead was an open lift whose door closed behind her when she pressed '2' on the panel. Judith was aware that she was now in what had been the university library until just before she had enrolled last autumn. When it moved to a concrete fortification on the edge of town, the open shelves and study areas had been taken over by the Psychology Department, while the stacks had been bought by the shadowy Oceanus Corporation for an undisclosed but reputedly enormous sum. The academics were far from happy that women's writings rumoured to celebrate masochism in a way any right-minded psychologist must condemn were housed on their very doorstep, but their tongues were mostly silenced by the funds the sale had created for the conversion of their quarters. Access

21

to the stacks had always been restricted; now it was by special permission only, which was granted almost never. So they can hardly complain that this scandalous stuff is thrust into people's faces, even those right next to it, thought Judith as the lift stopped and she stepped out into a small vestibule.

Opposite was a door marked RECEPTION and Judith knocked and went in. Just inside on the right there was a young woman with a ponytail sitting at a word-processor while to the left was a computer console with a bank of screens and keyboards. She got up and Judith noticed with approval she had on a high-necked sleeveless top and a short leather skirt, both in white.

'I'm Helen,' she said. 'Miss James is ready for you now.' She opened a door in the far wall and ushered Judith straight through, closing the door behind her. A raven-haired woman of about forty, all in black, rose to her feet and moved to the side of her desk, extending an arm.

'My name is Samantha James. You are Miss Wilson.' They shook hands and Judith returned the woman's firm grip. 'Please have a seat,' she said, indicating a small armchair on the right. The room was of moderate size with the same high ceiling as the outer office. The left-hand wall was filled from floor to ceiling with shelves of books, complete with a wooden stepladder to enable the top ones to be reached. In front of these was a tall teacher's desk with a sloping lid, but without any kind of seat by it. Apart from where Judith had entered, there were two other doors, a padded one ahead and a plain wooden one to the right.

'I have called you here because the responses you have made on paper suggest to me that you may me suited both to the work here and to the way we do it. So, Miss Wilson –'

'If you wish, Miss James, please call me Judith.' She took advantage of the slight pause, hoping it was the right thing to do.

'Thank you, my dear. So it shall be. Now, Judith, I do not intend to conduct a formal interview.' As the older woman was speaking, the younger began to feel more at ease. While Cat's medicine had worked a treat – and Judith wondered briefly what Miss James would think of her early morning preparation – her anxiety had inevitably risen again as nine o'clock approached. But the dark woman with the beak of a nose had such a penetrating gaze that any pretence seemed futile; and once dissembling was not an option Judith could only be herself, wherever that might lead her. With this woman she would be honest; not because she already trusted her, that didn't come into it, but because any other course was ruled out.

The director had been explaining that she would show the applicant where the collection was housed and where her working space would be. She continued, 'You may have been wondering about our name. These days it suggests to people the idea of vengeance, but the original Nemesis was a nymph-goddess who presided over a cult of ritual flagellation. A rather exciting figure, I find, with her brass-tipped scourge hanging at the ready from her belt, and well suited to represent our central concerns here. She is related to the Furies, which is presumably where revenge comes in, and it is perhaps no bad thing that the name does not immediately suggest the real nature of our materials to all and sundry.'

Miss James had let her enthusiasm show and Judith smiled, warmed by it. Now the director sat forwards, business-like. 'Very well, then,' she said, 'to practicalities. For the rest of the morning, I want you to do something that is in part a test – the last one – of your skills, and in part a trial run for what I hope will be the future.'

Judith settled back in her chair and listened attentively.

'I shall give you a short memoir to digest on discipline in a convent school of the 1950s. For the moment we leave aside questions of how materials of this sort are to be catalogued. From your reading I want you to do the two other things that are basic to the post you have applied for: prepare an abstract of 150 to 250 words for our database and make a list of points of interest, queries, problems – anything at all in fact that you think worthy of discussion. And I do mean what *you* think, not what you may guess *I* think or believe you *ought* to think. Is that clear?'

Receiving a nod, Miss James stood up. 'Then follow me, Judith.' She opened the door on the right and they stepped out into the stacks of the old library. Judith paused, looking up and then down with a lurch of vertigo. Ahead an aisle separated the bookshelves running off to both sides, while to left and right she could see through a gap the two floors of books above and, under her feet, levels below levels that disappeared down into darkness. The unsettling effect was made worse by the opaque glass flooring on which they stood. The director explained that the whole thing was a steel construction within the shell of the stone building whose purpose was to utilise all the available space without requiring those who would read items from the top shelves to teeter on long ladders. So four original high-ceilinged floors had been replaced with six more accessible ones.

She led the way to the far corner where there was an ornate spiral staircase which she motioned Judith to ascend ahead of her. She did so, at first uncomfortably aware that if the rumours were right, Miss James had an ideal opportunity to feast her eyes on an arse moving inside the thin and clinging trousers of Cat's choice. Oh, what the fuck, thought Judith with a surge of exhilaration at the strange environment she was in and the new challenges that were coming up. Let the lady *have* an eyeful. That was part of the idea, after all. And she continued on up to the top level that was labelled 5.

Miss James emerged from the stairwell behind her and pointed through the rows of books and boxes of manuscripts to an alcove at the end. When they reached it, Judith saw that a small space in the corner was clear of shelving and there stood a computer terminal and beside it a small table lit by spotlights on the wall above.

'If, after today, we both wish the appointment to be made, this is where you will work. The text I spoke of and a pad are laid out for you and I shall expect the results by 12.30, when Helen will take you to lunch.' With that she turned and walked back the way they had come. For the first time, watching her retreating figure, Judith realised that Miss James was wearing close-fitting knee breeches and long boots below her waisted silk blouse. Face to face, her eyes held you so that any other details of her form escaped attention but now Judith registered the powerful haunches and thighs. And I thought to impress her, she said to herself with a little smile, sitting down to the task at hand.

It was a typescript on A4 paper with the heading: *Le Couvent de Ste-Agathe, Bretagne 1956-8*. Underneath was a bracketed note: *The former pupil of the convent school was referred to me for psychological examination, which I conducted between January and March of 1962. The sessions were recorded but the quality of the tapes is poor so what follows is, after an interval of thirty years, a reconstruction rather than a verbatim record. I shall be content if I manage to convey the substance and something of the flavour of the tale told me then (with the exception, of course, that I am using English). Michelle Brown, PhD 1992*. Well, the actual writing is quite recent, she thought, but here's our first problem. No details of the so-called Dr Brown nor of the girl who was supposedly there: nothing at the beginning or the end of the document. Judith took up the pen and wrote on her wad of paper: '(1) Is this fiction? How can we tell?' As she leaned back in her chair the sun came out from behind a cloud and she became properly aware of what was in front of her. Her little table was halfway into the recess in the thick walls that held the window, whose length extended well beyond the top floor of the stacks, so she commanded a stunning vertical sweep from the rooftops of the houses across the quadrangle to the figures going about their business five floors below on the grass, almost straight down. Fuck, I could work in this place. Judith smiled to herself and shook her head, then turned over the first page to read. If, that is, I can stop staring at the view.

They were by no means all unhappy, the times we had in those last two years, though I have to admit they set me on the track that went so badly astray. Looking back on it now, I think we girls had little inkling of how our environment had become unusual, at least not until it all broke down. But unusual it certainly was, and the whole thing must seem very strange to someone who was not caught up in it from the beginning. One moment we seemed to be children – I know I was quite naïve at the start – and the next we were immersed in an adult world of sensuality.

It began when the old Mother Superior and two senior teachers took retirement all at the same time, with the result that their replacements had free rein to put their ideas into practice. The main thing they did was to install a completely new régime of discipline. Up until then, physical punishments had been a rarity and girls who broke the rules by talking in class or rowdiness earned lines to write or a stint scrubbing floors in the main convent building. The old head had a cane which she kept in her office, but it took really bad behaviour for it to be used. I remember once there was a girl who stole money and then tried to put the blame on her classmate. The teacher reported her and she got six strokes on the seat of her knickers in front of us all. It made her howl, but we already considered her to be a coward. In those days collecting a few stripes on the bottom wasn't a thing we dreaded, but it didn't take long for that opinion of ours to change! The new Mother Superior owned a whole rack of canes, many being heavy and supple instruments beyond anything we knew. She carried one of them with her wherever she went and was only too ready to use it. A girl could be bent over on the spot for nothing more than looking untidy. The drill was for the victim to pull her own pants down and hold her ankles while some vicious cuts were laid across the bared buttocks. This was a different proposition altogether from the old 'six of the best' and from that time on we moved around the school in fear of these impromptu doses of scorching pain. Thus a new hazard was added to our daily lives; but what really turned them upside down was the arrival of the birch rod.

From the outset, it was surrounded by ritual. Friday was decreed the day when all our crimes of the past week would be paid for, so a tally was kept in a large book of every offence and and the penalty it incurred. Once these had been added up, a list was read out in the refectory at five o'clock tea of the culprits and the chastisements they were to get an hour later. A long low room was set aside specifically for that purpose and to think of it still brings me out in goose pimples. It had a platform at the far end on which stood a waist-high block with a padded ledge each side for the knees and elbows of the girl to be whipped. To be named on a Friday was not good for the appetite, so the designated girls would often leave their meal early and head up the stairs. Those to be birched were required to line up by number of strokes to be given, which took much conferring and shuffling about. It didn't do to get the order wrong since any girls out of place would be given 'extras' after the listed punishments were over. The most severe were handed out first, the idea being that these were painful enough to induce penitence on their own. On the other hand, those sentenced to the minimum six strokes were supposed to benefit by watching the girls who writhed under a dose of six *times* six – an awful warning of how they would suffer if they continued to misbehave.

Each girl had to appear at the punishment room barefoot in her nightgown. This was a plain cotton shift that was tucked right up under the armpits, leaving the victim's bottom and thighs completely unprotected when she knelt over the block to be flogged. There were no fastenings on the device: a girl was expected to keep in place while her ration was dished out. However, there was an upper limit set of three dozen strokes for a single whipping, which we were all supposed to be able to endure without being tied down. But just to make doubly sure no one weakened there was an added threat: jumping up from the block would earn another full punishment first thing the next morning. The prospect of a repeat performance with flesh that was still very tender was so dreadful that over two years I never once saw a girl, whatever her pain, who did not manage to stay down. I came close myself to breaking near the end of a 'max' (as we called them) but the thought of being back in the same place before breakfast gave me the will to take the last few lashes and be done with it, at least for another week.

Of course, it was possible to accumulate more than the quota of thirty-six from one Friday to the next and when that happened the balance was handed out mid-week. There were perhaps fifteen girls over the block on a normal Friday and only two or three on Tuesdays as a rule. Further penalties could easily have built up by that time, so a girl *could* be back *again* the following Friday. I remember one wild tomboy who got a full dose twice a week for a whole month. With that treatment her hindquarters became red raw but she carried on untamed and was in the end expelled.

As soon as a girl's flogging was finished, she was sent off to bed to contemplate her misdeeds. It could be two hours or more ahead of our normal retiring time, and that was how the new disciplinary code began to do things to us that had not been anticipated. There were twenty-nine of us sharing a single sleeping area, all healthy and curious girls of sixteen or seventeen suddenly confronted with the regular sight of naked bottoms and thighs wriggling and squirming while they were lashed. Nobody was supervising the dormitory at this time and before long the girls who had been well whipped got in the habit of comforting one another. Alone on their beds as they were, those who began by stroking a friend's stinging bottom soon moved on to caress more private parts of hers. That was certainly what happened to *me* and I was a witness to many others doing the same things.

From eight-thirty onwards a sister was present while we took turns to wash in the bathroom then readied ourselves for the gas lamps being turned off at nine sharp. She slept in a cubicle at the end of our communal area but we soon found out that she was oblivious to small noises unless they were the sounds of voices. So as long as she didn't speak, a girl could creep into another's bed to continue the petting that had been started earlier when they were alone. There were a couple of anxious moments when a girl forgot herself at her peak, but each time a hand over her mouth stifled the cry and brought her to her senses before the sister was roused. In this way – and I had two regular bed-partners, myself – many of us got started on sex lives that were anything but normal.

It wasn't just that these were all lesbian passions that flourished in our dormitory. Without boys, what else could they have been? And maybe they might have gone the way of schoolgirl crushes we had before this time if it hadn't been for the corporal punishments that had set the whole thing off. The hottest affairs were between the girls who got a Friday flogging more often than not; that is, the ones who were strong-willed and disobedient. I was among them (I am afraid to say) and it was through us the punishment room itself acquired a strong sexual charge. Girls who were intimate with each other – just as much as conventional lovers are – watched their naked partner on the block and were really excited by what they saw. When it was their turn they twisted and spread their legs as lewdly as they could, pretending their movements were caused by the pain of the birch. And that was when things really began to fall apart. What they later called a 'disease' spread and more and more girls began to plan to be chastised to the tune of a dozen or even two dozen strokes so that they could make a sex display under its sting. So classroom order went rapidly downhill as even normally well-behaved pupils joined in the effort to appear on the Friday list. For some it may have been a kind of game, but I am sure that the girls I knew best were changed by it just as I was, even though I have not seen them since. What I know for certain is that now I am incapable of a full sexual response without some kind of corporal punishment in the situation.

Judith set down the stapled pages and gazed out of the window. She shifted position in her chair, uneasily aware of the dampness in her crotch that was the result of the images of nubile nakedness caught between caressing and whipping. It was made to sound as though it could be equally lubricious either way, at least once the two things had become connected. But birching is a *punishment*, she told herself. It fucking hurts. OK, maybe there are secondary effects, after the pain eases, like heat and tenderness. She could see how they might be sexy if you were a bit aroused to start with.

She picked up the script and looked at what was left. There were a few more pages that dwelled on the physical details of young female bodies moving under strokes of the rod and then a lyrical account of the narrator and a partner making love. She described an occasion – and left the impression there were others – when they lay face to face in the narrow bed, each fondling the other's chastised behind with one hand while the other was occupied between her lover's legs. It was graphically rendered and made the reader more disquietingly lubricated than she already was. Then the final two pages recounted the end of it all.

As we were to discover, the Mother Superior had become increasingly suspicious, so with her two close associates made a sudden check of our dorm towards midnight one Friday. She found three beds that were occupied by amorous couples and the game was up. The six of us were dragged off and locked in a large barred cell in the basement under close watch. In the morning we were told that many of the others had owned up to 'impure thoughts' along the lines of what we were caught *doing* and it was decided that the whole class was to be split up. Most of the pupils would be dispersed to other convent schools in the region but we six were to be expelled altogether, though not before each of us had been soundly thrashed for our 'outrageous conduct'. Four could then be returned to their families in disgrace but I and another girl were orphans who could not be dealt with that way. Instead, we were going to be sent to a reformatory school until we were twenty-one. Given our ages at the time, that meant we could expect four years of the harshest of institutional régimes without hope of release. The action was to be taken immediately, so still in our shifts we were marched through the corridors and up a flight of stairs that brought us to the familiar punishment room. It was 11 a.m. on the clock above the raised platform when we filed in and stood before the birching block. My heart sank to see that it had been fitted with restraining straps for arms, legs and waist and I was further cast down by the sight of the Mother Superior holding a long cane that quivered with each small movement of her wrist.

We were informed that we were to receive two dozen strokes apiece in the order we now stood. After the caned girl had recovered enough to leave the room, she would be despatched to her destination and the next would take her place over the block. The signal was given to begin. As the first victim was stripped of her garment and fastened down I felt some small measure of relief that I was next. While my knees were shaking at the prospect of being in her place, I had only to endure the sight of of one girl in extremis before my own torment would start. And once started, I told myself desperately, as night follows day, inevitably it would finish. Then my part in these beatings would be over and I would be on my way to a new place. However strict the system there, it was an unknown quantity and I could still hope for the best.

I watched the Mother Superior raise her flexible instrument and begin. Again and again it bit deep into the exposed bottom on the block. She was in no hurry, and let each stroke be fully felt before landing the next. My heart ached for the poor girl, but again I managed to find a little comfort in the fact that it would almost certainly be a less vicious deputy who thrashed me while the Mother rested after her efforts. At last the punishment was done and the bands released but the girl's legs would not carry her. She was left on the block for another minute while we stared in horror at the thicket of crimson weals that crossed her swollen behind. This time when lifted up she stayed up and clutched her shift as she was helped to limp unsteadily to the door. Then it was my turn to be secured, but after that there is a blank. I can no longer recall my own thrashing which, thankfully, seems to have been erased from my mind, though for months afterwards I would wake screaming from a nightmare that I was again tied down to be flogged without mercy.

The next memory I have is of two female staff from the reformatory watching me as I changed into my new uniform. I was still shaking from my ordeal and one of them assured me that I could expect my bottom to get worse treatment than it just had every single week if I was the least bit naughty. But they must have seen the tears come into my eyes for the other squeezed my arm and told her mate not to be cruel. They gave me trousers in a large size since I was so swollen and said not to repeat it but where I was going they didn't believe in girls getting thrashed like that. When we left I was so sore and throbbing I had to kneel between the two women on the back seat of the car – sitting down was out of the question – but their news had lifted my spirits and I was almost cheerful as I watched the convent disappear into the distance.

Well, it may all be a fake, thought Judith, but I want more. What happens to the girl at the reformatory, and where does she go next? If it is fiction, I'm hooked. She looked at her watch: it had just gone 11.30 and in less than an hour there was an abstract to write as well as notes on her responses to the material. She picked up the script again and flipped through its pages, trying to formulate a few sentences that would capture what it was all about. Not so easy, she thought. It's like a case history but there's no framework of analysis around it.

She decided simply to summarise what the text said happened in the two years specified at St Agatha's Convent School and leave everything else to her commentary. I could check whether there was any such place in Brittany if I really want to, she thought. The abstract was done by 11.50 a.m. and she began to write notes that soon spilled over on to a second and then a third sheet. It was simple enough to comment on the style (if there *were* transcripts, then they had been extensively reworked into prose) and the questions about language (there was no mention of translation, so was the narrator bilingual?) but Judith's own reactions she found much more difficult to dissect. Her wet knickers forbade her to deny she was aroused by what she had read, but she felt ill at ease with it. Much as she wanted to think the sexy descriptions of girls petting to climax in bed were what mainly turned her on, she knew that was not true. No, it was the whole nexus of naked intimacy, pain and sex that held her, fascinated, in its grip. And it wasn't just that moderate birching might stimulate as much as it hurt, for she had felt a real throb in her genitals at the severity of the canings. Nothing but pain in one of them, she thought with a shudder, but the idea still drew her.

The clock across the quad said 12.20 p.m. and Judith gathered up her papers. From her corner she noticed there was another spiral stair diagonally opposite to the one they had used to get up to the top, so she headed for it and went down two floors. She came out not far from a door that should, if she was right, open into the secretary's office. Judith was reaching for the handle when she heard a curious noise from the next doorway along and took a few steps in that direction. It was coming from the door into Miss James' office, which stood slightly ajar. She identified the sound almost at once though her mind refused at first to accept what it was. Judith's heart began to pound as she put her eye to the crack and confirmed what she had suspected.

Thwack! 'Ah!'

Thwack! 'A-ah!'

She had a perfect view of the scene. There was a figure draped over the tall desk Judith had noticed earlier. Its clothes showed it to be Helen, though her skirt was up round her waist and her face was not visible. She couldn't see the director except for an arm that was laying a two-tailed strap with some vigour across her secretary's bare bottom. Oh God, oh God, oh God. Judith's knees felt weak and all at once she became conscious that she was spying like some kind of Peeping Tom. She crept away towards the other door and steeled herself to turn the handle and go through. She made for a revolving chair in front of the computer consoles and sat down with her notes, waiting for her pulse to stop racing. There was not a sound through the connecting door, but then it was padded, as was the other. If that one had been shut she wouldn't have heard – or seen – what she just had.

Then the door opened and Helen came through wet-eyed, clutching the seat of her skirt. She saw Judith and started, wrenching her hands away. 'I'm sorry, I'm going to the toilet,' she muttered and carried on through. Miss James appeared in the doorway, saying, 'Ah, Judith, you're very prompt. I like to see that.' Then Judith followed the commanding figure into her room.

Afterwards she could remember little of what was said in the ten minutes of so that she sat with the director. She handed over her notes, that she knew, and she was aware of how Miss James had a higher colour than before and her eyes seemed particularly bright. When leaving she agreed to return at two for a short discussion, once her work had been read, and then she was handed over to a more composed Helen to be taken to lunch. Nothing was said either by the director or her secretary about what she had seen, and it was clear that as they ate, the latter wasn't going to volunteer any information, in spite of the obvious fact that she wasn't sitting at all comfortably. Judith's own ambivalence about the subject made it impossible for her to ask a direct question and they passed an awkward hour trying to find topics of conversation. The difficulties were exacerbated by Helen's evasiveness about her background. The girl was not much older than she was, Judith reckoned, but she found a way of blocking every enquiry as to what she had done or where she had been before Nemesis was housed in its present location.

At two o'clock Judith was sitting once more in the armchair facing Miss James. The traces of excitement were no longer present and the older woman sat, chin resting on her hands, staring at her young interviewee.

'If you want the position, it is yours,' she said straightening up in her chair. 'The abstract is more than competent and as for the rest, I am impressed that a person of your age is able to give expression to deep conflicts without rushing to close them off in a peremptory fashion.'

Judith looked down, embarrassed by this praise, then realised she was expected to reply. 'Thank you, Miss James. I really do want this job.' Feeling awkward, she plunged on. 'And I hope I can do what you expect of me.' Jesus, what am I saying? she thought. *I'll* end up over that desk at this rate.

'Well, that's up to you, my dear.' For an instant Judith was shocked at the apparent response to what had flashed through her mind. Then the director continued. 'I have only one rule: that you are here between nine and 12.30 each weekday. As you know, it is a full-time appointment, but how you put in the remaining hours I leave entirely up to you. If you wish to work evenings or weekends rather than in the afternoon, that is your business. However, in return for that freedom, I make it a condition of employment that you report to the office at nine o'clock Monday to Friday. Whether I see you personally at that time will depend on the work in progress. Is that understood?'

Judith felt the full weight of the older woman's gaze as she paused. 'Yes, Miss James.'

'Let me make myself quite clear on this point. The way I run things, the breach of a rule incurs a penalty – ultimately, of course, that of dismissal. But before that stage is reached I favour a payment for infractions that is more in keeping with one of the principal interests of our establishment.'

Oh, God, she means the strap. *That* strap, the one Helen was getting a dose of. Judith's mind whirled while the director continued calmly.

'But we can cross that bridge when, or should I say, if we come to it. For now, I shall just say that I think, and certainly hope, that you will benefit from being here just as your presence will benefit me. From my brief experience I take you to be a person who keeps the daring things below the surface. But you do so in a way that they are not suppressed and may emerge if given the opportunity. That pleases me, for it indicates a great deal of potential.' She stood up with almost a frivolous smile on her face. 'Perhaps your clothing today is a good illustration of what I'm saying. It is not obvious at first glance what's underneath, but a little close attention may uncover it.'

Judith could feel the heat of the flush that had risen to her face. Oh, fuck, she means the thong under my tight trousers. She saw it all on the staircase.

Miss James gave a short bark of a laugh. 'I believe you have just validated my example without any actual inspection being necessary. Shame, really. But one of these days, perhaps ...' She led Judith to the door before she could voice any of her turmoil at the recent remarks. 'At nine in the morning I shall give you a proper briefing on our collection and I shall have ready material for you to work on, some of which you may find to be of particular interest. *Au revoir.*'

She went back into her room, closing the door. Helen was at her desk, typing and Judith said: 'Er, see you tomorrow, then.'

Helen looked up and nodded, but her smile seemed rather forced. 'Bye.'

Judith went down in the lift and out through the security barriers. In the open she stood squinting in the bright sunshine. Then, amid the smell of freshly mown grass, she sat down on a wooden bench and breathed the summer air.

3

Manuscripts

'And you're telling me you *saw* her walloping the secretary's bare bum? What are you on, girl?' Catherine's scepticism was an obvious pretence and Judith laughed. They were sitting round the kitchen table at the end of the afternoon sharing a large bottle of ice-cold beer.

'But seriously, it fits with all the talk,' she went on. 'What's the girl like who was getting it?'

'Couldn't make her out. Helen, her name is.' Judith took a mouthful and swallowed it. 'I quizzed her for an hour over lunch but she wouldn't tell me anything. I mean, OK, she had a sore bottom and it didn't help that I'd seen her earlier coming out of the office in tears, but I was really trying to find a way of being sympathetic –'

'I reckon she goes way back with that scene.' Catherine cut in, tapping her empty glass. She reached for the bottle and topped them both up. 'Y'see, she arrived with the dark lady herself when the place started up. They never looked for a secretary from round here, not even on the grapevine like they did with your job. So what's the betting she's still shacked up with your boss but doesn't want to admit it? That's why she's being so cagey.'

'You mean she's the one the scandal was about, where Miss James was before?'

'Makes sense. And she's going to be really jealous of a new girl appearing on the horizon. Especially one waggling her arse in a tight pair of pants.' Catherine giggled and took another drink.

'Oh, God, the boss made a comment too. You and your satin thong. She fucking saw the outline of it, didn't she, when I had to climb up two flights of this spiral staircase ahead of her.'

'Well, you should be thanking me for getting you the job. I bet that flash of your assets was what swung it for you. But what about the normal gear for this number? You supposed to be smart?'

'Well, I asked the lady and she said she didn't tolerate jeans. But she's quite happy with shorts in hot weather –'

'– as long as they're in black lycra –'

'– and she can follow me up the stairs!' They both succumbed to an attack of the giggles, then Judith emptied the rest of the beer into their glasses.

'Well, here's to the new appointment,' said Catherine, and they drank. After a minute, she said: 'So what does the secretary girl wear, then?'

'Oh, Helen *looks* pretty neat. Today it was white leather miniskirt and top. But I get the distinct feeling I'm not welcome.'

'Well, two's company and all that. If I'm right and your new boss was, probably still is her mistress – that's like capital M, Mistress – she'll know *all* about what she fancies. You say she's unfriendly now. What's she going to be like when the lady J has you baring all for a leathering?'

Judith looked at her flatmate, shocked. She'd not mentioned Miss James' remarks about penalties for lateness, but, just like she had in the morning, Cat seemed to be assuming that corporal punishment was part of the deal. Not just reading about it, but taking it. Actually pulling her pants down and bending over . . .

Judith felt cold in the pit of her stomach while Catherine carried on brightly.

'I wonder what it's like? I mean, all this talk has got me quite curious. I was never spanked, not once, even as a kid. What about you, Jude?'

Judith shook her head, colouring. The last thing she wanted was to talk about herself. She wished Cat would change the subject, but she was following a train of thought.

'How painful do you really suppose it is? I mean, being hit with a cane must hurt like fuck, at least right when it happens. But even that maybe leaves you all hot and sexy afterwards. What d'you reckon, girl?'

Judith felt herself getting redder and redder. She had shared the flat with Cat since the beginning of the year and she'd never really talked about sex before. But since the bathroom display it seemed to dominate the girl's mind. A month ago she could not have imagined the orgasm treatment of that very morning. And look at Cat now, thought Judith, watching the bright eyes flashing and the curls bobbing as she talked animatedly. She's like a child getting enthusiastic about matches, thought Judith. She has no idea of how this stuff affects me.

Without waiting for an answer to her question, Catherine had plunged right on. 'I don't know what it is but these days I just keep hearing about all this s/m business. It's obvious that for a lot of people getting their backsides tanned is directly to do with sex. I can see how birch twigs might work, I mean there's the whole sauna thing, and that's kind of straight stimulation. But what I don't really get is the stronger stuff like your Helen, for example. I mean, the strap's made her cry, yet she stays around and comes back for more. That sounds like an erotic fix to me and I hate to think I'm missing out on something.' She stopped suddenly, eyes on the wall clock.

'Oh, shit! Here's me rabbiting and I'm due on in quarter of an hour. Thank fuck the place is only five minutes away.' She stood up and Judith breathed a sigh of relief that the conversation was ending. But there was a parting shot, albeit unwitting, as she went off to change. 'The sister's not too bad anyway over a few minutes one way or the other. Now if I had *your* boss, with my timekeeping, this pert little bottom here would soon be red raw. Oo-ooh!' Catherine put on a pained face and held the seat of her jeans. Then she burst into cackles of laughter and disappeared with a cry of 'See ya!'

At ten the next morning, Judith was installed in the top floor of the stacks in front of a pile of manuscripts. They were all stories of women's experiences of sadomasochism from different times and places and Miss James had just been explaining that *anything* on that subject matter qualified for inclusion in The Nemesis Archive. What they had put together was contained in the three upper floors and half of the second, so there was plenty of vacant space for the acquisition of new writing and fresh discoveries from the past. As the two women walked through the shelves, stopping here and there for the director to point out something of special interest, they talked of the points they had only touched on the previous afternoon. Judith felt she was clearer now about the two interlocking questions that had to be asked of every item, whether typescript or published volume. Was it biography or was it fiction; and was the author really the person claimed? The situation became more complex yet with the case studies she was to read since the author was not the same person as the narrator.

It was important for the collection that they were able to identify a core of material consisting of autobiographical accounts by women themselves of their involvement in s/m. A close second in usefulness were case histories that had been put together by a sympathetic analyst, and out-and-out fiction by women had a part to play in extending the range of masochistic fantasy. Standing as a kind of obverse of the core, there were the fake 'lives': first person writings by men under women's names. As with work avowedly produced by men about women, these sources could, in the last analysis, be of corroborative value only.

Judith's job for the week was to study the bunch of scripts on her desk with these issues in mind. They were part of a bequest that had recently arrived in the office and ranged in time from accounts of two gaol whippings of 1802 by the mere teenagers who suffered them to a chapter from the journal of a present-day submissive in LA which went into the theory and practice of being branded with her lover's initials. But whether the prison's switches or the red-hot irons were a real part of the experience of these authors or the figments of overheated imaginations was for her, the new Assistant to The Nemesis Archive, to try to determine. Feeling a glow of importance, she thought: let's begin in the present, and bent her head over the journal by one Viola Cruz . . .

The next three days flew past. Each morning and afternoon Judith sat down and took up a new manuscript, to be plunged into yet another world where punishment and sexuality were enmeshed. There was a back entrance to the stacks on the ground floor and at around one o'clock she used her key to go outside with a sandwich. Rather than face the trial of eating with Helen, she sat by herself in the summer heat. Behaving as an office worker lunching on the grass like the others, Judith could not forget the libidinous thread that bound her to the dark world within the nearby walls. For all she wore the shorts and crop top of a sun worshipper (with the approval of the director, no less), she saw herself transforming into a creature alien from the simplicities of strong light and hard-edged shadows, and it was with a feeling almost of relief that she returned to the murky greys that washed over her documents of penance and pain.

Two scripts focussed on the sadistic delights of judicial caning in South Africa around 1930, one by a nursing sister who had talked her way into administering the punishments she was intended merely to supervise in her medical capacity. The other was by a mysterious figure identified only as AKS who, the text implied, had at one time been a governess in England but had left under a cloud. Her memoir described in detail and with relish the whole spectrum of discipline from a six of the best right up to the exemplary thrashing of the naked buttocks of a mature woman to the tune of thirty strokes. There was one more that took the chastiser's perspective in this unrelenting way. It had stapled to it a note claiming it to be 'an unpublished MS by the notorious Austrian Edith Cadiveč' – she must be, Judith thought, for even I have heard of this lady – who rhapsodised about the effects of vigorous birching on 'naked girl-arses'.

These texts made no bones about the sexual excitement of wielding an instrument of corporal punishment. The remainder, though, which took the perspective of the one who underwent this treatment, were less likely to enthuse about its erotic dimension. No fucking wonder, said Judith to herself, shuddering at the idea of one of those canes biting into her bottom. There seemed to be more potential that way in the birch: in one instance there were memories of a governess in 1895 whose whippings were plainly experienced as exciting and for another there was the convent school – her first acquaintance of the batch – with the rod at the centre of the sexual games that grew up. But whether the victim was turned on or not, these materials began to have a cumulative effect on the reader of them as she sat alone at her desk in the corner of the top floor of the stacks. What repelled her about the idea of physical punishment was as strong as ever, the more so the more vicious its application, but her repulsion was more than matched by the thrill she now found in these tales of bared buttocks under the most exacting discipline.

The week's underclothes tell their own story, thought Judith as she picked up the last manuscript on Friday morning. After Tuesday, she had brought a change of knickers in her bag each day, only to find that when she went to replace the wet ones at lunchtime she had been unable to resist sitting on the lavatory to masturbate. She was so juiced up that a few deft strokes of the clitoris was all it took and the climax felt as though it would blow her head off. You've got to face up to this, girl, she told herself. You're fucking hooked on the stuff. With a sigh she turned back to her text and, genitals prickling anew, began to read about the public thrashing of nineteen-year-old Janina Čyprik in a town square in Hungary as late as 1905.

An hour later, Judith was trying to draw together the preliminary notes she had made on the authenticity of each document. The account she had just finished had convinced her almost at once in the vividness of its details. First there was the way the hem of the girl's shift had ripped when it was pulled up, catching the rough edge of the whipping block and the way the front of her thighs were full of splinters afterwards. Then the description of the first ash switch breaking after three strokes and its replacement lasting no longer rang true. Only on the third try was an instrument found that would serve for the whole punishment. And, finally, the relating of how, while her arms were gripped by a matron apiece, her legs were free since the restraining strap had perished with long exposure to the weather. She began to kick as her agony mounted, so a pole was found and pressed into the backs of her knees by two strong men until the sentence had been carried out. Thus four adults were used to hold down one teenage girl for this dreadful chastisement.

According to her own account, Janina remained conscious throughout but was far too frantic to keep any count of how many strokes she received. At the end she told how she was carried to her mistress' house (being an orphan in domestic service) and allowed to keep to her room for the rest of that day. A kind kitchen maid stole an hour off to bathe and anoint the wounds, but in spite of her continuing pain Janina was required to return to her duties the following morning. In all it was a month before her behind was free of the bruises the thrashing inflicted, and after a year there were still whitish scars where the skin had been lacerated which were no doubt with her for the rest of her life.

Judith sat staring but the view in front of her was unseen. Her head was full of images of the town square where, in front of a jeering crowd, four figures surrounded a screaming girl while a fifth lashed the already purple buttocks on which the welts were rising. She slid a hand inside the front of her shorts and hooked a finger under the oozing gusset of her pants. Then, with a start, she heard a door close and footsteps on the staircase. In a flash the fingers were out and dried on her handkerchief and when Miss James appeared she was writing some more notes.

The director looked hard at Judith, then a little smile came to her lips. She nodded at the Hungarian story. 'I read that myself when it arrived last week. A very affecting tale.'

'It is,' said Judith and awkwardly blurted out the things that had made her think it genuine.

'I agree entirely with your assessment, my dear. And its patent reality is what makes it such an intense piece of work. Anyone reading it must expect to need some relief from the strong feelings it arouses.'

Judith felt herself blushing furiously. Oh, God, she's talking about wanking; she *knows* what I was just going to do.

'So I should regard it as quite natural for a solitary student to indulge herself from time to time. However, I do not mean to embarrass you. I came to give you these. Open it.' She put down a box file and Judith lifted the lid with relief at something to cover her confusion. Inside was an untidy heap of foolscap sheets, some typed, others covered in scrawled handwriting. On top was one that said: *Dr Michelle Brown. Life notes and observations.*

'I know you were rather taken with our anonymous girl expelled from the convent school. This file was donated to us when the author passed on very suddenly in 1992. It is in complete disorder and the writing is almost illegible in places, but if you persevere you may learn here more of her fate. I'll let you get down to it.' And with that she was gone, leaving Judith, in a way that was becoming habitual, slightly stunned in her wake.

I settled into the reformatory very quickly. We were fed well and worked hard, either at carpentry and building or in the garden. It was a large area that grew all the vegetables and fruit for our own needs and the rest was sold in the nearby market. I liked that work from the start and once the stiffness from my farewell caning had eased my muscles soon adapted to all the bending and lifting that was involved. The institution was self-consciously 'progressive' in outlook in that it assumed that most wayward girls would respond to work that required some skills, a proper diet and some basic education. Most did and order was maintained, allowing for some rowdiness, even though the cane and the birch were outlawed. The first instrument was considered

47

too violent a punishment for a teenage girl and the second's requirement of nakedness of the buttocks too unchaste. As a very last resort a determined offender would be dressed in a pair of thin cotton shorts, put over the knee of the brawny Mina and spanked with a leather paddle in front of us all. It was hoped that the shame of a punishment as much as the pain of it would bring the bad behaviour to an end.

When I witnessed one of these rare events for the first time it brought home to me what was missing from my life. In our everyday world Mina was a solid presence whose reactions were slow and unexcited. But with a girl over her knee she was transformed. Her colour rose and her eyes shone as they fixed on the lightly covered globes in front of her. She smacked the paddle down again and again with a kind of joyful vigour, but in a rhythm slow enough to allow the flesh to bounce and ripple. I watched her and fell into a dream until the girl was released. She stood clutching her bottom while the principal lectured her once more, and I realised with a shock that I was wet between my legs.

The convent school was clearly to blame for this. The awakening of my teenage sexuality had been done with the stimulation of the birch on naked flesh in the company of young women similarly affected. And I pined for both of those things! It was wonderful, of course, no longer to fear a thrashing with the Mother Superior's cane, but a whipping with the twigs and the dormitory games that had followed were much missed. There was a girl I would have loved to take to my bed, a pretty redhead called Elise who had been a runaway and a thief. I knew she wanted me too, but our institution was very strong on chastity before marriage, which it was hoped a reformed girl would be aiming for after her stay at St Nazaire. The problem was that, being liberal, they knew a healthy girl between sixteen and twenty could well develop sexual feelings towards one or more of her fellow inmates, living closely together as we did. So our sleeping quarters were checked often enough to make a liaison there unworkable, and during the day we were never far from a member of staff. I had more opportunity than most once I became more expert in the art of cultivation. Then I was given tasks that would take me unsupervised to the edge of our territory, if I was lucky admidst the cover of fruit trees. Only once did I manage to get my would-be lover out there with me, but we had barely begun our passionate kisses when a girl appeared at the orchard gate. Elise had been missed and they would come looking if she did not return at once. Twice more in as many weeks she was found to have absented herself without leave and with a touching loyalty to me refused to explain where she had been. It was, we heard, that dogged silence more than the action itself that provoked the principal into consigning Elise to a session over Mina's knee.

As we assembled in preparation for the event, I was keyed up with excitement. It had been an erotic experience to see the paddling of a girl who was indifferent to me, so how much more so would be the chastising of my darling's bottom? At last she came in, barefoot in vest and shorts and stood before us, head bowed, while she was told that the stubbornness was going to be spanked out of her. The material of her clothing was a muslin fine enough for the ginger of her bush to be clearly visible, and when she had been positioned over the broad thighs of the punishing officer, it was obvious that we would see every twitch and spasm of her delightful buttocks under punishment as well as if she were naked.

I was aroused before the castigation began, and on the principal's instructions it was long and very thorough. Mina's paddle found and refound every inch of flesh on those proffered hindquarters from waist to flank to thigh and back again. The sheer protractedness of the discipline made even the plucky Elise break down in tears before it was finished, and I was nearly beside myself with desire. The recklessness of what I did next can only be explained by the imperative of lust and I still go cold when I think of it. After punishment, the spanked girl was put in a cell for a hour to reflect on the misdeeds that had brought her to that state. As was the way in our institution she was intended to remain there of her own accord; we had little use for locks and keys. Thus, on a pretext of returning to my duties in the garden, I slipped back in through a side door and tiptoed down to the basement. As I hoped, there was no one outside the cell and I opened its door to find my object. She was in my arms in a flash, then in a little I slid down her body, peeling the shorts off her glowing behind as I went, to plant my lips on her lower ones and suck the juices that were flowing. How often had I dreamed about this – the first real taste of my lover! Then our clothes were in a heap on the floor and we at last consummated our passion on the narrow bunk against the wall.

How we escaped detection I do not know, but we did. And indulging my desire for Elise's flesh emboldened me to seek satisfaction for my equally disreputable craving for discipline. So I concocted a plan. It was obvious that Mina was excited by the occasional paddlings she had to deliver and I longed to have my bottom warmed in that way. But I did not want to incur a spanking by the standard route. My work in the garden was successful enough to offer the promise of employment for me when my stay at St Nazaire was over, and I could not compromise the references I might get by bad behaviour. The question was: could Mina be persuaded that I was in need of some personal discipline without involved explanations being required? I was confident that she didn't think of spanking as sex, and as long as it stayed that way in her mind what we were doing could not be seen as a breach of chastity.

Then the idea came to me. I knew Mina regarded me with indulgence ever since they had collected me after my ordeal under the cane, and she was aware of the goings-on at St Agathe. Suppose I went to her and confessed that I had been trying to seduce Elise, to which, of course, she had not succumbed. Nevertheless I was the root cause of her naughtiness and therefore should be punished myself. But, more than that, I needed correction for all these impure thoughts I was having, perhaps even on a regular basis? That was how my mind was running, and as I describe it now the logic is flawed at best. But my little speech worked to perfection. Mina not only accepted my confession as a matter that would remain between the two of us, but she swallowed the idea that lustful thoughts could be driven out of me by the application of the leather paddle at weekly intervals. I had gambled correctly that, since she was oblivious to her own erotic pleasure in spanking, she would also fail to see my own lascivious interest in being on the receiving end of what she loved handing out.

For the next five – or was it six? – weeks I lay over Mina's knee on a Friday evening after supper while her room resounded to the smacking of leather on my thinly covered buttocks. I was in heaven. Of course the spanking hurt, and I was very tender the next day, but the fierce sting went straight to my loins and I climaxed without fail. My ecstatic writhings and cries on these occasions could have been caused by pain, so I did not worry unduly that they would lead Mina to see through my scheme. No, it was her own reactions that I was sure would be my downfall. I say *I* came to orgasm during these spankings; so did *she*, increasingly, as week followed week. Her thighs would judder and her gasps became out of all proportion to the effort of the chastisement, and I feared that it would not be long before realisation dawned. One day something would shift in her slow-moving mind and the spanking would be revealed to her eyes as the sexual act it so blatantly was.

That was the end of the page, but it clearly wasn't the end of the story. Judith had found three consecutive sheets stapled together under the title *M Bonnard 2: St Nazaire 1958–60* which brought the narrative thus far. At least she had a surname and an initial, though it was going to take a lot of patient work before the jumble of papers crammed into the box would yield a continuation. But that continuation she must have. Judith's interest in the story had grown to the point where questions of its probable authenticity were pushed aside. I'll deal with them later, she promised herself. I know it's very likely a fiction and written by a man, but for now I want to know what happens.

She turned her mind to M (Monique? Martine?), now presumably seventeen, who was shaping up to be a skilled gardener. It was the openness about her sexuality, thought Judith, that was so appealing. While she 'blamed' the birching mania of the convent school for inflaming the sensuality of the young pupils, she seemed able to accept the urges she has, whatever their origin, and act on them. OK, that last bit was complicated, but because of where she was and the rules of the place, not because of the desires themselves. With a sigh, Judith lifted out the contents of the file and spread them on her table. Would that she could contemplate her own inclinations and where they might lead with half of the reformatory girl's equanimity.

* * *

'Well, I can't be doing with that stuff at all, Marsha. Why are you always sticking up for it? I would've thought that s/m was the last thing a feminist ought to support.'

'Hold on now, Tanya. I wanna turn this round and ask you: why do you wanna stop people doing what they wanna do? What gives you the right to step in and say you can't do that?'

'I'm not saying "can't" to anyone, but surely being submissive in sex must undermine your independence. And from what I know it's all so gross. Bending over with your knickers down for six of the best from your master. I mean, puh-leez!'

Judith was feeling distinctly edgy in the midst of this argument that was taking place on Saturday night in a basement pub near to The Phoenix. At ten o'clock Marsha handed over the bar to a deputy and she and Judith had made a habit of a couple of drinks before any later plans supervened. But tonight Tanya was in tow and she was introduced as 'one of the orthodox persuasion'. It became clear that Marsha's use of that phrase was only half-joking at best, for their disagreement was basic. Then, as they sat down with their beers, what Judith had been fearing actually happened.

'Judith, Marsha said you're the one who's working at Nemesis with that woman,' said Tanya. 'How can you stand to be around all that stuff?'

'Well, I've only just finished my first week ...' Judith's words petered out lamely, and she saw the look of scorn appear on her questioner's face. Don't be so fucking feeble, she told herself. You've got to tackle this lady. 'OK, OK. I can't pretend I'm just doing it for the money. Miss James would never have taken me on if she hadn't thought I was suitable in some way. I find that "stuff", as you call it, quite uncomfortable, but something in me responds to it and I want to face up to that, not sweep it under the carpet. It's a real challenge –'

'Challenge? I don't see much of a challenge in all these women getting beaten and wallowing in it.' Then Tanya looked round at a man who was coming down the steps. She stood up, downed the rest of her bottle and took hold of her bag. 'I'd better head off,' she said. 'See you guys around.'

The women watched her take the man's arm and steer him rather quickly back the way he had come and out of the door at the top. 'Ha!' Marsha sounded bitter. 'See that. She's gotta make sure he's kept right away from these two pervy types. Who knows, maybe we'd infect him with ideas about putting darling Tanya across his knee.'

'Hey,' said Judith, putting a hand on Marsha's arm, 'don't take it to heart. After all, this is pretty dark territory: it should be no surprise people close their minds and back off. I mean, I've come far enough in a week to admit that reading about it turns me on but the whole idea still scares me to death.' She plunged into an account of the texts she had read and the unfolding story of the girl out of the convent school. 'You see the problem, Marsha,' she went on, trying to sort out her ideas. 'Lots of people could understand what she's up to without being into s/m. I mean, maybe she's a bit odd and all that, but obviously a spanking can be a very sensual thing if you forget about the humiliation side of things. So, yeah, this girl gets wet when her bottom's warmed up and it's not too hard to imagine yourself trying it out. But the Hungarian girl's flogging, that just makes people sick. And it makes *me* sick, too, only difference is I need a change of pants after reading it. So what does that make me?'

'Twisted, honey. Real twisted.' Marsha sat back and gave a belly laugh, looking more relaxed. 'What you gotta remember is that ninety-five per cent – ninety-nine per cent even – of submissives are into nothing more than the spanking that leaves a rosy glow. You're gonna get next to no volunteers for the whipping block in the town square except as a place in their heads. We're talking *fantasy*, sister, and you can't do without it even if you don't wanna actually *do* it.'

'Yeah, I suppose,' said Judith doubtfully.

'Wait a minute, now. Is all this angst just about reading stuff, or has the spectre of actual practice been shaking his gory locks?

'All too palpably to be a spectre.' Judith decided to come clean and recounted how she had seen Helen's bottom under attack and had been told to expect the same treatment if she transgressed. 'I mean, the boss must have left that door ajar deliberately. She knew I was due to come down and wanted to show me that she really does dish it out with the strap.'

'By the sound of it there's no one forcing you, Jude. What SJ has done is to give you one rule that you never need to break. If you're not late, nothing happens. In other words, the ball's in your court, sister. If you wanna plunge, she's given you the diving board. It's typical of the woman: very neat, very formal. But that's the worst of all in a way, isn't it? You've gotta make your own mind up what to do.'

Marsha signalled to the mini-skirted waitress and when she came with the beers squeezed her bottom. 'We were just talking about discipline, were we not, Jude? Well, I just wonder how long it is since this cute little rear end got a taste of leather.' Judith didn't know where to look. The waitress was new here, she was sure, but clearly not new to Marsha.

As she flushed and reached for her bottle the girl laughed. 'Don't be embarrassed for me, love,' she said to Judith, 'if I can put up with BEING GROPED IN PUBLIC –' her raised voice made several heads swivel and it was Marsha's turn to blush and drop her hand '–then it needn't bother you.' To Marsha she said, 'I'll see *you* later,' and pecked her on the cheek before moving on with her tray.

55

'Sorry. I get worse as I get older. I'm just feeling frisky with a tasty young date lined up.'

'I'm envious,' said Judith, 'though I'm still stuck on the guys. Or not, as the case may be. Do you reckon that's something else that's got to change?'

'Hey, that reminds me. Don't be in too much of a hurry to ditch your current sexual preference. I'll tell you why: because handsome hunk is back in town and will be around tomorrow night. I promised I would relay the information. As I remember, this one made a passable fist of pleasuring your ladyship the other week and I think he may be looking to repeat the performance.'

4

Refusals

It wasn't exactly what you'd call hunksville *yet*. Judith glanced up at the clock. Its hands pointed to quarter past eleven and she was leaning against the bar of The Phoenix considering the view across the collection of tables and chairs to the expanse of the dance floor beyond. Marsha had taken the night off and the new girl behind the bar was occupied with her fingernails when she wasn't serving customers, so there was no conversation to interrupt Judith's steady survey of the social scene in front of her.

There were *some* guys, all right, that might do at a pinch, but the better-appointed ones were all pretty tied up. Or tied down – it depended on how you saw it. Judith took a long swig from her bottle and returned to her scrutiny of young coupledom. Take Tanya over there, she said to herself, remembering her hasty departure from the s/m discussion. *Hers* isn't even allowed to look. She watched as a young black woman with a tumble of dark glossy hair hip-swayed past their table in a slinky dress, her bottom cheeks doing the toffee-chewing routine. His head swivelled to follow her progress while the jerk of Tanya's elbow into his ribs produced an 'Ow!' clearly audible at the bar. Judith smiled at the sideshow, but at the same time she was conscious that the undulating buttocks, so obviously naked under the clinging material, had given her a sharp tingle between the legs.

God, I'm really up for it tonight. Judith made a face to herself and emptied the remains of her bottle in one. She signalled to the barmaid, dropping a couple of coins on to the counter, and took the offered replacement from the magenta talons. Then she walked round the tables and stood just inside the disco area, facing away from the seated drinkers. The owner of the luscious behind was over on the left near the stage, swaying about in a loose group of women, black and white. As Judith eyed her she realised that she was being eyed back with a cool steady gaze. Then, before she had a chance to speculate that her randiness was making her see a come-on where none existed, she was deprived of sight altogether. A hand was clasped firmly over her eyes and there was the whiff of an astringent aftershave that she recognised at once as she felt teeth pressed, mock-biting, against the side of her neck.

She quelled her immediate impulse to tear away from the grasp and instead angled her head to offer the neck more completely. 'Take me, O master, make me yours,' Judith intoned, lugubriously. Then the jaws clamped tight, hurting, but before she could react Thomas had drawn back, grabbed her hand and was pulling her on to the polished wooden floor.

In a bare half-hour he was ready to leave and the brusqueness of his touch seemed to betray an urgent need. While Judith wanted sex too, she also wanted another beer and more time to become easy in the company of this very *un*-easy man. But seeing the instant restlessness her reluctance provoked, she gave in with as good grace as she could muster. Before they went she insisted on going to the ladies, knowing it would annoy him, but determined to assert herself in this one small particular. Once inside, the first thing she saw were the ripe globes of the black lady, jutting even more provocatively than before as she leaned over the wash basin applying a liberal coating of eyeshadow. Judith hesitated, not actually needing the use of a cubicle, and caught the woman's glance in the mirror.

'Sure you doing the right thing, girl?' She fitted the small brush back into its container and looked up again. 'I'm all alone tonight if you wanted to change your mind about partners. Name's Gwen.'

'J-Jude.' She stammered her own, taken aback by the direct proposition. 'I don't know, I mean, I can't *now*, oh, I'm not sure . . .' Judith looked down, tongue-tied.

'I don't mean you wrong to choose a man, sister. I like one myself – now and again, that is.' She took out a lipstick from her bag and removed the top. 'But that one you got, he's dangerous. And not in a nice-scary kinda way, neither.'

'I'll have to go.' Judith tried to break away but the power of the woman's sensuality was strong. 'Maybe if, maybe . . .' Again her speech died but this time she managed a move towards the exit.

'Later, Jude.' The woman had turned to face her as Judith reached the door. But she plunged on through, hearing the words: 'Just take it *easy*, honey,' before it closed behind her.

Once they were in his room, Thomas sat her down on the sofa. As if repenting of his impatience he produced a bottle of whisky, a jug of water and two glasses then sat down opposite. For a good hour they drank and talked. Rather, *she* mostly drank while *he* mostly talked, but Judith was quite content with providing the occasional comment. His conversation may have lacked warmth, but the alcohol was giving her that and his stories were making her laugh. By the time he had finished an account of his adventures and misadventures at the literary conference in Glasgow the previous week,

Judith was enough at ease to be getting quite turned on by the movements of his muscular body.

After one more dram – this time he matched her consumption – Thomas took her hands and pulled her gently to her feet. Nuzzling into Judith's neck he shucked up her short black dress and slipped his hands into her knickers. The hardness of his cock pushed into her soft belly as he pressed against her and she could feel herself lubricating in response. Then Thomas stood back. 'Please,' he said, 'I would like to try something.'

He moved aside the coffee table they had been using and in its place installed an upright wooden chair with arms, that he took from the corner. Then he guided Judith up to its high back and bent her forwards over it, positioning her elbows on the broad arms. Hers was alarmingly like the stance of one about to be disciplined, but mellowed by the whisky Judith let the twinge of anxiety dissipate. She felt Thomas's careful fingers folding up the dress, then the pants were drawn right down, and she lifted one foot after the other to allow their complete removal.

Then his lips and tongue were exploring the whole surface of her behind from flank to furrow to farther flank. The image of the rear end that had been in front of her in the ladies surfaced in Judith's mind: Christ, how she would like to do this to her! The incongruity of the thought in the face of Thomas's present activities almost made her giggle but, as Judith tried to restrain her slightly tipsy imagination, his hands started to work and her mind emptied. He stroked and kneaded rhythmically so that the masses of her buttocks were lifted, separated and squeezed together in turn. Then his thumbs were on her labia, spreading them, and she felt his breath on the wet flesh he had exposed. Letting go, he manipulated the flesh of her inner thighs until her clitoris throbbed and she began to make small writhing movements. Two stinging slaps pierced her but before she could cry out in protest his tongue was on her burning bud and his teeth nipped it and the impossible pleasure-pain racked her body in spasm upon spasm.

Afterwards he held her for a while, though she knew better than to try and kiss. She could feel his erection again and when his hands pressed down on her shoulders she knew what he wanted and dropped to her knees in front of him. 'Your turn,' said Thomas and Judith pulled back, bridling. How dare he tell her to do what she had been about to do of her own accord. But she wanted more yet from the night, so reined in her pride and reached for the fastening on his leather trousers. Under them he was naked and his cock sprang out at her once the zip came down. Taking hold of the stem, she eased back the foreskin and a gobbet of clear fluid hung there before she took the whole thing into her mouth.

Judith had done this but twice before, both times drunk and both times with men who made a pig's ear of fucking her. Now she was (relatively) sober and could recall the feel of this prick's hardness moving in her cunt until she came. So to have the thing between her lips was a kind of completion and the whole idea of it was making her ooze afresh with desire. Then Thomas cried out and Judith felt the organ pulsing and tasted the hot salt semen on her tongue.

'Swallow it –' he ground out the words between his teeth and grabbed her hair '–swallow it!' At the peremptory command everything inside Judith reared up in blind absolute refusal. She wrenched her head away and felt hair tearing at the roots, gathered herself, and spat the contents of her mouth at him. There was a second of frozen stillness where Judith took in the sight of the deflating, dribbling penis and above it the gouts of milky liquid she had sprayed amongst the black belly hairs. Then he smacked her across the face with the

61

palm of his left hand, hard. Judith staggered up and rushed at him; he lost his balance and fell back across the wooden chair behind him. In a single lunge she swept up her shoes and reached the door. Then she was down the stairs and out into the street. As she ran she thought: he can have the knickers, it's all he'll *ever* have now. Then at the corner the shock hit her and she doubled up and retched until her stomach was empty.

It was three in the morning before Judith opened the door of the flat and slumped down at the kitchen table. Her head ached and she still felt sick but worse than either of those was the insistent voice in her head, despite her common sense, that said: 'If you'd just taken your medicine, you'd be in his bed riding on a nice hard cock *right now*.' At that she felt the tears well up in earnest and Judith laid her head on her arms and sobbed.

Then Catherine's arm was round her shoulders, helping her through to the bathroom where, under the light, she peered at Judith's face. All she said was, 'Uh-oh,' and began to run the cold tap. Grateful to be spared a cross-examination, Judith gave herself up to her flatmate's care. The bruise was bathed and inspected then she was undressed and put to bed. Cat appeared with two pills and a glass of water. 'These will reduce the swelling.' As she swallowed Judith thought of her earlier refusal to do just that and nearly choked, tears pricking once more, but this time the medicine went down.

'Oh, God, Cat, I've got to work tomorrow,' said Judith helplessly. Her friend gave her a hug and fetched her own alarm clock which sported two large brass bells with hammers.

'Now lie down, Jude,' she said after winding it up and setting the time. 'I'm on at six so I'll see you when you get back.' Judith stretched out and closed her eyes, thinking sleep to be impossible; then almost at once she knew no more.

She woke with a start, the loud *tick! tick! tick!* from the bedside table unfamiliar in her ears. Something was wrong. Oh, fuck! The evening's events with the violent terminus of their lovemaking came back in a rush and Judith slumped back on her pillows, feeling sick all over again. Then she looked at the clock. Oh, fuck, fuck, fuck! Ten past ten and she had been due at Nemesis forty minutes ago. She leaped out of bed and splashed her face with water; then the bathroom mirror had another shock in store. If she set aside the turmoil of the night's memories and the self-castigation for sleeping through the alarm, her head was clear, yet the whole side of her face was discoloured. More a black cheek than a black eye, she thought, gingerly touching the sore area. Then, pulling herself up, Judith went back to the bedroom, threw on what clothes first came to hand and headed out of the door to face the music.

Miss James was not in her office when Judith arrived, so she fretted in her alcove for the rest of the morning, unable to settle to any sustained work. At 12.30 she went down the spiral staircase and opened the door to the secretary's office. Helen looked up, eyes widening at the marked face, then buzzed the intercom.

'Judith is here, Miss James.' After listening for a moment she said, 'Go on in,' and Judith was sure she detected a relish in the tone.

As she stepped into the inner sanctum, the door closed with a soft thud behind her. Samantha James raised her head from a pile of papers. 'What can I do for you, Judith?' she asked, the slight arch of one eyebrow the only indication that she had seen anything unusual in her employee's appearance. For a wild moment Judith entertained the idea of saying nothing about her lateness, but then she thought that even if

63

Helen didn't split on her she had no confidence in her ability to hide the misdemeanour from the sharp eyes now observing her.

'Miss James, I was an hour late this morning. I'm sorry. It won't happen again.' There, she'd got it out. Heart thumping, Judith felt absurdly elated, as if mere confession would wipe out the consequence of her action. The older woman stared at her for a moment before she spoke, and what she said brought the young woman's hopes crashing to the ground.

'Very well, Judith. I think you should take the rest of the week to work at home until your bruising fades. Thank you for telling me of your fault. Of course, I accept your apology, but you must realise that does not end the matter. I believe I was quite clear about the penalty I favour for what you have done, although you have the option to choose dismissal. Go and collect your things now; I shall expect you here at nine o'clock a week today to answer to me.'

The following morning, Judith sat at the kitchen table staring into her cup of coffee. Catherine's bed had not been slept in and she felt alone and miserable in the empty flat. There must have been a change of shift at her hospital placement that left her just enough time to get a short kip on the premises before she was on again. So there was no effervescent blonde presence to lighten Judith's mood as she contemplated the fact that in less than a week she must offer herself for corporal punishment or lose her job. She shook her head frowning as she thought again of how it was her pride that had led, if indirectly, to this situation, so what chance was there she could subdue it sufficiently to ask Miss James to strap her like a naughty schoolgirl?

Then Judith had an idea. She got up and retrieved from the bedroom the large box file she had brought home from work. Opening the lid, she removed the sheet that identified the contents as the notes and observations of Dr Brown and placed the untidy pile in front of her. *M Bonnard*. That was what she needed. More of the story of this intelligent young woman, unaccountably – as yet – speaking to a psychologist, who was so frank about the whole area of sexuality and discipline. Suddenly eager, Judith began to riffle through the collection of disparate and often dog-eared items. Then, in just half an hour, she came up with the prize: a sheaf of pages, this time handwritten in ink, that at first glance seemed to be consecutive. Scrawled across the top was *Marie B*. Marie. So that was her name. While there was no kind of introduction, Judith remembered the girl's interest in gardening and what she read made perfect sense.

The work was to be for two days a week at first as a kind of apprenticeship with the old man who had charge of the grounds of the house. As I learned more he would do less until, in perhaps a year or two, I would take over. Madame Dauvignon was the mistress of the house, a commanding figure whether on horseback or on foot in her habitual breeches. There was a husband, people said, but he had not returned from Paris in the last two years. I adored madame at once, not only because she had given me an opportunity few others would have countenanced, but for the way this handsome woman of forty treated me, a reformatory girl of eighteen, with total seriousness. She talked to me about her fruit trees, or the onion beds as if my views were of equal weight to hers, and I loved her for it.

After some three months it was early summer and my labour had doubled, though I was still resident at the reformatory. While I walked back at night across the fields, the postman delivered me with the mail and the newspapers in the morning. Then one afternoon I returned to the outbuilding that served as my head-quarters to find madame holding an object that was to change my life for a second time. It was a birch rod, a scrappy thing that she was examining with distaste. I learned that one of the kitchen maids and the housemaid had been caught in a state of undress with two boys from the village. The lads had run off before they were identified, leaving the girls to suffer for their actions. Madame had sent them to the wood to gather the materials for two rods which they were to bind themselves, but the results were the feeble instruments we saw.

Memories of the convent school came back in a rush and to cover my emotion I blurted out that I could do a much better job for her if she wished. Madame looked curiously at me saying that she thought the reformatory had no use for such a thing. She was right, of course, but I explained that the convent school I had been dismissed from (she knew of my scandalous past, which made her acceptance of me all the more wonderful in my eyes) had frequent recourse to the birch. I went on to say that we had been taught to put two cuttings from a lime tree in with four of birch to give extra strength and bite to the whole. My enthusiasm for this form of punishment must have showed for I noticed Madame watching me with an odd expression. However, she said nothing except that I should make two instruments in the manner I had described and steep them in the bucket of brine she had placed in the corner. She indicated a wooden trestle newly positioned in the centre of the floor where the chastisement would take place and told me to attend at noon the next day to witness it.

At the appointed hour I was waiting with the groom and the new stable boy when the miscreants were brought in between the cook and another maid.

Madame did not lecture the girls but said simply that in many households they would have been dismissed, so she expected them to submit to two dozen strokes each if not with good grace at least without a struggle. They curtsied, looking very contrite, then the first was led to the wooden frame and bent over it. Cook guided the girl's hands to the lower strut and told her to grip it firmly. Then she raised the skirt and petticoat and folded it down, leaving the whole area between the tops of the knee stockings and the small of the back completely uncovered. By this time my excitement was making me press my legs together. I had seen bottoms spanked in shorts at St Nazaire, but two years had passed since I had seen a girl's buttocks and thighs bared for the birch.

Madame took a dripping rod from the bucket, shook it and swished it down across the target. As the whipping proceeded, the initial gasps turned into small cries but the girl kept in place until the end. It was not a severe punishment but enough to streak the hind cheeks deep red and bring tears to their owner's eyes. The second maid was similarly treated and was equally stoical, though I fancied that the plumper flesh on display prompted harder strokes from the chastiser. My lustful condition was acute when the second birch was finished with and I was relieved when the maids were asked if they had learned their lesson and then dismissed with the rest of the company. Madame stood in the doorway for a moment and my heart lurched at how beautiful, how alive she was! Then she turned and stared at me and I realised suddenly that I must look as flushed and excited as she did. Madame took my arm and led me outside. In the sunlight she told me she would like me to move into the house, if that was what I wanted. I nodded, not trusting myself to speak, and she bade me go now and collect together my things so as to be ready for the trap she would send at four. I headed straight for the fields and as soon as I was out of sight of the house I lowered my trousers. Squatting down, I used my hand to release all the pent-up lust while in my mind's eye round buttocks twitched and reddened under the rod I had fashioned myself.

I was installed in my room by the end of the afternoon. It was on the ground floor at the back of the house, opening directly on to the yard across which my tools and equipment were housed, and where the birchings had taken place. I was thinking of these events sitting on my bed after supper when there was a knock and madame came in to see if I was settled. While I expressed my gratitude, she looked closely at me and I felt she could see right into the sensual images in my head. As if to confirm my fear, Madame went to the door and turned the key then told me to follow her. I watched astonished as she pressed a wall panel beside the fireplace whereupon a concealed doorway swung open. She led the way up a narrow spiral staircase and we emerged in her bedroom whose outer door she locked as she had mine.

My thoughts were in a turmoil as madame took my hands in hers and explained solemnly that there were some young women in this world who have a need for physical discipline and without it they do not thrive. She said she had formed the opinion that I was one such and proposed to act on it, provided, of course, that I consented. I was overwhelmed at her understanding of me and quite unable to voice my feelings. Madame, however, must have divined what they were for she went to a drawer and took out a martinet. Then she placed a dressing table stool in the centre of the carpet and told me to prepare myself. My boots had been left inside the door of my own room and I slipped my trousers down over my stockinged feet and stepped out of them. I knelt down and lay across the stool, pulling my shirt up under my arms at the same time. I was ready.

Madame began almost gently as if to let me get the measure of this new instrument, whose effect at first was like the bite of tiny insects. As her strokes grew harder I gasped and then cried out with the fierce sting of it, but at the same time it was wonderful to be bared and offered up to my beloved mistress. She whipped me until I was wet with tears, but I would have died rather than stop her. Afterwards I sat on her lap while she held me and stroked my hair until I had become calm, then I was dismissed back down the hidden staircase to my bed. When several days had gone by I was summoned again and we continued in this way for some weeks. Rather as I had once before lain across Mina's lap (a practice thankfully discontinued before that scheme of mine was exposed), what madame did was a kind of chaste lovemaking. Save for her hugs, and they were what you would give to a child, her only touch was to lay a cool hand for a moment on my burning flesh when the martinet had done its work. But I had the impression that she knew well what my feelings were and shared them but for some reason was deliberately holding herself back. In any case, it was all to change before the year's end, and in a way that would seal our –

Judith was startled out of her reading by the sound of the flat door banging shut and Catherine bubbled into the kitchen in a halo of blonde curls. 'Hi, Jude, and how's the shiner coming on?' She bent to take a closer look and Judith made an effort to pull herself back from the image of a bourgeois bedroom where a young woman gave herself up to her mistress to be whipped.

'Oh, my, that's a real beauty. Is it very sore?'

'No, it's not as bad as it looks. Cat, there's –'
She was about to launch into an explanation of what
had happened when her flatmate beat her to it.

'Jude, what are you doing home at this time of day?'
Catherine stood still, holding her shoulder bag and
Judith could see her mind working. 'Oh, no, *Judith*, you
didn't, did you?'

Her friend just nodded grimly.

'But that alarm would wake the stiffs in the mortu-
ary.' She shook her head in disbelief, then made the final
step. 'Oh, God, that means you broke the golden rule
and, and –'

'– *and* I've got to report for the penalty next Monday
morning. Or lose my job. Oh, Cat, what am I going to
do?'

In reply Catherine dumped her bag on the table and
fished out a loaf, cheese and four cans of Becks. 'The
first thing you're gonna do, girl, is share my lunch. I bet
you've had nothing all morning.' She pulled the ring on
a can and passed it over. 'Now drink this – nurse's
orders, better than doctor's – and stop panicking.
Monday's a long way off.'

They cleared a space among the spread-out papers
and Judith was suddenly ravenous. So for the next half
hour she wolfed down hunks of fresh bread and brie,
interspersed with gulps of lager while she was entertained with salacious tales of the intrigues among staff
and students at St Joseph's. When the food and drink
she had provided was all gone, Cat swept away the
débris and made a move to restore the manuscripts to
their former position. 'Ooh!' she cried out, lighting on
one particular page, 'is this to do with that convent girl
you were on about?'

'Yes,' said Judith. She shuffled through the largest
pile in front of her and produced another set of pages.
'And here's the second part of it. Why don't you have
a look and tell me if you think it's for real? But *now* . . .'

'OK, OK, you want to do some work.' Catherine took the hint and scooped up the two documents. 'I'll leave you in peace. I need a nap so I'll give you a report later.' With that she disappeared into her bedroom, shutting the door, and Judith turned her attention back to the interrupted story.

One warm summer's day I sat in my tool shed cleaning a hoe, when through the open window I heard shouts from the stables across the backyard. Then came a noise I thought I recognised, and when I heard it again and yet again, each time followed by a sharp cry, I was sure. It was the sound of leather striking flesh and it set my pulse racing! Madame's regular whippings had left me in a sensual state unrelieved by the lovemaking of the convent days and the thought of the stable boy's bare buttocks under the strap made me giddy. In a minute or two the noise stopped, then the boy himself ran past my window and pounded up the outside steps to his quarters directly above where I was at work.

Jean was around my age and had made advances to me before. These I had brushed aside, believing myself to be well fixed in my attraction to my own sex and particularly, of course, to my mistress. But in my heightened state I had to get closer, so I crept up the steps to his door, which was standing ajar. Through the gap I had a back view of him rubbing his scarlet behind, breeches round his knees. Then he turned sideways on and I saw his organ standing straight out in front of him, hard, and I was in the room beside him before he could cover himself. It grew even harder when I took it in my hand and I examined the first erect penis I had seen with some interest. After his initial shock at my appearance he let me do as I wished and as I squeezed him I inspected

71

the well-tanned bottom-cheeks that throbbed with heat under my other hand.

I don't know what came over me then for I dropped my trousers and bent forwards over the table, scooping up a finger of saddle soap that lay in a dish and pressing in into my behind. I had never been penetrated in that place before but I knew it would not make me pregnant and the idea filled me with a wild excitement. Jean responded immediately (I thought later of our old convent jokes about what boys did with boys when they couldn't get girls) and pressed his stiffness against the opening but my muscle was tight. Then he pushed hard and suddenly he was inside me and I felt his spasms almost at once. When he pulled out he lifted me up and began to caress between my legs until I was almost frantic with lust, then pushed me back down and entered me again. This time the thrusting was long and pleasurable and I came to a tremendous climax.

In this way my bottom was the centre of attention right through the hot summer: at weekends I bared it for Madame's loving lash and often twice during the week I bared it for Jean's stiff organ to probe. I could have continued like this with some satisfaction, but I knew that – however perverse it sounds – that my natural inclination was to make love with a woman. But without my intending it, matters were brought to a head one day in early autumn when we were discovered in the act of coupling. I was across Jean's table as usual, eyes closed as he thrust into me, when the door was flung open with a crash against the wall. It was madame and we sprang apart, frantically pulling up our clothes. Without a word she dragged both of us to the door and pushed us down the stairs and across the yard.

I had never seen my mistress so angry. She had become quite white and in an icy-cold voice ordered the startled groom to thrash the boy until she stopped him. She forced Jean down over a workbench and pinioned his shoulders, telling me to take down his breeches and hold on to his legs. I knelt and wrapped my arms tightly round his knees and pulled back, so that he was stretched between the two of us. It was a long, hard beating and I watched horrified as the buttocks right in front of me turned from pink to red to purple under the relentless strokes of the thick strap. Twice the groom looked at madame, as if expecting her to call a halt, but she motioned impatiently for him to continue. Eventually a trickle of blood started down the right flank, which had taken the brunt of the curling leather tip, and madame declared it was enough. Poor Jean, whose voice had almost gone with screaming, was helped up and escorted limping to his quarters.

Now it was my turn and I was led back across the yard into my own room. Madame went up the spiral staircase and returned with a martinet; not, alas, her customary instrument but one possessing much more substantial thongs. Her eyes still blazing, she ordered me over the stool, and I trembled with fear as I took off my boots and trousers. Once I was in place she stood in front of me, not as usual at the side, and gripped my head between her thighs. She told me to keep my legs tight together and began to rain down lashes on my buttocks, flanks and thighs. The pain was intense and while she whipped she cursed me for doing something that might put at risk my position and my opportunities. In the midst of my agonised screechings, I suddenly understood her fury: she thought I could be pregnant! So I yelled and yelled for her to stop, yelled that I hadn't done that, yelled that he wasn't in there, where it might make a baby.

Understanding dawned eventually. Madame threw down the whip, drew me up and folded me in her arms saying over and over how sorry she was, how she should have known I would be sensible and could I bring myself to forgive her. My pains were forgotten as I looked into the eyes of my beloved mistress and we kissed properly for the first time. Transported by emotion in the aftermath of my chastisement, I made her sit while I took off her boots. Then I unbuttoned her breeches and eased them down so that she could step out of them. Kneeling in front of madame, I pulled down her silk knickers and pushed my face into her thick black bush. It was soaked in her juices and I applied my tongue to the nether lips until she gasped out her climax. This was my only experience of the secret parts of a mature woman and their taste and scent went straight to my head. After a little she placed me over her lap and soothed my burning weals with an aromatic cream, her fingers playing all the while between my legs until I too reached my peak.

Later, back in my room, I thought of Jean, regrettably quite forgotten in my erotic excitement, and I slipped out to visit him. By the moon shining through his window – we dared not risk lighting a lamp – I could see his well-swollen behind that he said was too painful to sit on. But he was not in bad spirits and when I smoothed some of my own ointment on his cheeks he was soon hard. I let him come inside me for what would be a last meeting, as a kind of consolation for what he had suffered. I was expecting to be a proper lover to my mistress now that we had explored each other so intimately but, as it turned out – oh, God, I can't bear to think of it – that was not to be.

It was after midnight when I settled into my bed and drifted uneasily into sleep. I do not remember what woke me but I was suddenly aware of raised voices and they were coming from the half-open door to my end of the spiral staircase.

This last paragraph was barely decipherable and beneath it was an added line in pencilled capitals that had been inscribed forcefully enough to break its point. It read, I CAN'T GO ON WITH THIS.

It was the end of the narrative and Judith bit her lip in frustration. *Who* couldn't go on: Marie telling the story or the Dr Brown who was writing it? But more important was the question of what happened next. She felt sure it must be bad – there had been an early mention of disaster – and where did a psychologist come in? Well, if she had died – that was what Miss James said, wasn't it? – then the only hope of more about Marie was in the bundles scattered around her. Yawning, Judith laid her head on her arms and tried to think about how you could tell if this was a true story, short of tracking down the characters in it and getting their versions of events. It was undoubtedly erotic in the effect it had on her, but that didn't mean it was invented for the purpose. And even if it was pornography – in the sense of the author intending to turn the reader on – that still didn't mean that the things in it didn't actually happen as described. The convolutions of these thoughts proved too much in the sleepy mid-afternoon and Judith drifted off where she sat amongst confused images of embraces on spiral staircases and trysts with red-bottomed stable boys sporting huge erections . . .

She came to with a jolt, arms stiff and head muzzy. Cat was in the kitchen gesticulating with a bunch of papers. 'Hey, Jude, wake up! It's six o'clock, girl. I just read this and is it sexy or is it *fucking* sexy?' She squatted on the edge of the table in a T-shirt, dropped the pages and put a hand on Judith's wrist. It was warm and its owner was tousled from her bed. 'God, all those juicy young bodies being birched, and then afterwards . . .' Catherine's eyes were shining and she stood up, producing from behind her back an old gym shoe. 'It's all I can find. Go on. Take it. I've got to know what this discipline stuff is all about.'

Judith watched open-mouthed as her flatmate hiked up her top and bent over, holding her ankles. With her legs spread, the view was identical to the one in the bathroom that had stayed in her mind for weeks. But this time what Cat wanted was plain and Judith's heart sank.

'Go *on*, girl. Give it a go!' The doubled-up form swivelled to address her audience. 'Maybe that's what you need, Jude. Dish it out instead of take it.' Judith was rooted to the spot, appalled. She could no more take hold of the intended implement than she could have grasped a red-hot poker. But Cat was clearly consumed with excitement.

'OK, girl, OK. If you're not up for actual spanking, then just pet me a bit, huh? Like we'll pretend you've already whacked me and you're going to make it all better.' Judith's insides knotted in despair: why couldn't the girl see how fucked-up she was about all this? Then she found her voice.

'Oh, Cat, no, no, no, no! Don't you understand? I *can't*.' She dived across the kitchen, took one step to clear the small hallway then slammed the bedroom door behind her. She fell face-down and buried her head under the pillow, lying clenched and aching until she was sure her friend had gone to bed. Then, exhausted, she fell into an uneasy doze.

The rest of the week dragged by. Judith had no heart for deciphering the scrawl that covered most of the sheets in her box and Catherine had clearly taken offence. She was in and out of the flat with scarcely a word and for three nights she did not return at all. But with a grim inevitability Monday morning came and it was with a heavy heart that Judith let herself out of the building and walked in the direction of Nemesis. She had rehearsed a hundred times the performance required of her in the director's office but however she played it in her head it lacked the crucial scene on which the whole thing turned: the one where she dropped her trousers and draped herself over the tall desk. Judith could get it from the outside, so to speak, for she knew what Helen had looked like in that position, but she could not get her mind to compute the image with herself in the key role of disciplinee.

Standing in actuality before Samantha James, Judith knew for certain what she had feared all week: she could not redeem herself in the way demanded. There was no point in dissembling, so she took a deep breath and spoke. 'Miss James, I can't do it. I'm sorry, but I *can't*.'

There was a two-tailed tawse of black leather lying in front of her and the director picked it up in her two hands. She rose to her feet and came round the desk, holding the instrument out. 'Take it and feel it,' she said, a tall commanding figure all in black. Judith shrank back a little but in spite of herself did as she was told. It was warm and slightly greasy to the touch and the density of the thing shocked her. She could imagine all too vividly its supple weight smacking into soft buttock-flesh and gave a shudder. But along with the repugnance the punishment strap engendered in her was an erotic stab of arousal, and it was no doubt the latter that Miss James was aiming to produce. Judith made herself hand it back and looked up into the director's eyes, her insides churning.

'I can't.'

The older woman held the tawse by her side and moved back, her eyebrows raised. '*Can't?*'

'All right,' said Judith. 'I suppose I mean *won't*. I won't.' The word hung between them: it was indeed her refusal to submit, although a part of her wanted – and wanted so much – to present the lewdest nakedness to the leather's bite.

'Well, one day, perhaps you *will*.' Miss James walked away to the heavy door at the back of the room and turned. 'Please leave your keys with Helen on the way out. And you can tell her to come right through, since *her* appointment will now be a little earlier than I had planned.' So saying, she slapped the implement against her thigh and disappeared into the back room.

PART II

PART II

5

Fundamentals

'So, you're telling me that, in effect, you *quit*?' The bar manager of The Phoenix put down the glass she was rinsing and looked up. 'Honey, I wouldn't say that was exactly facing up to these inner demons we were talking about; more like turning your back, covering your eyes and praying they'll just go away.'

Judith laughed, though there was precious little to be cheerful about. She was drinking a much needed beer early on Saturday night to toast the eventual end of the week. It had been the second one in a row to crawl by: the first spent in fearing the worst and the next in regretting its occurrence. 'Oh, yes, I really fucking blew it.' Judith sighed and drained her bottle; at once there was a replacement beside it.

'On the house,' said Marsha, wiping her hands with a cloth. 'Get it down you and think positive, girl.'

'Not so easy,' said Judith. 'It isn't just being kicked out of Nemesis. Yesterday I got a note from my flatmate saying she was going to be away till the end of next month. In fact, she didn't exactly say she was coming back *at all*.' Catching Marsha's look, she added: 'I don't think you've ever met Catherine, have you?'

'Oh, yes, I have, Jude. I have indeed. Though from what you say I take it she didn't tell you?'

Judith shook her head, apprehensive at what was coming next. 'I've hardly seen her lately.'

'Well, she phoned me ten days ago asking about the s/m stuff I do now and then. We met up and had quite a talk.' Marsha glanced round the room which was empty except for a couple in the far corner and leaned closer. 'Jude, under her bubbly manner, that girl is really stuck on you. I don't suppose you had any idea, huh?'

'Oh, God,' said Judith. She wilted under the older woman's steady grey eyes, thinking of Cat's bathroom display and the sex 'therapy' before her interview.

'You know, you didn't even discuss with her what a bastard the hunk turned out to be. Imagine what she felt like, getting the whole story from me, when she was the one who looked after you at the time.' Marsha made a sour face and ran a hand over her cropped hair. 'So my guess would be she's retreated to lick her wounds.'

'Oh, God.' Stricken with guilt, Judith recounted the episode with the gym shoe. 'It's so pathetic, Marsha. I just ran away.'

'Shit, it's worse than I thought. No fucking wonder the girl is hiding from you, Jude. She really went out on a limb there and what did she get from you in return?' Marsha gave a loud snort. 'A slap in the face – instead of the one on the bottom she was angling for!'

In spite of herself Judith laughed again, but the image of Cat vulnerable and hurt cast her back down at once. Then the door swung open and Judith swivelled on her seat. It was the barmaid with the fingernails that had been the unwitting start of an eventful twenty-four hours.

'Hi there, Melissa,' called Marsha.

'Hi, folks.' The young woman turned her head as she went through to the back.

'Hey, Jude,' said Marsha, 'I have an idea. *If* you're going to try and sort yourself out, it's no good moping around in an empty flat all day, *or* spending money you don't have drinking too much beer. Right?' Judith stuck

82

out her tongue, but she was listening. 'So how about going for another job till you start back in October?'

As Judith opened her mouth to protest that jobs were few and far between, the barmaid reappeared and came over.

'Liss,' said Marsha, 'do you still need someone to take over from you next week?'

'Fucking right.' She pulled up another bar stool and sat down. 'I'll get a Pils before I go on, Marsha. And whatever you and your pal are having.' The Scots accent was strong and there was a tough manner to go with it.

'Jude. Thanks, I'll have another Becks. Is it, er, Liss?'

'Aye. The name I was given's a mouthful. Like the place I was working; was, that is, if I can find someone to step in.'

'Eumenides, Incorporated.' Marsha wrinkled her nose. 'In the old hall of residence that was done up a few years back. Melissa was a sort of general dogsbody for the boss – she's from the States, too – just the kind of thing to keep you out of mischief for the rest of the summer. Wouldn't you say, Liss?' There was something odd about her manner and Judith thought for a moment that a meaningful glance flashed between the two women.

But Melissa said breezily: 'I'll call round first thing Monday and show you the ropes. You'd be doing me a real favour to take it on.'

'That sounds ace,' said Marsha. 'Benefits all round. So there you are, Judith. How can you refuse?'

As promised, Melissa was on the doorstep at 8.30 a.m. The long magenta nails still caught the eye but now they were framed by an immaculate white blouse and a dark skirt, making Judith glad she had chosen the relatively formal, if close-fitting, black trousers she had worn to her last interview. Since they reminded her both of Catherine and the lost place at Nemesis, she was not in the best of spirits, but she tried to pay attention to what

Liss was saying as they walked. It seemed that she would be basically an errand girl for Ms Morris. Aye, you had to call her *miz*, everybody did, no exceptions. But she was a real lady and the pay was bloody good for what you did. But niggling at the back of Judith's mind as she listened to the chatter was the company's name: *Eumenides*. She couldn't get rid of the feeling that she had seen it somewhere recently, and its English version – the Furies – sounded more familiar than her scanty knowledge of Greek mythology should have made it. There was the worry, too, that Melissa's explanations about how she was needed suddenly at a German subsidiary of the parent outfit just didn't add up. How was a 'dogsbody' so important, and why hadn't it all been organised in-house? But her ruminations were cut short as they turned a corner and stood at the gatehouse of the converted St Mary's Hall.

Liss lifted a catch to open a small door in the expanse of wrought iron; the two young women bent their heads and went through in turn. Across the quadrangle they climbed a dozen steps and entered the main building through a set of revolving doors. Inside, an ornate staircase swept round to the right and away up into the glass-domed vault two floors above, but more striking than the architectural feature itself was the figure descending it. Her tall, spare build was clothed in a light grey suit and the ash-blonde hair hung in a bob that swayed slightly as she moved towards them. With the gleam of emeralds at her throat and the palest of lilac lips, the whole bespoke money and taste.

'Melissa, my dear! Good morning. And is this the young lady you are offering as a replacement?' There were the vestiges of a Southern accent that chimed with a certain languor in the movements, but the eyes that now fixed on Judith were far from lazy. She felt herself probed from head to toe in a way that had her blushing by the time she took the offered hand.

'Ms Morris, Judith Wilson; Judith, Ms Estelle Morris.' Melissa's introductions would not have been out of place at a formal reception.

'Now Judith – I may call you that, I hope? – I look forward to a proper talk with you later. For the present I am going to pass you over to my right-hand man in matters of internal administration. He will show you round and deliver you back to me. Ah, here he comes, with perfect timing. Mr Jennings, will you meet my prospective assistant, Ms Wilson?'

As the man in question crossed the hall towards them, Judith sensed Liss stiffen beside her. He was a grey-haired man of fifty or so with a pencil moustache, wearing a blazer and flannels. Her first impressions were not improved by his handshake which was clinging without being firm, nor by his free use of her first name as they greeted each other without in turn offering his own. Then he said to Liss, 'Such a pity you will leave without sampling my equipment downstairs.' It was almost an aside, delivered with a greasy smile, and she glared at him without replying.

'Will you come with me, Melissa?' Ms Morris spoke again, seemingly oblivious to the exchange. 'Since you have brought me a *very* presentable substitute –' she smiled at Judith who blushed again '– we have some final business to attend to.' Now it was Liss who reddened and her boss gave a little laugh. 'My dear, let us go before you look any more fetching. You make me quite impatient.' She put an arm around the young woman's shoulders and they set off up the stairs, leaving Judith puzzled as to what exactly it all meant. But she was not inclined to ask Mr Jennings for elucidation and when he bade her follow him through to the back she did so in silence.

Judith was quite glad when the 'tour' was over and they approached the door of the basement office. There had been nothing to see except a number of workers at their keyboards and a number of rooms containing boxes stamped EUMENIDES in large letters. Nor had her guide explained anything, taking the opportunity instead to deliver some homilies on the indisciplined upbringing of young women today, so Judith had interrupted to ask exactly what was the business that the company pursued. The question stopped his flow momentarily but she was none the wiser with the (she was sure intentional) vagueness of the answer that they dealt in 'information technology' and 'specialist goods'.

Now as they stood side by side Mr Jennings reiterated his belief in firm measures. With one hand he pulled a bunch of keys from his pocket while with the other he squeezed Judith's behind, quite slowly and deliberately in four or five different places. She froze: it wasn't the surreptitious kind of grope she commonly received in crowded public transport, but a systematic exploration of the size and weight of her arse. He made no comment but simply opened the door and stepped back, removing his touch. Judith was at a loss: she didn't want to cross the man on the first day in the place and, besides, the boss would no doubt expect him to report on her. But she could not help her dismay that the powerful and beautiful Estelle Morris should employ such a lieutenant. Then his phone shrilled and he ducked in ahead of her to pick up the receiver.

'Yes, Mrs Butler. Of course, Mrs Butler. Stay right there, I'll be with you very shortly.' He came back out and spoke to Judith. 'Please go in and sit down. I shall be five minutes at the most.' His manner contained no acknowledgement of anything untoward in his recent behaviour and he walked jauntily out into the corridor. Once the sound of his steps had died away, Judith sat down heavily in the swivel chair and stared about her. It was a plain office with two steel cabinets and a compact armchair in the corner. The surface of the desk was empty except for a letter about the central heating system and an open appointments diary. Resisting the temptation to scan through it, Judith looked up at the contents of a raised shelf at the back. Among the half-dozen books was one called *The Female Disciplinary Manual* and Judith took it down. Inside was the subtitle *An Encyclopaedia of the Correction of the Fair Sex*, though there was no author given. But the publisher's name at the foot of the page made her sit up – Eumenides, Inc – and as she investigated further the book fell open at a heading that set her pulse racing: *Using the Cane.*

Judith closed the volume with a snap and replaced it. She told herself that this man's predilections were no concern of hers, after all, she wasn't going to work for *him*. But the idea that his hand had been assessing her flesh for the purposes detailed in that well-thumbed chapter gave her a sexual charge she would rather not have felt and, uncomfortable, Judith got up. Then she noticed a connecting door to the left that stood ajar and, after a quick check that the corridor was quite empty, she stuck her head round it and peered in. It was difficult to make out much in the gloom so she plucked up courage, eased the door wide open and stepped inside. There was a smell of whitewash and Judith saw bare walls and a tiled floor, but what made her scalp tingle was the object in the centre of the room that was illuminated in the shaft of light from the doorway. She had not seen such a thing before, but the manuscripts she had perused at Nemesis had contained several descriptions that left her in little doubt of what she was looking at: it was a punishment horse. The device stood waist-high with a padded body about four feet long, and when Judith caught sight of the straps and buckles that hung from its four sturdy legs she knew she was right. Her imagination at once furnished her with a picture of a woman fastened in place, shrieking as a switch lashed her naked buttocks, and for a moment she was rooted to the spot in appalled fascination.

Then there were voices and steps approaching and Judith whirled round. Damn, damn damn! She was too late to get back into the office, so there was only one thing for it. Quickly she pushed the door to behind her and headed for the one she had noticed opposite. It opened and she was in a lavatory, and – with more luck than she thought she deserved – at the back of it a light glowed above the emergency exit. Pressing down on the bar she swung it out enough to reveal an empty passage beyond, but once having identified her escape route Judith let it swing back and quietly re-engaged the latch. She could hear the rise and fall of voices and was consumed with curiosity. What were the repulsive Mr Jennings and his 'assistant' up to? Holding her breath, she opened the door she had come in by, little by little until she could make out the words being spoken with her ear to the crack. By the sound of it they were still in the office, though with the connecting door standing wide.

'Well, Mrs Butler, the young lady seems to have gone. I tell you, this generation has no patience; we can only have taken the five minutes that I said. A good-looking girl too, I thought, but sorely in need of some of my special treatment.' Judith shivered at the emphasis on the word, then she heard the woman's voice.

'I quite agree, Mr Jennings. My late husband never let me go too long without getting down to what he called *fundamentals*.' She gave a fruity chuckle. 'Or to the bottom of things. He had a terrible weakness for puns. But, now, in the two months since he passed on so suddenly, I'm afraid that *I* have become as sorely in need as you say the new employee is. Although, of course, sore is exactly what I'm not.' She chuckled again and this time he joined in.

Then he said, 'Mrs Butler, as I told you earlier, I'll be most happy to remedy the situation in the way you suggest. Fundamentals it shall be. Would you care to choose an instrument?'

Instrument? Judith stifled a gasp as the penny dropped, then she heard the steel cabinet squeaking open.

'This one feels rather like what I'm accustomed to, Mr Jennings.' There was the sound of a cane being swished through the air. 'Yes, I think it will do very well.'

'A good choice, if I may say so. So, we may as well make a start. I am sure I do not need to impress on you the need for discretion about these matters, Mrs Butler. Our director is a stickler for what she calls decorum amongst members of staff.'

'Oh, indeed, I understand that, Mr Jennings. But we are quite private here, are we not?'

'Certainly. Ms Morris never ventures below ground level, so if we keep what we do here to ourselves she will not discover it.'

The voices had come much nearer, indicating that the speakers had moved into the next room. Judith knew that she should push the door quietly shut and make her getaway, but in the grip of an inner compulsion she did the opposite and eased it wider until her eye had a view through the slit. She was surprised to see that Mrs Butler was an attractive woman of around forty – God, what's she doing with that jerk? thought Judith – whose shining eyes and high colour expressed her excitement. She unzipped her knee-length skirt and removed it, and Judith held her breath as she saw that underneath the woman was naked save for the stockings that were held up by garters above the knee. There was a thick pubic bush revealed as she straightened then she turned her back and went to an upright wooden armchair that Judith had not noticed before. The woman placed it a yard or so away from the horse then bent forwards over its back taking a grip of its arms. Judith was open-mouthed at the sight of the full buttocks of a mature woman being presented voluntarily for the discipline of the cane.

'Are you ready, Mrs Butler?' Then as the questioner took up his position, Judith's view was blocked.

Fuck! She squirmed in an agony of frustration as she heard the swish and bite of the rattan in action. Then again. And again.

Zzzzz-crack! Zzzzz-crack! Zzzzz-crack! A-ah!

She counted six strokes, the last of which made the recipient cry out. Then there was silence, broken by a moan and the words, 'Please, don't stop just yet. Please.' The steady procession of sounds continued as before and while the cries were no louder, they were more urgent. Then she could see again and the sight took her breath away. Those magnificent globes were laced with vivid red stripes that turned darker where the cane's tip had bitten into the dimpled flank.

Judith straightened up, all at once aware of the danger of hiding in a room they might want to use at any time. But the spectacle was not yet over for Mrs Butler spoke again, her sexual need open and unashamed.

'My Teddy used to say, "Stripe her cheeks with the swishy one then bury the stiff one between 'em. *That's* fundamentals for you."'

Judith could see the dawning realisation on the man's face as he stuttered, 'You mean ... you mean ... you want me to –'

'Yes! Oh, yes! I *know* you're ready, Mr Jennings.' The voice was thick with passion and his hand went to the zip at his bulging crotch. Judith froze as she saw the ramrod of an erection in his hand and the woman doubled right over the chair. She had a glimpse of its oozing tip touching the exposed anus, then his body once more obscured her view. Insides churning at what she had seen, Judith was at last galvanised into movement. Forcing herself to be gentle, she turned the handle and leaned on the door while she released it. Then in the corridor she walked away from the clunk of the emergency exit closing at her back, fingers crossed that it would be drowned out by the noises in the punishment room itself. There was a side entrance to the left and, outside, she leaned against the wall with her heart pumping and the ecstatic cries of Mrs Butler in climax still ringing in her ears.

A while later she remembered that she was to have been 'delivered' back to the boss. Inside the building again Judith climbed the stairs very slowly to the directorial suite, waiting for her composure to return. Pinned under the nameplate that read ESTELLE MORRIS she found an envelope labelled *Judith Wilson*. In it was a note that read simply: *Called away. Please return at nine o'clock tomorrow if you want to work for me.* For you, definitely, said Judith to herself, managing a smile, but as for the rest . . . Then, bathed in relief that there was to be no interview, she clattered down the stairs out into the fresh air of the quad and escaped through the gate in the direction of home.

On a beautiful morning in early August, Judith was making the same journey, though in the reverse direction. Ten days had passed at the Meni (as she had learned to call it among her peers) in which she had taken memoranda to staff from the boss, delivered their replies and other internal mail and carried envelopes of instructions to a nearby warehouse which then often required the delivery of a package to an address elsewhere in the town. If the transactions were decidedly mysterious, the whole was rather charmingly old-fashioned, although the errand boy's bike with its handlebar basket had been updated to a scooter with capacious panniers. One thing only grated, but it grated sorely: her dealings with the building superintendent, Patrick Jennings. For a start, he insisted on being 'mistered' while calling her 'Judith' and, worse, contrived to make observations about the failings of today's young women at the slightest excuse. More and more, these contained leering innuendos about sexual behaviour and, what really stuck in her gullet, were combined at every opportunity with his grabbing at her bum. She could not believe that the director would condone such conduct and brooded on how she might engineer his comeuppance.

But this Wednesday, as she crossed the quad and began to climb the stairs, her thoughts were on how Ms Morris had wanted 'a special chat', now that Judith had 'settled in'. As she raised her hand to knock on the inner door, it opened in a waft of subtle perfume. 'Come in, my dear, come in. You'll have to excuse me for a moment: I need to deal with a matter downstairs. But make yourself at home, please. I have left a book of drawings on the couch that relate to what I would like to discuss with you.' So saying, the elegant figure in cerise closed the door behind her and Judith went on in to sit down, the new grey trousers she was sporting for the occasion seeming suddenly humdrum.

The volume referred to was leather-bound in a large format, and she picked it up curiously, opening the pages at random. What she saw made her draw a sharp breath. It was a line drawing of considerable detail and apparent expertise that depicted a young woman bent over, gripping her ankles while in the foreground an arm held a cane in readiness. Judith read the initials *E.M.* at the foot of the page then noticed the girl's half-turned profile. God, it was Debi from Accounts – and she was recognisable by more than the face, too. With a grin Judith studied the rather distinctive double crease under each buttock that had caught her eye in the flesh just yesterday. But what does it mean? Does the boss fantasise about her staff getting caned? Well, no big deal. She remembered with a pang how Cat's arse had figured in her own masturbation fantasies. But what if it's *real?* Well, the figure stood unsupported – none of the basement furniture she had seen – but the more she stared, the more the wrist and hand looked like the one that belonged to the odious Mr Jennings.

There followed other renderings of disciplinary scenes where the subjects were not identifiable, though all were female and all clothed. One, though, showed a girl with her skirt raised to display a knickered rump at the very moment of the cane's impact; and Judith lingered over it, feeling the response in her loins. Next were a series that featured an older woman in a long skirt. First she wielded a birch while the young victim knelt, bared, over a pouffe; later she was equipped with a cane and the girl bent over a chair wearing a slip that had been tucked in between her thighs and clung to the contours of the buttocks. These were more impressionistically done and they had a sado-erotic potency that drew Judith into its disturbing grip. Absorbed yet repelled, she started up bemused when the door opened.

'Sit down, my dear, sit down. I see my little sketches were entertaining you.' Estelle Morris stood looking at her employee as if considering what to say. Judith lowered herself back on to the sofa, blushing, still holding the book in her hands. 'My intention was not to embarrass you, Judith, but I see that I have. You will now be aware,' she went on, 'of my interest in the subject of corporal punishment; one I had hoped that you might share.'

'Oh, I do,' said Judith, 'it's just that I can't –'

'– can't yet accept your feelings?' The director sat beside her and pointed at the illustration on her lap. 'As you no doubt guessed, dear, this is a scene from my youth, some – in fact, I should say many – years ago. Right through my teens I was educated by an old-fashioned, very English governess who did anything but spare the rod. It left its mark on me, and in more than

93

the obvious way.' She smiled and Judith relaxed a little. 'As you can see, it was mostly very decorous. When I had been positioned for punishment, she would insist I should be grateful she was going to use the cane. I didn't feel grateful, of course, but she had a point. Unlike for the birch, there was no need to be shamingly bared; I can assure you that a thin garment properly stretched affords no discernable protection from a good cane stroke, and all of Miss Whitfield's strokes were, needless to say, good ones.'

Ms Morris stood up. 'But I did not bring you here to listen to an ageing woman reminisce. What I wanted was first to tell you that there are a few of my young staff – some recorded in this very book – who take part in a disciplinary régime of my devising. The chastisements are carried out discreetly in the basement, where Mrs Butler prepares the recipient and Mr Jennings administers the caning.'

In trepidation, Judith put down the book. God, where was this leading? She felt a lurch of panic at the idea of being herself beaten by the man who lost no chance of exploring her arse by hand.

'My dear Judith, don't be alarmed.' Her boss put a hand on her shoulder, smiling reassuringly. 'I did say a *few* of my girls are involved and I was not proposing that you should be one of them. But I am going to suggest that you witness one of these events: I think you owe it to yourself to give these inclinations a little more head. Now, in just a couple of minutes Sandra Bright from the Catalogue Department will arrive, expecting to be sent for discipline. I should like you to accompany her – I can assure you she will not mind being watched by someone who has a special interest in these things – and then you can do something else for me. I believe that girls like Sandra have a deep need for corporal punishment, but while having *their* good at heart I make no secret of the satisfaction *I* derive from its infliction.

94

'A videotape is occasionally made of a session, with the chastisee's knowledge, as an inducement to the chastiser to follow proper procedures. Now I want you, if you will, my dear, to remove the recording once the caning is finished. Keep it for the present: I suggest you take the rest of the day off to digest what you will see. I have had suspicions from time to time that a tape may have been edited or – God forbid – copied for other uses; but if I know it is in your safekeeping I shall be content. So, Judith, what do you say? Will you do what I ask?'

Just at that moment there was a tap on the door and at the director's command a girl with ginger hair entered. With no time for reflection or discussion, Judith said simply, 'Yes, Ms Morris, I'll do it.' In her head was the thought, What have I to lose? but it was undermined by the foreboding that just a few steps into these waters might take her well out of her depth.

Sandra kept her eyes lowered, and though it was explained to her that Ms Morris's assistant would be going as an observer, she made no acknowledgement of Judith's presence. *This* Sandra was a different person from the forthright, opinionated cataloguer who strode about in her domain on the first floor. The submissive demeanour she now presented was such that even her height seemed diminished, though Judith had judged the girl easily as tall as Ms Morris. It was as if, like a novitiate who was in preparation for a transforming ritual, she had withdrawn from the usual conditions of her existence, and would remain set apart until the business in the basement was done.

Then the director continued, 'Well, Sandra, I'm afraid that Mr Jennings is going to be rather strict with you this morning. Your work has been very slovenly of late, so you will ask him – very politely, of course – to lay a round dozen of the best – his very best – across the seat of your trousers. Is that quite clear?'

'Yes, Ms Morris. I promise I'll be good in the future.' Her voice was subdued, almost tearful, but when they were dismissed she led the way out of the office and down the stairs with a firm step. Following, Judith wondered at the steady resolution with which the girl approached what was going to be, undoubtedly, a most painful experience.

Mr Jennings and Mrs Butler were both waiting and the young women were ushered into the small office. 'Take a pew, Sandra,' he said with a wave in the direction of a small armchair in the corner. 'You may as well enjoy sitting comfortably while you still can. Mrs Butler will attend to things next door while Judith and I choose an instrument. Now, tell me, girl, what is the ration to be today?'

'I am to ask you for twelve strokes, Mr Jennings. Twelve of your very best, please.' Her face was almost without expression, the eyes fixed on a distant point ahead. In contrast, the man about to execute the sentence made no secret of his enthusiasm.

'Twelve, eh? *Very* good. And they will, indeed, be just that. Very good ones indeed.' He chuckled and rubbed his hands together. 'Now, Judith, come here and examine a few of my choice specimens.' Quelling a surge of distaste for the man, she went forwards as he opened the cabinet doors and took out one of medium thickness. 'Try it. Go on, it won't bite. Not you, that is. Not yet.'

Judith tried to ignore his unpleasant little snigger and, gripping the cane at the handle, swished it through the air twice. The feel of it took her by surprise – it was almost alive in her hand – and she did it again, imagining a posterior on the receiving end. Then she removed another more slender rod, but rejected it as too light and insubstantial.

'Try the top shelf.' As she reached up, he was right at her back and his hands grasped her two buttocks and lifted them. In a low voice at her ear he said, 'If I had *my* way, I'd treat these beauties to a demonstration.'

Judith jerked away from him and stood, fists clenched. Red and angry, for a moment she struggled for control; then Mrs Butler was in the doorway.

'The top shelf, Judith. I think we'll use one of the new ones.' The brazen tone dared her to make a scene and Judith fell back into her appointed role, vowing to find some way of getting even. Still fuming she took down a three-foot black rod, thinner than her first choice but actually more weighty. She slashed it viciously down from above her head and was gratified to see Mr Jennings jump. 'Steady on,' he said with a forced laugh, 'this one needs careful handling. However –' he took it from her and bent it between his hands, recovering his equilibrium '– with proper use, this piece of modern technology might just fit our requirement for twelve of the very best. I read that it contains an epoxy-resin core bonded into a hard rubber sheath: the idea being to give high density with great flexibility. Quite formidable, I'm told.' He tapped the thing on the palm of his hand with a grin. 'But we don't have to take anyone's word for it. Let us go and put it to the test right now.'

Sandra's faraway gaze had been replaced by one of consternation at the evil black implement that had been adopted for use on her backside. Watching the girl, Judith was feeling a guilty excitement at the severity the impending punishment seemed to have taken on. This wasn't something she was reading in a story, even a true one. Nor was it like eavesdropping on Mrs Butler getting a dose. While that was quite gripping (even though Judith couldn't actually see anything) it was really a bit of foreplay to the buggering that followed. What was coming was different. She had been officially sanctioned to view the deployment of the cane in a piece of serious purgative discipline.

In the chamber Mr Jennings showed her how the video recorder worked, this time to her great relief keeping his distance. Judith noticed the machine made no noise, and placed as it was there was no visible indication that it was running. She saw also that there were several new tapes in a pile, unwrapped ready for use, and the germ of an idea began to grow. When they emerged from the back of the screen, there was an upright chair placed to the front right of the punishment horse and Mr Jennings motioned towards it. Judith took her seat while he moved to the other side, cane held in his right hand. Sandra stood against the padded top while Mrs Butler took a firm grip of the waistband of her fawn trousers, then yanked them tight up into the crotch and pushed the girl forward. When she reached obediently down to grasp the front legs of the horse, the taut buttocks bulged under the stretched material and Judith's attention was caught by the outline of a dark triangle at the top of the cleft that betokened the scantiest of underclothing. Next the older woman ran her hands over the prominent cheeks, patting and squeezing as if they were a pair of cushions she was plumping into shape. The young woman gasped and wriggled at the indignity, and was rewarded with a sharp slap that resounded off the bare walls.

'Keep still!' snapped Mrs Butler. 'Any of that during punishment and there will be extras.' She said the word with relish and stood back with a satisfied air. 'Sandra has a fine well-fleshed bottom, as I'm sure you can see, Mr Jennings, so you may give of your very best – or worst, depending on one's point of view.' She smiled at him, eyes gleaming and as he moved forwards, the bulge of his erection was blatant.

Judith shifted in her seat, feeling her own genital response; then it hit her that these two would be up to their games once the girl was dealt with. Well, if so, *she* could play one of her own when she took the tape.

The man tapped the cane against the thin fabric of the girl's trousers and there was a sound that could have been a choked-back sob. 'Are you ready, Sandra?'

It wasn't really a question, but she replied with a faint, 'Yes' and he raised his arm up in the air and began.

The whole thing could only have lasted five minutes, six at the most, Judith reckoned later. As it was she seemed to have moved sideways into another dimension where a puppet show replayed the same movements in slow motion. The black rod sliced through the air with a buzz and the figure's head jerked back and made a noise. Then the legs did a strange little dance and the hips writhed, making the afflicted buttocks jiggle and bounce for a while. In the final part of the sequence, the torso slumped back on to the horse and the head went down, leaving the movements of the posterior to decline into sporadic quiverings. But each repetition was not quite a replay, for the noises got louder and higher in pitch and the vigour of the dancing and writhing grew. All that was truly constant was the hands' clasp round the wooden legs, though it was obvious that the increasingly energetic response of the body to the rod's impact would, in the end, unstick them from their place.

But that end did not come since the twelve strokes had been delivered and Mr Jennings drew back, lowering the cane to his side. Coming out of her abstracted state, Judith found her pulse racing and her crotch awash; guiltily, she exchanged a glance with Mrs Butler and saw in her the same arousal. From the horse the young woman came slowly upright with much wincing. She stood, flexing her cramped fingers for a moment before putting the hands with care to her maltreated backside. Then there was one last piece of ritual to be enacted.

'You have taken your correction quite well, Sandra.' It was Mrs Butler speaking and the girl raised her tear-stained face to look at her. 'It is quite a privilege to have sampled the new instrument, which I'm sure you'll agree is most effective. So, now, what do you say?'

Judith saw the girl's eyes widen with incredulity that the pain she had undergone could be considered a privilege. But then the spark of resistance died and she lowered her head.

'Thank you for caning me, Mr Jennings. I won't forget it.' At his nod, she turned and walked stiffly out through the door.

Once she was gone, Judith went straight behind the screen that concealed the recording equipment. As she pressed the button marked EJECT, she heard snatches of a low, urgent interchange behind her. First his voice, questioning: '. . . fundamentals, Mrs Butler?' then hers: 'Sshhh . . .' and, lower still '. . . please, yes, oh, please . . .' That decided her and Judith put in a blank tape and pressed RECORD. I'll give you fundamentals, Mr Groper, she said to herself. Just wait till your boss sees what's going on to this.

Then she heard him saying, '. . . too harsh, Mrs Butler. Come and choose another,' and when she looked round the room was empty. There was a plastic card lying beside the video machine and, suddenly inspired, Judith grabbed it. Heart in mouth, she took her chance to dive into the bathroom and wedge the thing into the catch of the emergency exit so that it would open from the outside later. Clutching the record of Sandra's ordeal, she emerged into the office to find the superintendent and his assistant at the steel cabinet. He held a thinnish length of rattan instead of the brutal black rod and they looked flushed and excited, though plainly discomfited by her appearance.

Ignoring all that, Judith waved the tape at them. 'I've taken this, so I'll be away, then,' she said briskly and, without waiting for any reply, made off down the corridor.

At the main door Judith decided to deliver the recording before she went home, rather than take it with her and bring it back. At the top of the stairs she entered the

100

outer office and went to knock on the door of the inner sanctum. But it was not quite shut and she heard from within Ms Morris's voice, uncharacteristically soft and soothing.

'Oh, my poor dear, you must be *so* sore. Just keep still, now. This will help.' Judith put her eye to the crack. God, I spend my whole life snooping these days, she thought, but curiosity demanded to be satisfied. What she saw gave her a jolt but it was perhaps not so entirely unexpected. Sandra was leaning over the director's desk on her elbows, the light trousers and a wisp of black panties down round her thighs. Judith smiled wryly to herself: so much for *decorum*. Ms Morris held the girl close to her side with one hand on her bare hip while the other took ointment from an open jar beside them. The purple weals left by the caning stood out shockingly against the fair skin and on the lower curves of the cheeks had coalesced into a solid swollen band. The sight produced an immediate sharp pang between Judith's legs and a rush of guilt that she should be so turned on by the girl's pain. So she turned quickly away, dropping the tape quietly into the in-tray and tiptoed out, leaving behind her the sounds of Sandra's 'oohs' and 'aahs' as the soothing cream was applied.

6

Feeling the Heat

The mirror wasn't at quite the right angle, so Judith
stuck out her leg and pushed it with her foot. Then she
resumed her position over the chair and inspected the
curve of her behind once again. The grey trousers were
moulded to her skin and the sight was a fair approxi-
mation to the appearance of Sandra on the horse, save
for the present intrusive outline of underpants. Judith
contemplated with a shiver the deliberation of it all. Not
only did the girl present herself for the beating and stay
in place through it, but she had carefully dressed in a
tiny pair of briefs that would not be in the way of the
cane. Sighing, Judith straightened up and stripped
slowly. At the end, as she took down her more
substantial knickers, she felt the gusset slick with her
juices and sighed again. Highly stimulated by what she
had witnessed in the morning, she was also unsettled: a
simple act of masturbation was not going to do the
trick.

Judith thought again of the severity of the rubber-
sheathed instrument. From the marks she had glimpsed,
Sandra would be stiff and sore at least until the
weekend. But how did she feel once the immediate
agony had passed? Did she get turned on by it and
wank? God, maybe the boss did the job for her when
she was bent over the desk. It would be so natural for

the fingers spreading the cream to dip down lower and
... 'Shit!' Judith swore out loud and kicked off the
soggy pants that were round her ankles. These reflections were making some kind of action urgent.

She rummaged in the cramped corner-cupboard of
her tiny bedroom and emerged holding a wooden
clothes brush. It wasn't very heavy and Judith slapped
the flat back of it against her open palm, considering. A
mere month ago if she'd had such an idea – which was
unlikely – she'd have shied away from it, mortified.
Now, after reading the manuscripts at Nemesis and
viewing the display at the Meni she felt less shamed by
the reality of her desires. Resolved, Judith bent back
over the chair and raised the brush in the air.

Smack!

'Ow!' She rubbed herself, wriggling. Fuck, that hurt!
Then, thinking of the travails of Sandra, Judith told
herself sternly not to be such a wimp. She gritted her
teeth and, sticking out her behind, brought the implement down firmly six times to the left buttock and six
times to the right. The sting was astonishing, but after
the first shock it was endurable; so she delivered a
second dozen whacks and then a third, trying to cover
the whole area of her bum. Then she craned her neck to
see the result in her mirror. Both cheeks glowed red and,
thrilling to the heat of them, Judith laid on another
batch as hard as she could. Now she really burned with
the smart of it all and there was a fierce throb in her
clitoris. Judith dropped the brush and put one hand to
the hot soreness while she slipped the other between her
legs. Two deft strokes with the middle finger and all the
pent-up arousal of the day exploded in spasm after
violent spasm until she subsided gasping on to her bed.

After a long hot soak in the bath it was still only one
o'clock, and Judith pulled on a black T-shirt and sat at
the kitchen table with a sandwich and a beer, towelling
her short dark hair dry. She felt curiously calm after the

excesses of the day and ate hungrily. As she sat back and drained the bottle, the red spine of the box file caught her eye. It had lain untouched on the shelf since her traumatic dismissal from the archive and Judith got up on a whim and took it down. Lifting the lid, her fingers detected a flap that she had not noticed before and closer inspection showed it to be a pocket that contained two pieces of paper, one of them a folded sheet of yellowed newsprint. Suddenly alert, Judith opened the cutting and read the date: *19th May 1962.* She scanned it twice before she saw the paragraph that was headed *Meurtre de Mme Dauvignon.* Even Judith's grasp of French could make sense of the first sentence: *Suspecte Mlle Marie Bonnard est arrêtée et tenée à Rennes.* The remainder seemed to say that she had not been charged at present, with the implication that she was likely to be before long.

Judith was staggered. Marie kill the woman she called her 'beloved mistress'? Impossible, surely. And yet . . . She remembered that last sentence she had read, about the husband returning. Maybe if he'd pushed Marie out, she would have been so consumed with jealousy that, that – No. No fucking way. She might kill him in that case, but never her. It must be a trumped-up charge. Resisting the impulse to search the remaining contents of the file – that was several hours' work that she was not going to begin now – Judith picked up the other sheet she had taken from the lid. On it there was a message that read: *Cherie – Quand tu liras ceci, j'aurai me perdre en rigueur. Ce qui tu trouve dedans, c'est à toi. Je t'embrasse, M.*

Beyond the obvious affection of the opening and close it made little sense to her; but it had been handwritten on headed notepaper that bore the name Michelle Brown PhD and an address that Judith recognised as being on the other side of town. Who was there now, she wondered, seven years after the demise of the lady

She took the tape, switched off the machine and remembered to remove the piece of plastic from the exit on her way through. Then she was out of the building and across the empty car park into the back street quite safely, but it took until she was halfway home before the heart stopped thudding in her chest.

Home, though, was not the immediate destination and at 6.20 p.m. she stuck her head round the swing door of The Phoenix.

'Hi, Jude!' called out Marsha from behind the bar. 'Come and keep me company till I get some damn drinkers in.' Once installed on a stool, Judith shrank back a little from the older woman's gaze. 'Hey, you look done in, girl. What has the elegant Ms Morris been doing to you? All right, all right. Don't tell me, I don't wanna know.' Marsha plonked a bottle down in front of Judith and picked up the tape that lay on the counter. 'So, are you going to tell me what this is, or shall I guess? Does it perhaps show a smart young office worker getting the seat of her pants well dusted with a springy cane?'

Marsha chortled delightedly as Judith felt the colour flooding into her face. She took a long swig of beer and said: 'OK, OK, wise guy. I don't know how much you know about the Meni –' the bar manager made a 'who, me?' face, then ducked the fist aimed by her customer '– and I don't want to know just now. As you observed, Marsha, I've had a busy day and I'm fucking knackered. OK? But the vid is for you.'

She swallowed some more from the bottle while her friend waited. 'Will you take a look at it for me? It should have on it some sexy doings between Mr Bastard Jennings and his assistant. Now, I know you're completely unshockable, Marsha,' said Judith deadpan, taking her turn to avoid the mock punch with a giggle, 'but, more to the point, I don't even have a telly, so I'm depending on you to tell me what you see. And what I need to know is will it upset the aforementioned elegant director?'

'Jude, what are you hatching here?

'Well, I do know that the Groper-in-chief was concerned that she didn't find out, so maybe I can bring him down a peg or two.' Marsha had on the expression she acquired when she was going to tell someone they'd got it all badly wrong and Judith put a hand on her arm. 'Not now, Marsha. Just have a peek at the evidence, and we can fight about it on Saturday.' She slapped a fiver down in front of the doubtful bartender. 'And now, change of subject. We're both going to have a drink while you tell me the latest scandalous gossip that's going about this miserable town.'

At eight o'clock Judith was back in the flat, slumped at her kitchen table. The beers had gone straight to her head and she ached to see Catherine's guileless face smiling at her again. There was only one thing for it and she reached for the pad that lay on top of the box file. *Dear Cat*, she wrote, then stopped. If she's really pissed off with me, that's too familiar. So she amended it to *Dear Catherine* and sat chewing on the pen. Maybe she should write about what had happened since she started at Eumenides, just as if she was sat right here and they were chatting. Go on, she told herself, do it in rough first and then see what it's like.

For a while Judith scribbled furiously until she had covered two whole A4 sheets; then she revised it until the writing was almost obliterated by deletions and subsequent additions. About to begin on a fair copy, she suddenly stopped short. What the fuck am I doing? I mean, it makes a good story and it would make the girl laugh if she were here; but she's not here. And she's not fucking here because you let her down. But Judith's diatribe against her own reprehensible behaviour ran out of steam almost at once because she knew in her heart that she couldn't bring herself to spank Cat or bed her now any more than she could then. And to tell her funny stories about the s/m delights of the Meni was just dishonest if she didn't face up to that fact.

Judith crumpled the scrawled pages into a ball and lobbed it across into the bin. She got up and found on the shelf a photo Marsha had taken of her perched on a bar stool at The Phoenix, clutching a bottle. On the back she wrote: *Drowning my sorrows! I REALLY miss you. Please come back soon. Jude xxx.* Then she slipped it in an envelope, stamped it and addressed it to Catherine Milton at St James's Hospital.

Outside the air was cool though it was still not completely dark. At the corner, Judith posted her message and walked slowly through the deserted park opposite, lingering in solitude by the pool on whose surface shimmered the lights from the converging paths. Back in the flat she shed her clothes in a heap where she stood, climbed into bed and fell almost at once into a deep sleep.

It took most of the next two evenings to put the bits and pieces of Dr Brown's writings into some kind of order. Frustratingly, the effort added no new information at all about young Marie, but it did throw up some oddities about the psychologist, not least that the thesis which earned her the PhD was not completed until 1990. It was called *The Suffering Position: Female Masochism after Freud* and the title alone supported the idea that its author was equipped to assess the desires of the ex-convent girl. But those sessions that she had turned into a convincing narrative were supposedly conducted in 1962, decades before Michelle Brown was any kind of doctor at all.

Strange, too, was the fact that her version of Marie's early life was so compelling. For a second-hand reconstruction of a story told to her thirty years before, it was remarkably – even unbelievably – fresh. And then there was the note Judith had found inside the lid of the box file. If it went with the contents – *ce qui tu trouve dedans* – then it must have been written to her erstwhile boss as director of Nemesis. However, it had to be said *chérie* was not a mode of address that sprang to mind for the stern Miss James, and on top of that the thing simply didn't read like the letter from someone dying who was leaving their last fragments to an official archive. But then who else could it be from if not Dr Brown?

These questions echoed in Judith's mind on the Saturday morning as she made her way through the terraces near the city centre into an old inner suburb of detached houses that were now badly dilapidated, many divided into squalid flats or bedsits. She was heading for Randolph Drive, though what she hoped to find getting on for a decade after Michelle Brown's demise was far from clear. It was precisely that uncertainty which had stopped her using the phone number printed on the headed notepaper opposite the address: she wanted to have a look at the house before deciding what to do.

The street identified itself as a cul-de-sac and, finding number one to the left and thirty to the right, Judith guessed that the number fifteen she wanted would be more or less at the dead end itself. Now that her goal was not far off, misgivings mounted and she slowed her pace. While she could pretend she had expected to find Dr Brown herself, what was she doing on the doorstep instead of on the phone? Any appointment that explained her actual presence would need to have been made years ago.

Then she saw it facing her as the road swung in a sharp curve ahead and stopped. Unlike the others she had passed on the way the hedge had been clipped and the gate – its wood weathered but painted – stood open

110

to reveal an old estate car in the drive. The place was shabby rather than neglected and it had a friendly down-to-earth feel that was enhanced by the rows of cabbages that grew where an unkempt lawn was the rule. Encouraged, Judith made her way towards the house but she demurred at the steps up to the front door. In keeping with the air of the place, she wanted a less formal entrance and took a path that led towards the back, at the same time deciding to jettison elaborate lies in favour of a simple declaration of interest in Marie Bonnard. After all, the most likely outcome was that the person she spoke to would know nothing of any use to her.

At the end of the side wall was a sash window, the lower half of which was raised. Judith peered in and was just about to pass on round the corner when the door burst open.

'Get your hands off me, you swine! No, don't you dare. Don't you fucking dare!'

Judith caught a glimpse of a woman struggling in a man's grip before she flattened herself against the wall. He was saying nothing, but her voluble complaint continued.

'If you lay a finger on me, you bastard, I'll – No! No!' There was the sudden creaking of a chair and a series of loud slaps. 'Ow! Ow! Ow! That fucking hurts!'

God, was she being battered? I've got to do something, thought Judith, and dropped down to peer in at the bottom edge of the window. The sight made her gasp, for the cursing lady was over the man's knee, skirt up and the slapping noise was being made by his palm coming down with force on her bare bottom. That was surprise enough but it was nothing to the surprise when the victim jerked her head round, looked Judith straight in the eye and gave a broad wink that made Judith wonder if she had really seen it. As the spanking continued she swivelled back and resumed her vocal responses, although now the cries were more like moans and there was no further abuse of her partner. What was happening was obviously a kind of ritual rather than an assault.

He was a burly man with a black beard and clearly so engrossed in his task that Judith had no real concern that he too might catch sight of her presence. The woman was an attractive, slightly blowsy dyed blonde whose generous flesh bounced and rippled delightfully under the heavy smacks and now that Judith was recovering her equanimity it was a spectacle that was making her lubricate freely. Then abruptly it stopped and she was on her knees in front of him with her hand on his trouser zip. The leather skirt was still rucked up and the watcher glimpsed scarlet hind-cheeks before she ducked back out of view. God, she's going to suck him off – and I bet *she* swallows every drop. At this thought Judith got wetter still, even though the outcome of her own foray into fellatio was all too fresh in her mind.

The sun was warm on her back and the young woman felt unaccountably at ease, hunkered down against the red brick of the wall. She was beginning to sink into a reverie, hand on crotch, when there was the sound of a door closing from the room and a voice just above said: 'Well, well, well. I reckon you'd better come in, my duck.' Judith straightened up and a strong arm helped her climb over the sill. Once she was inside, the big blonde looked her up and down. 'I would say you must be that girl who started at the archive.'

Judith examined the speaker in her turn. She looked thirty-five or forty, and was visibly braless under a stained T-shirt. The lack of knickers had already been revealed; now the worn leather miniskirt was back in place, clinging to strong thighs. The outfit was completed by thick woollen socks rolled down to heavy workmen's boots and the whole effect, which might have been simply sluttish on a lesser figure, was of a powerful and free sensuality. Somewhat overawed, all that Judith managed to reply to the question was, 'Yes'.

'But you're not there now, are you, dearie? You didn't last very long.' Her speech was slow, with a warm rural burr, and the tone was anything but critical. Still Judith flushed and cast around for some way of accounting for why she had left. But before she could speak, the woman held out her arm. 'Sorry, I don't mean to pry. My name's Jeanie.'

'Judith.' They shook hands with a firm grip.

'Well, Judith, first things first. Am I right in thinking you rather enjoyed what you saw just now?' She gave a wide grin and carried on. 'Maybe you fancy some of the same yourself, do you? My Bill could help out, now; he'll give you a lovely hot arse, my duck. Will I go and give him a shout?' Horrified, Judith stepped back and the other woman burst into uproarious laughter at her discomfiture. 'Just my little joke. Don't take offence. But, seriously –' she took hold of Judith's wrist '– I got really going there knowing you was watching. Bill, he didn't have the foggiest. Typical man with his brains in his cock; once it's hard there's only one thing he thinks of. Here, put your hand here, feel how hot he made me. D'you like that, now, my lover?'

Judith's embarrassment had all but gone as she let the sexual magnetism of the woman do its work. Never before excited in this way by a female body, she stroked the flesh that burned under the faded leather and her loins began to throb urgently. She dropped to her knees, both hands cupping the ripe buttocks and nuzzled into the thighs, pushing the hem of the skirt up with her nose.

'Oh, yes, oh, yes –' Jeanie's voice was deep with passion '– my cunt is so ready for this,' and she spread her legs and bared the whole of her genitals. Entranced, Judith gazed at the naked lips that, engorged, seemed to pout directly at her. The inner labia glistened wetly and

113

below there was the gleam of a gold ring, while out of the upper folds stood the hard bud of erectile tissue. The young woman leaned forwards and pushed her lips into their slick nether counterparts, revelling in the heady musk laced with sweat and piss. This was the strong meat of an older woman's arousal and it put what she knew of her own anodyne secretions to shame. Jeanie's hands now held the back of Judith's head as she ran her tongue around the prominent clitoris. Fluids dribbled down her chin and, awash with tastes and scents, she made tiny nips with her teeth until the body she held on to jerked and cried out.

They clung together while the spasms subsided; then Judith felt the strong arms under hers, raising her up. Jeanie kissed her wet face as if thirsty for her own exudations. Then she took hold of Judith's trousers, undid the fastening and lowered the zip. Her hand slipped down inside the knickers and two fingers slid easily into the brimming vaginal opening. Judith gasped out and doubled up as her own clitoris responded to the probing hand which Jeanie held firmly in place while with the other she pulled down the clothing at the back. Then she caressed the young woman's behind, one finger finding its way into the anus as the other hand continued working in her cunt. Impaled from front and rear, Judith climaxed in an explosion of sensation that made the room spin and her shouts seem to come from a great distance.

An hour later, the women sat in the large kitchen before a spread of home produce. There was a plate of smoked ham, a mushroom quiche, a dish of pâté and fresh loaf of crusty bread together with a jug of cider to wash it all down. They had showered and Jeanie had changed into a stretch brown dress that, while clean, made an even more louche exhibition of her full figure. Judith wore only her shirt, while the washed knickers dried on a rail in front of the stove. They ate hungrily in silence for a while, then Jeanie explained that Bill was away with a delivery of cabbages.

'Just as well, Judith, while you're dressed like that. One glimpse of that arse and he'd be chasing you through the onion beds.' She drank deep and got up to refill the jug from a barrel out in the scullery. Putting it down, she asked: 'D'you want to see round, dearie? This'll keep till we come back in.' At the back of the house every inch of space appeared to be used: in between the various outbuildings Judith saw row after row of peas, beans, carrots, and leeks flanked by two whole patches of potatoes. Then there was a large hen house and a small orchard at the back in which was tethered a pig. The whole thing was a haven of fertility in a surrounding area of rundown decay.

Back inside, though, Judith began to be puzzled. Caught up since her arrival in a sensual whirl of spanking, sex, food and drink, she had almost forgotten why she had come to this address. Unsure how to begin, she toyed with her refilled glass then said, 'The garden must have been here a long time.'

Jeanie sat back and looked across at her. 'Twenty years – and more,' she said, 'though twenty years is how long I been here.'

'But how, I mean, what . . ?' She tailed off, not really knowing what to ask or how her questioning might be received.

'You want to know how I came here, what I came here for? Well, if I tell you something, then you can tell me something back. All right?' Judith nodded. 'I was just sixteen when I come here –' the accent was growing noticeably broader as she spoke '– and that was when my – er, when the doctor took me in. I were adopted, see, and then she took me back. Well, I don't mean *back*. I mean she took me *on* to work in the garden she was making and I been here ever since.' Jeanie looked flustered. 'But what about you, Judith? You didn't come here to see *her*, did you?'

'No,' said Judith, glad of a straight enquiry. 'No, I was told she was dead. Seven or eight years ago?' The older woman nodded, but she still looked uncomfortable. 'I came because of something she wrote – about a girl called Marie Bonnard. I think she was charged with murder back in the sixties.'

'Oh, I can't tell you nothing about that.' The tone was final but Judith had the idea that there would be more to come another time, if not right now. So when she was offered a refill of her glass in exchange for the lowdown on her brief time at Nemesis, she gladly accepted. The story took another three drinks to tell as Judith began with Cat's pre-interview 'therapy' and went through the incident of Helen's bum to end with her own sorry demise. After what they'd done earlier, Judith felt able to tell all and she was pleased to see Jeanie become relaxed and warm once more. When she finished the older woman sat shaking her head.

'You're in a bad way, my duck,' she said slowly. 'You've got a girlfriend you won't make a *proper* girlfriend and you've got a mind to have your arse tanned – but you keep running away from it.' Jeanie stood up, looking decisive. 'We've got a good hour till *he's* home and I think you'd better run along before then. I've taken quite a fancy to you, Judith, and I want to try something. Will you trust me?'

Apprehensive, but exhilarated by the cider and by Jeanie's potency, Judith allowed her hand to be taken and herself to be led over to a wooden chest that stood against the wall. The older woman sat on the end of it, hitching her dress up, and pulled Judith down across her lap. Her shirt lifted into the small of her back she lay bottom up with her bare thighs pressed into Jeanie's own. Somehow, miraculously, her insides were not knotted in a seizure of panic and she waited.

116

'Good girl. That's how you should be. Nice and easy. Now I'm just going to have a nice feel of your very pretty bum.' One large hand held her firmly by the waist; the other stroked and patted, squeezed and lifted, fingers dipping the while into the furrow between the cheeks. Judith became so aroused that she began to thrust her buttocks up into the exploring hand as if begging for heavier treatment, and when the first smack came her gasp was of pure pleasure. A small flurry of light spanks to the undercurves of her bottom was all it took and she came deliriously, grinding herself into the bare flesh supporting her body.

Judith slipped off the lap on to her knees and tried to spread the solid thighs but Jeanie stood up and pulled her to her feet. 'That's the car I can hear coming up the drive, my lover, so you'd better make yourself scarce. Don't worry, he's all right, and I'll get a good fuck out of the bugger later. But I don't want him to find you here.' She took the pants from the rail and picked up the rest of Judith's clothes. 'Here, go through and get dressed in the front porch. Then you can let yourself out when he goes round the back. Now you watch how you go.'

Outside, the bright sunshine on her face was all wrong. Instead of the four o'clock it actually was it felt like the four o'clock in the morning when sexual pleasure must give reluctant way to sleep, and Judith walked slowly home through the Saturday afternoon strollers as one set apart, half-expecting to be not even visible to their daylight eyes.

Trial – and Error

'So you're saying this isn't going to make our fortunes as a porn vid?'

'Honey, she gets a cool swishing and she's got a peachy big butt, so that's say six out of ten, maybe seven at a pinch. But when he sticks her you don't even see which hole he's in, only his ass blocking the camera, and he keeps his fucking pants on! So that makes a total score of three, tops. I make better tapes than this every weekend. Talking of which, it's time you came along to star on one – and we'll have *your* sweet ass good and bare. Now *that* would have to be worth a few bucks!' Marsha hooted as Judith went red, wrong-footed by the lady's deadpan humour.

'I'm sorry. Don't get mad, Jude. I can't resist getting a rise out of you. Just remember I'm not letting on *what* I do between Saturday night and Sunday morning, but I'll tell you it's usually with just one lover. That's l-o-v-e-r. I want you for a *friend*, girl.' The voluble American pecked quickly at Judith's cheek, conciliatory, and Judith smiled. It was impossible to be cross with Marsha for long. Together they picked up the drinks they had just bought and were carrying them over to the corner table when Judith spotted a familiar black face on the steps down into the basement bar. For a second she was blank, then it came back. It was the girl who tried to pick her up in the Ladies before, oh, God, before . . . It was a full month ago yet to think about it still made her sick. Gwen, that was her name. Judith called it out and the young woman looked across and waved.

She bought a beer and came over, and Judith did the introductions. 'I've seen you around,' said Marsha, looking from her to Judith and back with a twinkle. 'The Phoenix folk are following me about on my night off.'

When they were sat down, Gwen took a sip of her drink and said to Judith, 'So that guy you were dating got up to his old tricks again.' For a moment Judith gawped – how on Earth did Gwen know what had happened to her that night? – then the penny dropped. 'Didn't you hear? He's been done for assault – some lady up north – and it ain't no first offence neither. So the bastard'll be going down for sure. Good fucking riddance.'

'For a while,' said Marsha.

'Then you didn't hear he got me,' Judith said.

Gwen looked horrified. 'Jesus fuck. Me and my big mouth. Oh, honey, I had no idea.'

'Don't worry about it. Just a bruise. But it was a shock I could have done without. And it led to me losing the job I had.'

'Oh, fuck. You were at the archive, yeah? The place the feminists wanna close down?'

'Some *so-called* feminists,' Marsha put in with a snort.

'I don't get it. How could him hitting you put you out of work?' Gwen continued.

'Well, only indirectly. Oh it's a long story, let's just say I was late the next day and there were consequences.' Judith saw Gwen had a curious look that was asking for more. 'OK, OK. Much as I'm caught up in all this discipline malarkey, I just couldn't – wouldn't – take a leathering from the boss. So I had to leave.'

'Wow! So she practises what the stuff on her shelves preaches, eh? Hey, that's cool. Kinky stuff. It kinda gives me a funny feeling to think about it. And that's funny-nice, I mean. I ain't never done it, but offering your bare bum up to be slapped is a fucking sexy idea.' She stopped and put a hand to her mouth. 'Honey, you lost your job over this and I'm rabbiting. Fuck, I'd be chicken, too, when it came to the point of pulling my pants down.'

Judith looked away. How was it everyone else could be so at ease with this subject when it tied her up in knots inside? Then with relief she saw a second figure she knew at the far end of the bar and seized the opportunity to switch the conversation into different channels.

'Hey, Melissa! Over here.' Heads turned at her raised voice, then she said, half to herself, 'Wait a minute, she's supposed to be in Germany. That's why I took over.'

Marsha stood up, looking for once distinctly sheepish. 'Er, Liss is with me for a couple of nights, then she's back to Bonn. Stay where you are, I'll go and get a round in.'

Judith smiled at the hasty disappearance; it was rare to see her friend embarrassed. So here was this weekend's lover for them all to see: they'd had their Saturday night and Sunday morning and by the look of it there was another night to come.

When the two of them came through with the drinks, Judith could sense Gwen's keen interest. The sexual rapport between the wiry American with the iron-grey crew cut and the Glaswegian blonde with the startling red fingernails was an almost material presence at the table and while Liss muttered to Marsha in a low voice, gesticulating, Judith felt breath in her ear and a hand on her thigh.

'Cor, see them. Makes my knickers wet to watch. You wanna follow their example out the back, hon?' Startled, Judith swung round, only for the black girl to dissolve into giggles. 'You should see your face, Jude. But it ain't really a joke, you know that.' She gave the bare flesh below the short skirt another squeeze, then Melissa leaned forward and spoke to Judith.

'How you getting on at the Meni? I hear you care for the janny even less than I do.'

Judith laughed. 'He'd hate being called that, the way he fancies himself as *superintendent*.'

'Aye. That'll be superintendent of young lassies' bums. But he never got his paws on me. When he tried it on I stuck a nail file in his ribs. Let the shit believe it was the point of a knife. Kept his fucking distance after that.'

Gwen's eyes were popping out. 'Jeez, Jude, are you safe working there? I mean, what is it this outfit actually does?'

'Good question,' said Judith, looking at Melissa. 'It's some weird deal altogether. All I know is I deliver stuff from this depot two streets away. There's books – some of their own publications – and then there's, well, straps and, er, things. All securely wrapped and I haven't dared have a proper look yet.'

Melissa exchanged looks with Marsha and again Judith had the feeling they knew something she wasn't being told. All Liss said with a shrug was, 'No use asking me. I was never given the big picture at all, just what I was doing.'

Who do you think you're kidding, thought Judith, with you swanning about their European branches?

Gwen was clearly fascinated. 'So you're taking supplies of your actual *implements* –' she stressed the word with relish '– to all the discipline freaks around the area? I like it, sister. I would say that's a step on from just reading manuscripts.'

Judith smiled at her enthusiasm, but before she could press Melissa to spill more of the beans about the mysterious Eumenides company, a group of the university's more orthodox feminists sat down at the next table. Marsha may have affected loathing of their company but it was clear the attraction of a bit of verbal fisticuffs outweighed it, especially when the beer was flowing.

'Your recruits get younger every time, Marsha. You sure these are old enough to drink?'

The lanky redhead meant *them*, and Judith felt Gwen stiffen beside her. She stood up and took the black girl's arm.

'Time to do your eyes, girl, and I'm bursting with all these beers. Come on.' Inside the ladies she said: 'Marsha loves a barney, but I don't want to get into it. I'm too confused in my own head to join a scrap. And you looked ready to deck Carrot-top.'

'Too fucking right.' Gwen leaned forward and examined herself in the mirror, her camouflage combat trousers tight across the prominent rump. 'Actually, the make-up will do. But thanks for getting me out of there, honey. We don't really wanna get barred from this hole.' She straightened up and they looked at each other without speaking. Judith could feel that her own sexual attraction had returned.

'Got to pee.' She dived into a cubicle just as another woman came in to use the mirror. When she emerged they were alone again and Gwen said, 'I think we know how we feel, right? Thing is, there's a guy staying at my place next couple of weeks and I kinda said, well, I sorta promised . . .' She broke off with a grimace. 'To be honest, it's a fucking mess and I'll be glad when it's all over. *No* chance will it work out. But I don't wanna make you an offer when I ain't properly free.'

Judith was touched by this plain speaking and turned on more than ever. Following her out of the lavatory, she tried to keep her eyes off the firm protuberances of the girl's behind and her thoughts away from what they

122

would feel like under her hands. Shit. First Jeanie, now Gwen. Women were obviously becoming the business in her life.

At the table the argument was raging, though Judith judged they were a few drinks away yet from the stage of gratuitous insults. The tape was lying by her bottle and she picked it up, raising her voice to explain that Gwen and she were going to leave them to it. Marsha winked lewdly and was straight back into the fray, but Liss leaned over and spoke.

'I shouldn't really stick my oar in, but I'd be careful if I were you, hen. You may think you know her nibs quite well, know just how she's gonna take it when she gets this from you, but . . .' She shrugged and emptied her glass of vodka. 'Whatever. It's not *my* funeral. Who's for another?'

The two young women walked side by side through the park before their ways diverged. By the pool they stood and kissed for a while then stopped as if by mutual decision.

'I'm off work, Tuesday,' said Gwen. 'Any chance I could see your place?'

'The boss is away all week. Hey, why don't you come out delivering with me? There's room on the back of the bike.'

'Fuck, that'd be great. Will I get to see some of these imp-lem-ents?' Gwen drew the word out.

God, she is hooked on this topic, thought Judith. 'It's 16 Markham Street, top flat. Be there at 8.30 and we'll walk over to St Mary's. OK?'

On the Tuesday at 9.15 Judith came back outside with three packages, two of which were metre-long tubes taped shut at the ends while the other was a smallish cardboard box. 'Well, even I can guess what those two are,' said Gwen, 'but what's the third one? Hey, it's quite heavy. Go on, Jude, let's have a look.'

'No way.' Judith shook her head firmly. 'They're very keen on things being properly sealed till they reach the customer. However, if you're patient you may get to see what's in the box.' As they walked round to the garage she explained that it was to go to a model school out in the country and they were to wait while it was inspected in case it didn't suit.

In the garage, Gwen was impressed by the shiny red Vespa. 'Wow! These things are cool.' Judith stashed the items in the paniers, the ones that could only be canes sticking up obtrusively. 'We'll get rid of those first,' she said, before we head out of town. 'Put this on.' She handed over a helmet and thought it suited Gwen a treat, dressed as she was in a leather jacket, black stretch leggings and boots. Then they both climbed on and, with the feel of the black girl's body pressing into her quickening the pulse, Judith started up and drove them out into the back lane.

As they reached the main road Gwen yelled into Judith's ear, 'When you get your test, then?'

'Don't ask silly questions,' Judith said over her shoulder and as she did a nifty right turn almost under the wheels of a double-decker bus she heard from the back a shout of 'Fucking hell!' and what sounded like: '*Now* she tells me.'

The long packages were dropped off in suburban streets, the first to a shifty-looking man who looked even shiftier when he saw it was two young women who had brought his order. The second was taken by an older woman who was anything but embarrassed by their presence or by what they had brought. She opened the tube on the doorstep and swished the cane several times appreciatively, seemingly careless of what the neighbours might think. Gwen was goggling at the sight, but since the item seemed acceptable Judith grabbed her elbow and steered her out of the gate, claiming they had a busy schedule. Who knows what kind of trial the woman might want if they hung around.

It took the best part of an hour to reach the final address after a wrong turn that petered out at a farm entrance, but eventually they swooped into a driveway past a sign reading MANNERLY MODELS. At the baronial entrance Judith rang the bell and the door opened almost at once.

'Ah! The delivery from Eumenides. *Entrez, entrez, mes chéries.*' He was a slim, well-muscled man in his forties with a shock of black hair and discreet, minimal make-up. In a silk shirt open to the waist and satin trousers that sheathed his thighs, he bubbled over with conversation as they followed him into the entrance hall.

'I'm afraid I'm not Mannerly. Courteous at all times, I hope, but not mannerly.' His laugh had a manic edge. 'Place is named after a distant ancestor of mine, an aristocrat, no less. Queer as a coot. Lovely man. Used to pick out a stable lad at the end of the day, leather his sit-upon then bugger him silly. They all adored Lord Mannerly, used to vie with each other for the privilege.' Eyeing his somewhat startled audience, he let out a heavy sigh, as if in mourning for those paradisal days long past. 'However, our girls are very lovely and I do get a little bottom-warming in now and then, if nothing else. Which is where you come in, darlings, so please follow me.'

He led the way through a small gymnasium where three young women were exercising at the wall bars, past a dressing room where several others were sitting in front of mirrors, into a classroom that contained perhaps a dozen desks. Then he stuck his head back out of the door and called: 'Ladies! When you're ready, *s'il vous plaît.*'

He took the package from Judith and began opening it on the table at the front of the room, talking all the while. 'I should have said that my name is Boswell, but they all call me Bozzy, so please follow suit. That is

Bozzy, not Bossy, though I'm sure I am at times. *Mes jeunes filles* can be so scatterbrained.' Tittering, he took out the contents, which uncoiled into a strip of what looked like leather and weighed it in his hand.

'I needed this because my pupil – ex-pupil, I should say – Marlene cut my old one up into little pieces and threw it in my face. Took a kitchen knife to it as if it were some kind of vegetable to be chopped. Then she walked out.' By this time the students had all appeared and Bozzy turned to them. 'These young ladies have kindly brought me my new strap and I was just telling them about Marlene's outrageous behaviour. *Très, très folle*, given all the opportunities of work your Bozzy is going to find for you. I mean it's not as if I ever really *hurt* your sweet bottoms, do I, darlings?'

His question was obviously rhetorical and the aspirant models pouted coyly to each other in a way that went straight to Judith's loins. Meanwhile, the director had examined the strap minutely and spoke again. 'They told me that this instrument has a rubber core under its leather surface and it certainly feels a little heavier. So I think we require a trial. After all, I can't buy something that might be *too* painful for my dear pupils, can I?' He appealed to the class who chorused, 'No, you can't, Bozzy,' in what was clearly a well-practised response.

'So what we need now is a volunteer to undergo the crucial test.' He scanned the occupants of the desks but each one had acquired an interest in a fingernail or the cuff of a sleeve; in fact, anything at all that would keep her from meeting his gaze. 'Now, I wonder . . .' he said, and turned to look directly at Judith. She was not aware of reacting strongly, but something about her face must have given him pause for he passed quickly on to Gwen. 'I think I have the solution. What if our second delivery girl here – such a lovely young woman of colour – were to offer herself so that we can conclude the purchase, wouldn't that just be so appropriate?'

There was a full second's silence and Judith could see Gwen trying to decide. Then she straightened up and said: 'OK. Right. So what is it I'm in for?'

'Oh, well done, darling. *C'est bien, nest-ce pas, mes filles?* Just a little six of the best with our new friend here. Nothing to it. Of course, to simulate the conditions of its normal use, you will have to take your trousers down.' Gwen pursed her lips but did not demur. 'If that's agreed, then, just come over here with me.'

At the front of the room beside the large table was a tall teacher's desk. It stood on its own without an accompanying chair and as the purpose of it became clear Judith recalled in a rush the time she had seen its twin at Nemesis with Helen bent over it for a dose of Miss James's strap. That seemed an age ago, yet it was little more than a month. Then she had been horrified and bewildered. Now, observing Gwen being prepared for similar treatment, she was more excited than scared. When the black leggings were lowered to the top of her boots, Judith's pulse quickened some more. The bad girl's got no knickers on *again*, she thought, as Bozzy began to enthuse about what he had uncovered.

'Oh, I say. What a treat we have in store, girls! We have such a lovely bottom here for a demonstration of our new instrument. *Now, ma chérie,*' he carried on, running his hands over Gwen's posterior, 'spread your legs just a little more and go right forwards. That's it. Wonderful. Exactly as it should be – a charmingly *full* rear presentation.' It was indeed quite a sight, the rich rounds split by a dark furrow that ended in the black-frizzed fig of exposed cunt, and Judith felt proud that the behind which had so taken her fancy was the object of such unqualified admiration.

'Very good. Now *you*, darling –' here he turned to Judith '– if you'd be so good to come round the back – *c'est ça* – you can lean over and hold your young

127

associate's waist. Not to restrain her, you understand, I'm sure she means to cooperate fully with us, but to give her the reassurance of your touch. A little moral support. *Parfait*. Now I think we can begin.'

As Judith watched, heart in mouth, the man took the broad, two-tailed tawse and brought it down across the whole breadth of the target. As the buttocks bounced she felt the body tense under her hands and there was a semi-stifled 'Fuck!' from beneath her. At the second stroke the hips jerked and the vocal response this time was loud and clear: 'Oh, fuck!'

Bozzy laid down the strap on the table, looking very angry. 'Now, I must insist, such language simply will not do. It is the one thing I cannot countenance, especially *that* word you used. I am going to start again from the beginning and this time I expect more self-control. *Qu'est-ce que tu dis à ça?*'

Later Judith wondered why they didn't just get up and walk out. However, at the time it seemed quite appropriate that Gwen should say, in an uncharacteristically small voice, 'I'm sorry,' and that the leathering should continue. Towards the end of what had become eight strokes, her legs kicked and she cried out, but there was no more swearing. When it was over, Gwen leaped up and clapped her hands to the injured parts but once again Bozzy was not impressed.

'Stop that and pull up your clothes!' he said sharply. 'We don't allow any rubbing, do we, girls?' The prompt reply was in unison and this time almost gleeful.

'No, Bozzy, we don't!' The would-be models' flushed faces and bright eyes made it clear that while none of them were keen to *be* strapped, they all found the spectacle rather pleasing. Seeing, too, the bulge in the director's satin pants, Judith wondered whether he was quite as queer as he made himself out to be. Perhaps, at least, there would be willing hands, or a mouth even, to bring about his detumescence.

These speculations were supported by the haste with which they were now escorted from the building, not in fact unwelcome since Judith was in the grip of needs of her own. 'Get on – quick,' she said starting up the Vespa and with Gwen clinging very tightly to her body they careered down the drive out into the country lane. At the first gate they came to Judith pulled right off the road and stopped. Inside the field she removed her friend's belt, tugged the leggings down and knelt behind her to kiss the hot cheeks. But when she moved to part them for a more intimate investigation with her tongue, she was rebuffed.

'Hey, I told you I'm not free,' said Gwen, pulling her up. 'Not yet, any road. Let's just do *this* for now.' And opening Judith's waistband and zip she pushed her fingers in under the matted pubic hair.

Half an hour later they emerged and, as she wheeled the machine back on to the tarmac, Judith was thinking it was as well there had been no passing traffic. Who knows what a driver might have done, eyes fixed on the sight of two young women, bare-arsed and kissing passionately each with a hand between the other's legs. As she started up and Gwen climbed on at her back, she said over her shoulder, 'Well, girl, d'you remember you were dead keen at the weekend to see some imp-lem-ents? I'd say you found out a lot about one of them.'

'Too fucking right!' was the answer in her ear and, laughing, they sped off between the high hedgerows.

Judith opened her eyes and peered at the clock. 8.05; loads of time. She stretched luxuriously, wisps of a dream still clinging to her consciousness. Gwen was in it again, just as she'd featured every night since their adventure as delivery girls, though they had agreed not to meet in the flesh for another week yet. Judith snuggled into the bedding and tried to recover the image: there was a long T-shirt that she was trying to lift up, but each time Judith got close to exposing her delectable bum the girl twisted away with that laugh . . .

Oh, shit! She sat bolt upright, suddenly wide awake. Horribly awake. It was Monday morning and today was the day. After vacillating all week, on Friday afternoon she had written a note to Ms Morris and sealed it in a large envelope along with the video of the janny and his helper *in flagrante delicto*. The word Melissa had used for him brought her warning to mind: that the boss wasn't going to like it. And if the mysterious Liss, who swanned round Europe for Eumenides and was plainly an intimate of Ms Morris, told Judith to be careful, she should have listened. Fuck, what had she done?

The clothes she had put out the night before were on the bedside chair and Judith got out of bed with a heavy heart and began to dress. The crisp white blouse and black skirt that wasn't, for once, too short or too tight gave her image in the mirror a conventional smartness she normally eschewed, but this time it seemed appropriate. The condemned girl ate a hearty breakfast, she said to herself, buttering a piece of toast and stirring a strong mug of coffee, while thoughts of Mary Queen of Scots and the executioner's block floated into her head. Judith gulped down the steaming liquid looking at the clock and shook herself, almost angrily. Jee-sus girl, get a grip! The worst that can happen is that you'll be out of a job for the second time this summer. Big fucking deal!

Walking in, Judith's spirits lifted a bit. Maybe she had gone out on a limb, but something had to be done about that bastard Jennings. When he discovered she'd taken Gwen out last Tuesday he berated her for letting an outsider get information about the corporation's activities. He'd cornered her in the garage putting the bike away and threatened to tell the boss unless she'd accept correction from him there and then. He'd had the nerve

130

to produce a cane and suggest that if she stretched across the bonnet of the van beside them and took a dozen of the best he would forget about the whole thing. Judith picked up a heavy spanner from the bench and told him that if he came a step nearer she'd lay him out cold. He'd fucked off pretty sharpish after that, but she regretted the action before he was out of the door. He'd never been well-disposed towards her, but now she had made a real enemy.

It was that incident that had really decided her to leave the tape for Ms Morris on the Friday night with a note that complained about Mr Jennings' other lapse of decorum in groping her behind at every opportunity that presented itself. As Judith crossed the quad, it occurred to her that maybe she was still deciding what to do and they wouldn't discuss it at all until later in the week. Then, climbing the stairs, she wondered if perhaps the boss hadn't even had a chance to see the tape yet. However, once she was through the outer door of the director's office, voices sounded clearly from within, and in a gut-wrenching instant knew her thoughts for the idle wish-fulfilments they were. It was Mr Jennings and Mrs Butler, here in advance, and together with Ms Morris they formed a reception committee that was waiting just for her.

At the inner door, which stood very slightly ajar, Judith hesitated. If she turned round now she could come back in the afternoon when Ms Morris would be alone. Then, as she dithered on the threshold, her fate was sealed: the door opened and the director herself was right before her. Without a word she took hold of Judith's arm and drew her into the centre of the room. When she turned to close the door, Judith saw with a pang of anxiety that she locked it and dropped the key into her jacket pocket.

'We have grave matters to deal with, and I wish to ensure we are not disturbed.' The superintendent and

131

his assistant sat at opposite ends of the large sofa, and it gave the young woman standing in front of them no comfort to see them nodding keenly at Ms Morris's remark. Neither in fact looked the least bit grave, and the director had a high colour and a glint in her eyes that made Judith's nervousness grow. This was not at all how she had imagined the encounter that would result from the delivery of the video recording.

Then, as Ms Morris began to speak, it became clear that the contents of the tape were not her prime concern and Judith's heart sank. 'Now, I understand that last week you brought an outsider with you on your delivery round without seeking anyone's leave. Is that correct?' Judith began to attempt an explanation but was instantly silenced.

'Answer me, please. Yes or no.'

'Yes.'

'And yet you must have realised that this was a potential compromising of our clients' confidentiality?'

'Yes. I'm sorry, but you weren't here, and Gwen wouldn't –'

'Be quiet. I'll ask again: do you accept that you were wrong? Yes or no.'

'Yes.'

'In that case, when Mr Jennings offered you the opportunity of summary discipline to wipe the slate clean, you should have accepted, should you not? Instead of which, you threatened him with violence. I consider such behaviour quite outrageous!'

Judith was rendered speechless by the construction that the director had put on the events in question. That she could regard the leering groper with his cane as an agent of on-the-spot justice was so at odds with the truth as to make her head spin and she gaped foolishly. However, Ms Morris was not looking for a reply.

'And what makes the whole thing ten times worse, in my view, is your effrontery in lodging a complaint

132

against Mr Jennings of what is sexual harassment, no less. You, my girl, have been with us barely three weeks and you have the nerve to attempt to blacken my right-hand man's name in this way. Shame on you! I need hardly add that Mrs Butler confirms that no behaviour of the sort you allege has taken place in her presence.'

'But, but, but –' Judith was finding her voice '– but what about the video?' As soon as she'd said it, she realised her blunder: it was something that should have been raised only when she had the boss to herself. As it was, her question seemed to set the seal on the occasion and Judith stood aghast as Ms Morris's tirade reached a climax.

'When I received it, I called Mr Jennings and after we had spoken I gave it him to burn. The only fit end for such a thing. How dare you!' The lady's colour was now even higher than before and her eyes blazed. 'I am going to do something now that is obviously long overdue. I am going to put you over my knee and spank your bare bottom red raw.' The last words were said with a quiet venom that rooted Judith to the spot. She flinched as the director reached forward, grasped the hem of her skirt and yanked it up over her waist.

'Hold that!' she snapped and signalled to the couple on the couch who got up and lifted a long wooden chest into the middle of the floor. Then they returned to their seats, leaning forwards for a good view, as Ms Morris sat on its padded top and dragged the shocked girl across her lap. An elbow pressed the back of Judith's neck, forcing her face into the rough tweed of the cushion, and the forearm pinned her back while the other hand tugged the knickers down round her thighs. Then began a series of hearty slaps at intervals that were measured to punctuate the stream of verbal censure.

'This (*smack*) is what little Judy (*smack*) should have had (*smack*) a good dose of (*smack*) when she was small

133

(*smack*). Then (*smack*) we should have had (*smack*) less of the trouble (*smack*) that has earned her (*smack*) this spanking (*smack*). This is for disobedience (*smack! smack! smack! smack!*) and this for rudeness (*smack! smack! smack! smack!*); this is for spying and telling tales (*smack! smack! smack! smack!*) and this (*smack!! smack!! smack!! smack!!*) is for all Judy's naughtiness.'

The pace and intensity of the onslaught on her behind had moved up a notch, yet while she jerked with the pain of each blow, Judith lay unresisting. It was as if her mind, unable to rationalise the humiliation of a punishment that was being inflicted to the undisguised relish of the audience, had disengaged from the possibility of evasive action. For a minute or two the spanking continued without commentary, save for Judith's own gasps and cries; then there was a pause and Ms Morris spoke again.

'At last this *naughty* bottom is getting what it deserves, but I think we have some way to go yet. So what does bad little Judy have to say, now?' There was a further volley of slaps that made Judith yell in earnest, then: 'Is Judy sorry for her bad behaviour?'

Appalled, Judith heard herself say: 'I'm sorry.'

'I'm sorry, *ma'am*.'

'Sorry. I'm sorry – ma'am.'

'Not sorry enough yet, I see.' And the chastisement continued, now in a grim silence.

'Oh, please, please. Ma'am, I'm sorry. Ow! Ow! Ple-e-e-ease!'

The whole of Judith's posterior was now so tender that a touch would have been painful. But, if anything, the director's smacks were growing harder minute by minute and any remaining shreds of self-control vanished. Judith howled and pleaded for it to end, all without effect, and she slumped sobbing across the implacable lap. Then, through the tears and snot of a thoroughly spanked teenager, Judith became aware that something else was happening. Oh, God, she was wet. The hot throbbing hurt of her buttocks was matched by a pulsing in her loins that was growing with each new slap and making her hips thrust into the fine weave of the director's skirt.

Appalled, Judith realised that she was going to come. In thrall to the mounting sensations, she had a horrid certainty that the watchers had recognised her state, and through misty eyes she could see them both eagerly attentive. Then, as the spasms took hold of her and the spanking hand seemed to follow their rhythm, to a remote part of her mind there came the beginnings of knowledge. Ms Morris had intended this: somehow *she* had known what Judith herself did not. Then even these glimmerings of understanding were wiped out as the abject Judy, cringing under the leering gaze of Mr Jennings and Mrs Butler, convulsed in orgasm.

Afterwards, she slid off Ms Morris's lap on to her knees and held her bottom, snuffling. Dimly conscious that the couple were leaving, the next thing she knew was that Ms Morris was in front of her.

'Get up!' she said sharply. 'Get up, girl. Look at this.' Judith stood slowly and saw the damp stain that was indicated on the director's dress. 'Look what naughty Judy has done now. And, tell me child, what happens when Judy is naughty? Well?' The voice was raised and Judith felt panic.

'She – she gets spanked. Ma'am. But I've just been spanked and I'm so sore . . .' The tears started to flow in earnest once again.

'Stop that nonsense at once!' Ms Morris lifted her skirts and sat down again, patting her thighs. 'Over here. IMMEDIATELY!'

Judith jumped, heart fluttering with anxiety and obeyed. 'Please, ma'am, I'm sorry, I can't bear it –' she began as soon as the smacking started, but she was cut short.

'SILENCE! Any more of that, Judy, and I shall call Mr Jennings to come back, this time with his cane. A bad little girl like Judy would benefit from a real thrashing, don't you think?'

'Oh, no, ma'am, please, I'll be quiet.' Desperately Judith stifled her sobs and submitted to her fate. Now the spanking hand worked at the junction of buttocks and upper thighs, and once more Judith found herself lubricating freely. And as each blow connected with the wet, swollen lips of her cunt it was not long before she was again racked in the throes of her climax. When it was over she lay panting for the few moments granted before she was jerked roughly to her feet.

'Come with me.'

Judith stumbled weakly after the commanding figure who led the way through two doors into a small bedroom. On a tallboy was set out a glass of milk and a round of sandwiches.

'Stand here and eat. I shall return in five minutes.' As the key turned in the lock behind the departing director, Judith was suddenly ravenous. When she finished there was barely time to look round at the narrow bed against the wall before the door opened again.

'Strip and put this on.' Ms Morris held out a short, frilly nightdress. When Judith was re-attired the woman held up an oval of thick leather whose handle was bound in twine. 'The remedial treatment necessary in this case – which has only just begun – is beyond the capabilities of my own hand. So here is Judy's very own instrument, which will be kept by her bed when it is not in use. In the morning, she will warm it between her thighs so that it is good and supple for the first spanking of the day. But now it is time for the last. You will see that a pouffe has been placed by the side of the bed. Kneel on it and stretch across the covers.'

The last spark of resistance gone, Judith obeyed and as she took up position the baby doll garment rode up to the small of her back, leaving her posterior completely exposed. She felt tears coursing down her cheeks and heard a little wheedling voice that could only be her own.

'Please, ma'am, please, not too hard. Judy's bottom hurts so much . . .'

'It will be as hard as necessary to correct a naughty girl's misbehaviour. No more, no less.' The tone was dispassionate, without pity, and a hand explored the tenderised flesh on display. Then there were six resounding slaps, each of which wrenched an agonised shriek out of her, though she had no spirit left to take evasive action.

'Get up and get into bed. Remember my instructions for tomorrow.' Again the key was turned in the lock and Judith lay face down, unwilling to pull the covers over her inflamed, throbbing buttocks. Then, even as her brain tried feebly to encompass the enormity of what was happening to her, the blackness rolled up in a tidal wave and she knew no more.

8

The Way

Judith stirred and reached over to the bedside table. The instrument – her instrument – wasn't there. There was a surge of panic and as she made to sit up she nearly cried out with the stiff soreness of her lower half. Falling back on to the pillows, she remembered she was at home. It was Saturday morning and she was in the flat until the resumption of treatment on Monday. She knew she should have been relieved, but without the ritual of the first correction of the day she felt stricken and eased herself, wincing, out of bed. At the dressing table Judith examined her rear view in the mirror and observed how the residues of discipline had painted the flesh in rich dark purples fringed with a dirty yellow.

Her lip trembled at the sight, yet she craved more and the clothes brush already used for that purpose lay directly to hand. It was a moment's work to position an upright chair and steady herself over its back, then she brought the flat wooden surface smartly down on the centre of her left buttock. The sensation nearly caused her to drop the brush but Judith bit her lip and waited until it subsided a little; then she forced herself to continue until each cheek had received six of the same. She felt weak with the pain and effort, but it had done the job and her cunt oozed. Back in bed Judith's mind drifted while her hand moved in the slick folds between her legs.

In the distance a buzzer sounded a long note, stopped, and sounded again. It was the outside door, downstairs, but she didn't want to see anyone. Not just yet. The juices were in full flow around her stroking fingers and there was only one thing Judy wanted to do right now ... Suddenly she came to and there were figures in the half-dark room.

'Jude, Jude. Wake up. It's eight o'clock at night, what are you doing in bed? What's going on?' Marsha. It was Marsha speaking and then, bewildered, she saw blonde curls as the other woman sat beside her and cradled her head.

'Judith, it's me, Catherine. Cat. Oh, girl, what have they been doing to you?'

As she had done once before, Judith put herself entirely in the trainee nurse's capable hands. Then she had been pierced with anxiety before her interview at the archive; now she was frozen into a semi-childlike state and the significance of the two women's peremptory incursion into her bedroom withdrawal would be appreciated only later. Judith was dimly aware of a hasty consultation, after which Marsha disappeared, then she gave herself to Catherine's ministrations.

First there was a hot bath with an oil that made her sluggish senses start to wake as she lay steeping. Then, wrapped in warm towels and patted gently dry, she was placed face down across her bed on a clean sheet and a heap of fresh pillows. The afflicted parts bared, Cat took an aromatic salve and stroked it, little by little, into the bruised flesh. While she worked she said no words, either of sympathy or reproach, and Judith found her numbness transmuting into tired relaxation.

When the fingers brushed her genitals, Judith reared up in a kind of reflex to prolong and extend the contact but Catherine stopped her. 'Later,' she whispered. 'Now you must rest.' The bed was rearranged and Judith was installed, fragrant and sleepy. She took the two capsules offered and on command swallowed them with water, then she sank back all at once exhausted. Within moments her mind was drifting and just before she was gone a voice said softly, 'You'll live, girl; but this was not the way.'

Judith woke mid-morning to the sounds of activity in the kitchen and they both ate a substantial breakfast. Afterwards she was placed again over pillows for an inspection and massage, then Catherine produced the two dildos she had left in her bedroom. In a short-lived relapse, Judith demanded petulantly that the brush be used but she was refused. Pouting, she submitted at first with bad grace to the stimulation on offer; however, under Catherine's deft movements her body soon responded and for the first time in a fortnight she reached an orgasm that was not partly the result of corporal punishment.

Then they dressed and walked out into the park. Sitting on the grass, Judith soaked up the hot sunshine that seemed like a material signifier of her emergence out of the mental fog of the past week. Now it was over she could scarcely comprehend the continuous flow of pain into sex and sex into pain, nor did there remain more than a dim recollection of the infantile state of mind that had accompanied it. She noticed that Catherine was looking at her thoughtfulness with a degree of concern and pressed her friend's arm with a smile; then they both lay back in the warmth of the afternoon and dozed.

Much later, back in the flat they made supper and drank some beer in the same companionable silence that had prevailed all day. Eventually, as it became quite dark outside, Catherine said, 'Jude, you know what you've got to do tomorrow.' There was no answer, so she went on. 'Melissa is coming here first thing and she'll go with you to hold your hand.'

Judith struggled to say first how grateful she was to be rescued and then how sorry she was for upsetting Cat a few weeks before. But she couldn't find the words to describe what exactly she'd done by refusing to play the spanking game: her uptight reaction then seemed very foolish after the past week's events. However, the young woman who had been so assured in organising Judith's care now wouldn't meet her eye and she floundered, not knowing what it was she wanted to express.

Still looking down, Cat said, 'I'm seeing someone just now, a guy – well, he kinda wants to be a girl.' She gave a giggle and looked up embarrassed from under her ringlets. 'So I've got to head off early, as soon as Liss comes. OK, Jude? I'll be in touch, er, to make sure you're all right.' She finished lamely and Judith felt pierced by a sense of things lost between them through her past equivocation. Though they sat for a while, Catherine talking of intrigues in the new hospital, the feeling persisted until bedtime and Judith passed a restless night.

It was nine o'clock when Melissa arrived behind the wheel of a car in an expensive pearl-grey suit with short blonde hair subtly streaked with violet. The fingernails were paler and shorter and the mode of speaking had been trimmed to the cut of the image. This is the result of a few weeks in Bonn, thought Judith as they eased through the morning traffic, but she wished she had heeded the less manicured speech in the pub. Liss explained that she had been contacted by Sandra from the Catalogue Department, and before the name brought a face to her passenger's mind it evoked a startlingly clear image of a tightly trousered rump that jerked under the blows of a black rod.

'You see, Jude, she feels like she's chosen her way which is to get a good dose of discipline every few weeks. Now, bending over to be caned by the fucking janny would no be my choice, but that's her business.'

Judith noticed how mention of Mr Jennings had caused the accent to flare up before the professional demeanour reasserted itself. 'But she didn't think that you'd *chosen* anything, so she was a wee bit worried. Some of these masochists, they kind of bond with someone who sees them get beaten. And that's what she's done. She was really looking out for you, Jude, and she went to I don't know what lengths to get hold of my number.'

Judith was still feeling guilty about Cat, so the idea of another young woman forming an attachment she might betray was disconcerting. But there was no time for reflection; they had arrived in the rear car park. 'Just remember I'm here to back you up,' said Liss. 'But you know *you've* got to do it.'

When they reached the outer office on the top floor, Judith stood for a moment with her hand on the door knob of the inner sanctum. Her palms were damp and her head ached, but she opened the door and leaned forwards, clearing her throat. Ms Morris stood up at once from her desk.

'You *bad* girl, you are late. Look at the time.' She reached for the paddle and slapped it on her hand. Judith's stomach knotted with apprehension but she forced herself to speak.

'Ms Morris, I have come to resign. I'm afraid it's all been a mistake . . .'

At first there was angry disbelief on the older woman's face; then Judith opened the door wide and Melissa stepped into the room behind her. The effect was an immediate demonstration of the young Glaswegian's improbable authority and for the first and only time Judith saw the director of Eumenides Incorporated totally at a loss. Her mouth opened and closed as she looked from one of her visitors to the other, though no words came out. But then she put down the piece of leather and shrugged, and Judith could not but admire how quickly self-possession returned.

'I think I should own that the mistake was mostly mine. Do you think we could perhaps return to the situation as it was? I should be pleased if . . .' She faltered, looking at Judith's expression of incredulity at the idea she should continue working with the superintendent whose position she had tried to sabotage. 'No, I suppose not,' she said with a sigh and scribbled a line on her desk pad. 'Very well. It can be your final job to take this to Accounts on your way out.'

For the next two days Judith mooched about the flat in a less than happy frame of mind. While the note she delivered had seen her handsomely paid, her visit to Cataloguing to find Sandra had misfired. She had wanted to express her thanks for what had been done for her, but the usually forthright girl had blushed and bolted as soon as Judith approached. Having tried to do something that would help make them 'friends', she'd no doubt deepened Sandra's crush on her. To make matters worse, she was chafing under a vow to deny herself the comforts of masturbation, or continuing experiments with the clothes brush that were likely to instigate it, in an effort to break fully from her week of juvenile subjection.

That was definitely not the way. It's what Cat had said and she was right. There was no choice about it, she had to leave Eumenides, just like she'd had to leave Nemesis before it, with the result that she was out of a job for the second time this summer. Where did she go from here? Judith paced up and down, out of the small kitchen across the hall to her bedroom and back. She avoided Catherine's room altogether, knowing that to see its empty state would make her feel worse, even though the sight of the closed door – always open when her friend was staying, except when she was asleep – conveyed already the bad news about her absence.

As she moved restlessly about the apartment, Judith's thoughts turned back to the convent girl who had been

143

so unashamed of her masochistic desires and to the doctor who had set down her story. Marie Bonnard and Michelle Brown: what had happened at the trial of the first and how did the second get involved? The more she pondered, the more questions came to mind. There was the note to Miss James of Nemesis that had addressed her as cherie and then spoken of being lost. What was it exactly? She took down the file from the shelf, opened it and retrieved the sheet. *Quand tu liras ceci, j'aurai me perdre en rigueur*. When you get this, I shall be lost in rigour. It had to be something like that, unless it was an idiom of some kind. What on Earth did it mean?

Judith sat down at the table and looked through what she had of Marie's story once again. It was a compelling tale running as it did from the birchings and dormitory sex of the convent school through the reformatory training to position of gardener with Mme Dauvignon. And then, just as she was dallying with the stableboy Jean and had become her mistress's lover, disaster. The husband had returned and then there had been a murder. Memories flooded back of her brief time in the archive immersed in those dark manuscripts, oblivious to the figures that passed in bright sunlight across the quad below her window. What she read there had opened her eyes to her own needs without showing her how to satisfy them. With Miss James, she had just seized up in panic at the idea of the strap, and then with Ms Morris she had collapsed – abjectly – into an infantile state. It had been most powerfully erotic, but she couldn't live like that. There had to be another way, a way through those two reactions, and somehow Judith couldn't shake off the idea that Marie held the key to it.

But how? The information that she had said the girl's story ended in *disaster*. That was the actual word she used, or rather the word that had been set down in Dr Brown's narrative. As Judith sat and pondered, it struck her more forcibly than ever that there were oddities here. It wasn't what she'd first thought – that the whole thing might be an invention, an erotic fantasy, possibly penned by a man – for now she accepted (without knowing quite why) that it was a true account. But it was an account of events of nearly forty years previously, supposedly recalled by the writer who had interviewed Marie at the time, in 1962. That's what it had said on the (properly typed) title page at the beginning of the first section.

Right, said Judith to herself, let's be logical about this. We know that the doctor didn't actually get her PhD until 1990, long after the interviews that she says provided the basis of the narrative. Now that was written in 1992 and it's very vivid after such a long time, but there were tapes, even if they were poor ones, so maybe they would jog the memory. But unless she was quite aged – and the death being unexpected argued against that – she would have been a young woman too in the early 60s. And that really didn't make any sense. There was no way an unqualified young woman who was no relation was going to be allowed access to a murder suspect.

Dawning awareness of where the train of thought was heading made Judith's scalp prickle. There was Marie Bonnard 'interviewed' by the English-speaking Michelle Brown (on more than one occasion); the young French gardener and the doctor-to-be who later (much later) plants a flourishing garden in England. Could it be? Yes, it had to be. Suddenly Judith was certain. Same initials, same age: they were one and the same person. There never had been any *interviews*; the manuscripts she had were recollections by the woman herself. But then, but then – oh, no! – it meant that if Dr Brown had died, then so had Marie.

Judith sat and stared at the pages in front of her, shocked. For the first time she realised that at the back of her mind she had assumed that Marie Bonnard was alive, and not only alive but traceable. Faced with the prospect that the woman was neither made her understand how important that idea had been to her, even though, as in the past week, it had been buried deep under the fierce demands of the moment. As a kind of last resort had been the barely examined thought that the girl out of the convent school could guide her in some as yet unimagined way. But now she had arrived at a conclusion that would rule out the possibility and she felt stricken by it.

There was one small beer left in the fridge and Judith jerked the top off with a bottle opener, flicking it into the bin. She was halfway through its contents before she saw the flaw in her reasoning. While she had no doubt that there was one person not two involved in the story, what that meant was that the second individual was an assumed identity. Not exactly a fiction, since there had been a Dr Brown who had acquired qualifications and established a house and garden, but an identity that had been created *and could therefore be destroyed*: The 'death' of Michelle Brown didn't necessarily imply anything about the demise of Marie Bonnard, only that the alias had come to the end of its useful life.

She stood up and swallowed the rest of the beer, cheered but aware that it was only a negative conclusion she had made. There was perhaps no reason to think Marie was dead, but nor was there any evidence to show that she was still alive. The note now made more sense, of course. It was a parting note – from M for Marie – to say she was leaving her alter ego to become lost – *se perdre* – but how, and where? Did it mean, being in French, that she had gone back to her old country? Judith sighed and tossed the empty bottle into the bin. There was only one obvious place to get some questions answered and that was at the doctor's old house, from Jeanie. Would she be less reluctant to talk if she knew what Judith now understood, or at least thought she understood? Well, there was only one way to find out, and she had a phone number on the headed paper in front of her.

Just as she was reaching into the pocket of her coat for some change, the outside doorbell buzzed sharply right beside her. Keyed up by her reflections, Judith recoiled and it was a moment or two before she spoke into the intercom. There was no reply and after a pause she repeated the question, 'Who is it?', still to no avail. Downstairs, she picked an envelope from the mat that bore her name in a big, loose scrawl, but from the top step there was no one visible who might have delivered it. The message inside was – as Judith realised only later – deceptive in its apparent simplicity: *Friday at noon if you want more. J.*

The next morning Judith got up late and pulled on an old pair of jeans and a sweatshirt. Over coffee she made herself consider some of the implications of Jeanie's note. First, there was the question of her address. Judith was sure she had not left one: details like that had been interrupted by the return of the man and she had taken off in a hurry. But the woman knew she had worked at Nemesis, so it was a good bet it had been got from the archive. Maybe the secretary would have passed it on; but no, Helen had hated her, so it must have been the boss herself. Miss James – the lady whose strictness she had walked out on – *she* had given the information to Jeanie. That was certainly food for thought.

Considering the content of the thing was less pleasant, for while its ambiguity (surely deliberate) opened the possibility of gaining information about Marie it did not rule out entering another situation like the one she had just been saved from. And that was something Judith very much *did* want to rule out. For now. No, for good: the thought of the large woman's power gave her a fluttery feeling of panic and she started up from the

147

table. Get a grip, girl, Judith told herself, but without much effect and she decided to venture out. Perhaps the bright sunshine would quell these dark thoughts.

In the park it indeed seemed rather silly that the warm and sensual Jeanie could be a threat. 'But it isn't just *her* that scares me,' announced Judith to the ducks on the pond, 'it's what *I'm* capable of doing in the presence of that strength.' She glanced quickly round, but there was no one within earshot and shook her head with a grimace: time to find someone who was actually there to talk to. Judith looked at her watch. It was three o'clock and while The Phoenix would be shut, Marsha might be there and she could get in down the side alley.

Ten minutes later she found the back entrance of the pub open and went in along a short corridor that led past the toilets. Then, about to pull open the door into the bar itself, Judith heard voices and something about the tone of them made her draw up. She couldn't make out everything, but some phrases came through clearly.

'I told you I ain't sure I'm interested no more . . . anybody who could do something like that . . .'

'Well then, honey, just let me . . . mmm . . . and again . . .'

The second voice was Marsha's, no doubt about it. Puzzled as to what was going on, but reluctant to burst in, Judith strained her ears and what she heard made her go cold. The other woman was Gwen and now every word was audible.

'Hey, girl, hold on now. It ain't Jude who was standing in your way. Last night was great, but it's a one-off, right? Cos I'm tied up, right now – just like I told her when I fancied her, before all this shit she pulled last week.'

The meaning of the words hit her like a kick to the stomach and Judith slumped against the wall. Then her shock began to turn to anger. So-called friends! She decided that she was going to break up the cosy

148

tête-à-tête of the lovers – even for one night only – and returned to the heavy back door, this time closing it with a bang that vibrated down the passage. Then she marched straight into the bar calling out a loud 'Hi!' as she did so.

Two pairs of startled eyes swivelled in her direction. The women were perched on bar stools so close together that the black girl's knee was pressed between the American woman's thighs. 'Hi,' said Marsha, jerking back and jumping rather quickly down, while Gwen said nothing, dropping her gaze.

'Girls, I've got to make a phone call,' said Marsha looking from one to the other. 'I'll be back in ten minutes, OK?' There was no response to her query, so with a half-shrug she went out through a side door that led to the office. Judith pulled the vacated seat well back and sat down, staring at the girl left sitting opposite.

Eventually Gwen raised her head and spoke, though without meeting Judith's eyes. 'I suppose you heard some of what we were saying.'

'Yeah.' Judith let her hurt show. 'Thanks for all your support.'

'Kid, I was sorry about what happened, but how *could* you do it? How could you let her take you over like that?' Embarrassment fading, Gwen's habitual pugnaciousness was breaking through. 'What the fuck would've happened if they hadn't come to sort you out?'

'Fuck. D'you think I'm any happier than you are about what I did?' She glared at Gwen but felt strangely better for their angry sparring.

'OK. Let's put it this way. I get the appeal – or I thought I did – of sticking your arse out for a walloping. I mean, I did it myself when we was out together and that was fucking sexy. It hurts, sure enough, but showing all your assets like that and getting licked with that piece of leather – cor, it could go to a girl's head. As well as her bum.' She giggled and Judith

149

thought with a pang how gorgeous she was when something turned her on. However, Gwen pulled herself up and put on a solemn face.

'But to let yourself be treated like a little kid . . .' She let the words hang in the air then put her hands up, palms out, in a truce-like gesture. 'OK, Jude. Whatever I reckon to all this, I'm still not free, so that's it for now, anyway.' Gwen got down from the stool and picked up her bag. 'I gotta dash. I told them I'd be at work half an hour ago to do a late shift. Look, girl, I know where you are and in any case I expect I'll see you around.'

With that she was gone and as if waiting for her cue Marsha appeared behind the bar and took two beers from the cold cabinet. 'Honey, she wasn't yours, and as you probably guessed, she isn't mine – even for the few more nights I wanted. Hell, that's a fast turn around even by my standards. Too fucking fast.' She uncapped the drinks and pushed one bottle towards Judith. 'Don't let's fall out about this. At my age I've got to take what chances I can get, especially when they're as delicious as our young black friend.'

Judith spluttered into her beer. Not only had Marsha bed the girl she lusted after herself, she had to rub it in. Such shamelessness could well be a ploy, thought Judith, but if so it was one that worked, and her waning annoyance soon evaporated altogether when the American woman went on to ask for a report on her health and presented a sympathetic ear to the worries about Jeanie it contained. Two hours and several drinks later Judith left feeling much better, buoyed up by alcohol and Marsha's reassurances. It wasn't until she was passing through the park on her way home that Gwen came back to mind. At the thought that she was slipping away from her, Judith sat by the pond and shed a tipsy tear, though she took care this time not to address the ducks.

* * *

The next day, at the appointed time, Judith made her way round to the back of the house in Randolph Drive. Before she reached the door it opened and Jeanie ushered her into the kitchen.

'Come in my dear, come in. I'm glad you could make it but I'll have to warn you there'll be no hanky-panky today. You see, his lordship's about and he can't abide the idea of me doing things with another woman. It don't stop me, of course, but I do have to wait till his back's turned.' The speaker winked broadly and chuckled, making the full breasts with their prominent nipples swell under her cotton top. As before she was clad in a short skirt that clung to her broad hips, though the boots had been replaced by sandals more appropriate to the hot weather.

'Anyways, I don't suppose that it's my body that was the first thing on your mind, was it, my duck?'

Judith half-shook her head, self-conscious at the arousing memory of her lips pressed to the wetness between those sturdy legs.

'But I would like a look at the state of you, Judith. I hear that you've been in the wars and we've got five minutes, grace, I'd say. Come here, now; it's a good excuse for me to get another look at that pretty arse of yours.'

Jeanie sat down by the table and Judith faced her, fears forgotten, wondering how the information had reached this far. Where she lived was known at Nemesis but her submission to Ms Morris? The older woman opened Judith's ancient pair of threadbare jeans and peeled them down round her thighs. 'Maybe I was wrong that you didn't come for sex, dearie; you know what they say about a girl who leaves off her knickers. It's certainly true about me.' She laughed again and Judith was thankful to be turned round with the result that her blushes were hidden. Jeanie was quite right, of course: there was a kind of sexual bravado, wearing a garment whose ripped seat would show plenty of bare flesh if she bent down. She must be recovering . . . But now hands were exploring the remnants of the bruises inflicted by Ms Morris, which were no longer painful, if still quite dramatically coloured.

'You're well on the mend, Judith, though I dare say it was all very sore, eh?' She nodded, feeling her juices beginning to flow with all the appreciative attention to her buttocks. Then, as Jeanie's hand began to wander down from the mottled cheeks into the space between the legs – a move quite unresisted – there was a noise out in the back scullery and Jeanie jerked away.

'Quick, girl, pull up your trousers and sit down. It's himself come in.'

No sooner had she done so than the door opened and Bill stood there. He was only marginally taller than Jeanie but he looked enormous framed in the narrow entrance to the low-ceilinged room. Judith's heart skipped a beat when she saw the tawse clenched in his fist, but he ignored her and fixed on Jeanie, black beard bristling.

'Right, woman. Time to settle up.' He whacked the leather hard across his palm and came into the room. 'Out to my workshop – *now*, or I double the dose. I might just do that anyway,' he went on, still giving no sign he was aware of the existence of a third party. 'I'm really in the mood to give you what for.'

Jeanie stood up with a stricken look on her face that was belied by the surreptitious wink she gave Judith. 'There's something for you in the big envelope on the shelf: you can read it now. I'll be back,' she said, turning to the man, 'well, er, in a while . . .' There was an intense look that passed between them, then he took her arm and pushed her out ahead of him into the scullery.

Judith sat transfixed, hearing the outer door bang and footsteps crunching on the gravel path. They must be heading for one of the outbuildings and she had a

152

sudden image of the buxom lady stretched across a wooden bench. God, she would love to spy on the proceedings, but dismissed the idea for fear of landing on the receiving end of that substantial piece of oiled leather. Judith winced at the thought and tried not to pay attention to the response of her already primed loins.

She got up and went to the doorway. There were faint noises in the distance that could have been the sounds of bare flesh being strapped, but Judith pulled the door shut firmly and took down the envelope Jeanie had indicated. She took out the bundle of papers and placed them on the table, pulling up a chair to face the entrance, but what she saw on top put all thoughts of the ongoing chastisement out of her head. It was a letter to Dr Brown written back in 1991, not long before she 'disappeared'. The name of its sender – Elizabeth Marshall, PhD – meant nothing but Judith gaped to see that it was headed *Oceanus: Special Projects Division*. The text ran as follows, and Judith was pleased to find an immediate confirmation of her guess about the Brown-Bonnard identity:

Dear Marie,
I hope I may call you this, in view of your stated intention to resume your old name.

As you know, we have now established an experimental recruitment base fronted by our (fully legitimate) IT business here in Chicago which we call *Eumenides*. Early results, however, are a little disappointing and Estelle Morris from our board has persuaded us that English girls are likely to provide more suitable material. Hence we are negotiating to relocate in old St Mary's Hall in your vicinity in the year 1993–4.

Our collection of specialist materials is growing well and we have decided to adopt the name *Nemesis* for it (another child of Oceanus in myth and in fact!). Looking ahead, the archive will require its own premises and it has come to our attention that the university is seeking funds to erect a new library before the end of the decade. Our informant tells us that the stacks at present housing a proportion of its collection would be ideal for our purposes and I am working on a proposal to take over the building.

But, most importantly of all from your viewpoint, the application you made for the financing of a retreat in Brittany has been approved in full. Our accounts department will forward details of the transfer of funds within the next few days. Congratulations! (I have been *une peu méchante* in keeping this news till last – perhaps at a later date I can expiate at your hands?)

Most sincerely yours, Elizabeth.

Judith put the paper aside and stared into space as she tried to assimilate the information. The Archive and Ms Morris's company were both part of the same Oceanus Corporation and – of course! – the Eumenides were just the Furies by another name. She recalled now Miss James's little lecture about how the original Nemesis was a nymph-goddess related to them and remembered now that the first letter she had from the Archive bore the company name at the top. The signs were there; she had just been too blind to read them. As Judith shook her head at her past obtuseness, a second implication struck her with force. It had been no accident that she had become involved with both the offshoots of Oceanus in the town. Each time it had been Marsha pulling the strings; she had been coolly directed into the two local s/m scenes, one after the other. And no doubt Marsha was the informant referred to in the letter – someone without formal connections to the corporation who could advise on the conditions for setting up new outposts. Judith laughed out loud at one more case of the American woman's brazen cheek, though she smarted at the recognition of her own easy manipulability.

A second letter was dated January 12th 1993 and at first Judith read its addressee as *Jeanie*, though a second glance showed it to be inscribed to *Ma chère Jeanne*. It was short and to the point:

It is done and I shall write no more. I hope you can understand. In an emergency you may contact Thérèse Marchand at 10 Rue des Vierges, Vannes, who will send me a message.
The Way is open. Adieu, M.

Oh, God, that word again. In her mind Judith replayed the voices: what she had done was not the Way, while Sandra had found her Way under the cane. Capitalised, the term took on a new significance as the end of a quest and she tingled with the sense of impending revelation. Marie Bonnard had found – had constructed – her Way; could it also provide the Way for Judith Wilson, who sat lost in silent thought at the kitchen table of this strange suburban house?

She came to herself in the realisation that there was complete silence. Whether the sounds from out back had come from Jeanie getting 'what for', they had stopped. She was likely to return any minute and Judith looked quickly at the remaining sheaf of papers in front of her. This appeared to be a single document with the title *The Problem of Masochism*, dated on its last page 1980. It must be some kind of plan for what the thesis was going to be about, thought Judith with rising excitement, and she began to read.

Some of what Freud says in wrestling with the subject over the years is today frankly laughable. For instance in 1925 he suggests that some cases of the 'common' [?] female fantasy of a child being beaten may well be simply an admission of masturbation, the 'child' standing in for the clitoris. This makes no sense until we understand his view that a need for clitoral stimulation was something a sexually mature woman transcended in a commitment to vaginal orgasm. But underneath such absurdities there is the valuable notion that the internalisation of suffering is the very foundation of an inner space that we call the self –

Judith broke off. The silence was beginning to feel oppressive and concentration was difficult as her thoughts strayed to what the couple of the house were doing now. OK, she said to herself, assuming a nonchalance she was far from feeling, the spanking is done so afterwards they fuck. Big deal. The lady'll be back soon. But the image of an unfeasibly long and thick cock embedding itself between two large scarlet mounds insinuated itself into Judith's mind and produced an immediate response in her cunt. 'Damn!' she said out loud and began to flick through the typescript in an attempt to banish it. Then her eyes lighted on the phrase *my time in prison* – oh, God, there it was, Marie had been convicted of killing Mme Dauvignon – and Judith read on.

What happened to me there illustrates the point. I had – from as far back as I can remember – been sexually excited by spanking, though of course the negative emotional circumstances surrounding such an event in the household mitigated against enjoyment of it. However, by the time I was receiving the more formal institutional punishments of the convent and the reformatory, I was able to reach orgasm over a warder's knee and even once under the birch (though I had been primed on that occasion by the

156

sight of another girl being well whipped). At this point I was becoming aware of a need that was left unsatisfied by these experiences. What I longed for was a kind of atonement that I had hoped my substantial prison term might satisfy. But it was not enough, or perhaps not even the right sort of thing at all.

It was in my third year that Agnes took over as supervisor of our wing, though she was scarcely older than I. She quickly formed an attachment to me and it soon transpired that she too had an interest in corporal punishment (though it, of course, played no part in prison life). So I seized the opportunity to cajole her into caning me in the seclusion of her office but the experiment was a failure. The very feelings for me that allowed Agnes to be persuaded into the activity made it impossible for her to hurt me to the degree I was seeking. On the occasions that she did – most reluctantly – raise on my flesh weals that truly burned and throbbed she was unable to refrain from casting the instrument aside in order to caress and comfort me.

It was becoming clear that my need to suffer, to take suffering into myself, would require the agency of an absolutely strict, impartial being. While my relationship with Agnes gave us at times great pleasure, I was growing desperate to pass beyond the sexual stimulation of moderate chastisement to the rigours of purgative flagellation.

The bang of the outside door brought Judith back to her surroundings with a start as Jeanie came into the kitchen, looking flushed.

'Well, that was some session,' she said, standing by the sink with miniskirt hoisted up behind to allow the massage of visibly scarlet globes beneath. 'The devil got into him today all right and the strap just weren't enough, were it? No, he had to go for the riding crop as well. I can tell you, girl, I don't feel like sitting down yet awhile, though it's always worth it for the afters.' She gave her guest a slow smile, and it was as though the scorched arse she was holding imbued the whole body with a radiant sensuality. Sore but sexually content: how easy it was for some, thought Judith with envy. There was a basic homeliness and wholesomeness about Jeanie that belonged in a different world from Marie's driven search for penitential severity, and while Judith warmed to the easy openness of the earth-mother figure before her, she was coming to the uncomfortable realisation that she herself must take the harsher route.

As if responding to these thoughts, Jeanie's expression turned serious. She pointed at the manuscript on the table and said, 'You can take that away with you, my dear. It's well above my head, always has been. But I'll keep the letters, so if you want the address in France then you'd better copy it out.' The address – she could *use* the address. God, she could *go there*. With an adrenaline rush Judith suddenly knew what she had to do, though the idea of it made the pit of her stomach go cold. Jeanie stood looking at her for a moment then plucked a cushion from the wooden chest and placed it on the seat opposite the girl.

'I can't be doing with all this standing,' she said and lowered herself gingerly into place. 'We need to talk, my duck.' She leaned forwards on her elbows, wincing slightly as her weight shifted in the chair. 'I dare say you'd guessed the doctor didn't actually die before you even saw that letter. She just went back to being the one you was looking for and back to the place she came from. And you'll have some idea what she went back to do. But maybe you haven't sorted out yet where I fit into all this.' She raised her eyebrows and Judith nodded, picking up the note to *Jeanne*.

'Yes, dearie, that's me all right. That's my actual name – the name I was given. But you see I was looked after, right from birth, over here, by her cousins and they wasn't keen on the idea of a French name, so that's how it got turned into Jeanie. I'm used to it now, anyway.' Judith stared, uncomprehending. Who was the woman talking about? *Whose* cousins brought her up from birth?

'You haven't got it, have you, Judith?' Jeanie was looking flustered, even impatient. 'She couldn't look after me in prison, now could she? All those years . . .' She dropped her eyes and there was an emotional silence. Then in a flash Judith understood. Marie had been pregnant at the time of the murder and she had given birth to a daughter, a daughter who was sitting in front of her right now. Jeanie – *Jeanne* – was Marie Bonnard's child. At a loss for words, Judith put out her hand and laid it on the arm of the woman opposite, who was still gazing down at the table.

At first she carried on speaking without looking up; it seemed clear she was going to finish the story. 'So I never saw her – my mother – till I was sixteen. *They* didn't tell me anything. I suppose it was with good intentions – to keep the shame of it from me, or some such – and the first I knew of it was when she was released. And when I found out I was really wild and I came here as soon as I could. It wasn't like suddenly having a mum, of course, how could it be? But she taught me about growing things – I was never any use with books but plants, now, that were something else – and we got quite close over the years. A lot better than it might have been, if you think about it, eh?'

Judith had a lump in her throat and she could see the speaker was misty-eyed. But Jeanie sat up straight and managed a grin. 'That's it, really. There's nothing else I can tell you – I don't even know where the money came from to buy this place, even though it's been signed over to me. And my mother never talked about what happened to her mistress. All she would say was "I was the cause of it" – she blamed herself and that was the end of the matter. But I still don't believe she could kill anybody.'

An hour later Judith walked slowly back into the town. While Jeanie could not – or would not – intercede on Judith's behalf with her mother (whose second 'loss' she was plainly not reconciled to), she had made it clear that the address in Vannes was for Judith to use as she saw fit. It was up to her how she pursued her preoccupation with the person of Marie Bonnard and her masochistic quest. However, while she went through the motions of considering possible courses of action, Judith knew there was only one way. This was no time to be faint-hearted: she must go to the address in Brittany and thence, if she could, to the nearby retreat spoken of in the letter. Only too aware that her courage might evaporate overnight, she determined to act before she had a chance to think better of it.

Passing The Phoenix she slowed, thinking that Marsha might be there before the bar opened at five, but she couldn't face the prospect of Gwen being around, in spite of what she'd said. In any case the time for discussion was over and, when she thought about it, she hardly felt like confiding in the American woman who had not levelled with her. Judith knew that without Marsha she would not be on the verge of taking a big step, but the lack of honesty rankled and she quickened her pace down the street in the direction of home.

The next thirty-six hours flew by. Saturday morning was spent in the library, poring over all the materials she could find on her destination, and the afternoon in the travel agents working out the way to get there. In the end she opted for the train that would take her right to Vannes and bought the necessary tickets. On Sunday Judith packed a large bag then sat down at the kitchen table with a pad. Marsha deserved to know what she had planned, so she wrote: *Gone to Brittany (I'm sure you'll know why!) Love, Jude.* Then she addressed an envelope to Sandra Bright, Catalogue Department, Eumenides, St Mary's Hall and put in a note that said: *I think of you under discipline as I go to find my way if I can. I shan't forget how you saved me. Judith xxx.* It was rather naughty of her, Judith thought, but she smiled as she sealed it then went downstairs and posted the letters. Hoisting the strap of her luggage on to her shoulder she set off towards the station for the London train and, thence, in the morning, the express across the Channel to Lille.

PART III

9

Into the Order

She cut through a cobbled alley with the cathedral's
bulk at her back and came out in the middle of Rue des
Vierges but courage failed at the crucial door of number
10. With a grimace at such lack of resolution, Judith
passed on by the half-timbered façades to an open space
at the end of the street and sat on a bench. As at so
many times during the long train journey, she doubted
the wisdom of arriving without warning, although she
knew it would have been intolerable to wait out the days
at home for an invitation which might well, in the end,
have been refused. And appearing unannounced gave
her the advantage of surprise. So it was too late for
second thoughts and, moreover, it would soon be
getting dark. If she were not welcome at the address – a
distinct possibility – then she would need to find
somewhere for the night. Assuming an air of determination she was far from feeling, Judith got to her feet,
shouldered the travelling bag beside her and began to
retrace her steps.

There was an old-fashioned bell pull in the door
frame and Judith used it, hearing a faint ringing
from within. There was no response and, reaching
again for the handle, she noticed that the door was not
fully shut. It yielded to a push and Judith leaned
forward.

'*Allo? Y a-t-il quelqu'un?*' She was too nervous to shout, and was not surprised by the continuing silence. Judith stepped in and put down her luggage in the hall, looking about her. At the end of a short passage was a kitchen, also empty, although a kettle emitting wisps of steam on the range showed it to have been recently occupied. The leaded windows looked out over a narrow courtyard at the back and through a small window on the other side Judith saw a woman speaking on the telephone. Her head was turned away, hair tied in a ponytail and something about her was disconcertingly familiar. Then she vanished from view and, just as Judith was wondering whether to go and knock on the door opposite, it opened. The figure that emerged was swathed in a purple cloak, though with its hood down there was no mistaking those features: it was Helen.

Judith drew back and peered round the edge of the curtain, pulse quickening. The last time she had seen this young woman was the day she dismissed herself from the Archive by refusing to take the strap from Miss James. During Judith's short time at Nemesis, Helen had been unfriendly at best and it didn't take a genius to work out that her arrival in Vannes was not going to improve the girl's temper. As it was, she did not look happy: the mouth was set in a thin line of displeasure and the brow was furrowed. With relief, Judith saw that she was not heading in her direction but towards a door on the left, so she made a snap decision. There was only one thing for it: Helen's presence here must be to do with the 'retreat' – or whatever it was – so Judith had to follow her. That way she might find a more sympathetic ear than she could expect from the young woman she was watching.

It was a heavy piece of timber that had closed with a thud as Judith crossed the yard, forcing herself to adopt a steady, business-like pace in case other eyes were watching. Then the latch opened easily under her trembling fingers and the door swung back without a sound, revealing a flight of steps that descended into darkness. So far, so good, said Judith to herself, and taking a deep breath set off down.

At the bottom there was a sharp right turn and some twenty yards off a form was just visible in the gloom. Then light streamed out, making a sharp silhouette of Helen's figure, frozen for a moment in the doorway while she pulled out the key. Without so much as a glance behind her she marched on and Judith sprinted for the narrowing band of brightness. Squeezing through she let the lock click into place at her back and saw the passage stretch on into the distance, lit at intervals by wall lights. The keyring held firmly in her quarry's hand pointed to the presence of a second locked door somewhere ahead. Shit! With no cover of any kind along the bare walls she would have to keep close in order to penetrate the security of wherever it was they were going. Praying that Helen would remain as preoccupied as she now seemed, Judith crept after her, thankful for the runner of carpet down the centre of the worn flagstones that allowed her to move silently. Eventually a further right turn gave on to another door, this time with a glass panel through which she could see a T-junction ahead. Helen turned left on the other side and again being closer gave Judith time to reach the door before she was locked out.

The corridor beyond was panelled and several doors opened off it. She hesitated for a few moments, watching Helen's feet disappearing up a set of stairs at the end, then she took a step forward, determining to keep up her pursuit. But when she reached the top step it was too late: her quarry had vanished. Judith leaned against the wall surveying the passage that stretched ahead and those that ran to left and right. Which way to go? It was impossible to decide. Then there was a sound behind her and she whirled round. At the bottom of the stair she had just climbed were two figures cloaked much as Helen had been and one was beckoning her to approach. Both hoods were pulled well forward, but a glimpse of fair hair and a smooth cheek was reassuring enough to draw her back down and follow them into a side room. It did not take long for Judith to realise her mistake. As the door she had come through banged shut, the tricksters were gone in a giggling swirl of material through the door ahead and she was locked in between the two.

There was a metallic scraping noise and Judith's eyes came open. She sat up blinking at an outline in the bright doorway. God, she must have slept, in the end. The shouting and hammering had quickly seemed futile and pacing in the dark even more so and the last thing she remembered was curling up on the bare floor.

'Please follow me.'

Judith struggled stiffly to her feet and was led up the stairs to another room that was lit by daylight from a high window. Deliverance from the cell in which she had spent the night had come from a woman in a long black dress with a high collar who wore her grey hair scraped back. Now she proceeded to pour out a steaming liquid from a jug on the table.

'Sit and drink this before you speak. It will make you feel better.' The English was clear, if strongly accented, and Judith was relieved that her school French was not to be put through further tests.

She took the large mug and sank down on the bunk. It was coffee, rich and dark, and she sipped at it in grateful silence, trying to collect her thoughts. Plainly she had got into the retreat that Marie Bonnard had been funded to establish and been locked up for her pains. Thinking back through the twists and turns of the underground passage, she concluded that she must have passed right underneath the main body of the cathedral itself. Then she noticed her travelling bag beside her on

168

the floor. She had left it in the house on Rue des Vierges, just inside the front door and she had left *that* standing wide open. In it, along with her own travel documents, were all the papers to do with Marie, so anyone who had examined its contents would now know not only who she was but of her interest in *them*.

'My name is Sylviane and I am *la gouvernante* – How do you say? – housekeeper, here. I am in charge of *les domestiques*.' The dark eyes and wide-eyed gaze gave a strength to the rather plain features and Judith thought she would not like to be a member of staff who had failed in her duty.

'I know that you are Judith and I apologise for the searching of *vos bagages*. But we did not know with whom we were dealing at first. Some are saying that we still don't . . .' The last was an aside that tailed off, then Sylviane resumed. 'I must also make apology for the locked door. You are of course free to leave at any time, though not to wander as you please. That is why you were confined overnight.' As she finished speaking there was a chatter of voices outside and a sharp tap at the door.

'*Entrez, mes enfants. Bon. Restez là.*' At a glance the couple who came in could have been taken for children, dressed as they were in skimpy white T-shirts and shorts. While that impression was reinforced by their cherubic faces, a little flushed and topped by a tousle of fair hair, there was a look in the clear blue eyes that told a different story. It dawned on Judith that they were certainly beyond the age of consent; and that was not all. At first sight they could have been identical twins but as she stared she realised with a jolt that what she had seen as pre-sexual, androgynous creatures before her were actually of different genders. It was quite a subtle thing: the lips of the girl a little more pouting, the hips slightly more curved and – yes – there was a just discernable roundness that signalled diminutive breasts. These were all in themselves minor differences of bodily

169

configuration, yet together they triggered a disconcertingly major shift in perception.

'*Donnez-moi l'instrument,*' said the housekeeper with a stern look which was at once mirrored in the expressions of the youths as she took from the boy the cane that he produced from behind his back. '*Bon. Maintenant préparez-vous pour la correction.*' Turning from them she apologised. 'You will excuse me. My young assistants know only a little English.' On another occasion Judith might have explained that she had enough French to understand the simple commands given, but as it was her attention was caught by the two figures who, in what was clearly a practised drill, bent forward and grasped their ankles, presenting a fetching view of cotton-clad posteriors.

'Let me explain,' Sylviane went on. 'I imagine you do not recognise them but these are the ones who locked you in last night. It was their first occasion of dealing with an uninvited visitor and I am afraid that they thought their action to be – how do you say – a fine joke. It was not until this morning when your bag was brought to me that I learned of your presence and now they are to be disciplined for their impertinence. I shall give each of them what you call, I believe, "six of the best" then we shall inspect the results. You will decide whether they receive more.'

With that the housekeeper took up position on the lefthand side of the culprits. '*Êtes-vous prêts?*' she demanded and there was a subdued '*Oui, Madame*' from both her staff. Judith watched with dry mouth and quickening pulse as the cane swished down three times across the boy's behind, producing three audible gasps; then Sylviane leaned forward and administered the same treatment to the marginally plumper cheeks of the girl, with a similar effect. The process was repeated, though this time the strokes were visibly harder and the gasps became small cries.

170

'*Ne bouges pas!*' She spoke sharply as the girl made to move, then stepped across and lowered the shorts of both her victims. 'Come and examine *les fesses* and give me your decision.' The housekeeper took Judith by the arm and drew her near, running her fingers as if by example over the punished flesh. Judith followed suit, touching the raised red cane tracks whose colour seemed to grow darker under her gaze. She felt strong prickings of lust – with the wry thought that male and female buttocks excited her equally – and knew she had to see more. Sylviane looked at her and it seemed she divined Judith's state of mind.

'*Bon. Je vais répéter le fouet.*' Judith nodded and at the complaining noises from the youths the housekeeper raised her voice again. '*Silence! Restez à bas ou je ferai le retour.*' At this threat of a repeat of the whole there *was* silence and Judith held her breath as the cane sliced into the now naked curves. When it was over the recipients were ordered again to keep their positions while the angry weals that laced their bottoms were subject to a further and leisurely inspection.

'*C'est fini.*' The older woman stepped back and Judith watched as the pair straightened up and turned with pained faces. They were like mirror images of each other, thought Judith, save for one thing, and her attention was drawn by its semi-erect state. The boy had noticed it too and reached down to touch his member, which at once stiffened further in his grasp. Sylviane, however, intervened.

'*Arrêtez,*' she said shaking her head. '*C'est n'est pas le bon moment. Une autre fois, peut-être. Allez, allez – au travail!*' She clapped her hands and the youths pulled up their shorts and scuttled out of the door, their high spirits quickly restored now that the punishment was over. The housekeeper, though, looked a little embarrassed. 'You will excuse them, please? They may perhaps – ah – entertain you later if you wish it. Like young animals they are full of sexual play and some here use

171

them that way. But *Maîtresse Bonnard* does not approve for we are *rigueuristes – vous comprennez?*'

Sylviane looked enquiringly at Judith whose mind was, for a moment, completely blank. Then she recalled the phrase *'perdre en rigueur'* from the first letter of Marie's that she had seen, and the essay she had brought with her had something about rigours in it.

'Our aim, though not all reach it, is to leave desire behind and with it guilt. By submitting to discipline it is possible to take these feelings and *surpasser* – How do you say? – transcend them.' Her eyes shone and she put a hand on Judith's arm. 'But you will learn later, if you want. For now I have been neglectful of my duties.' She walked to the far wall and pressed a button whereupon a centre panel swung open revealing a bathroom beyond. 'You must want to shower and change your clothes. If you still wish to discover more of our place here – ' Judith nodded vigorously to the query in her tone '– then you should dress in the brown robe you will find behind the door. What you wear underneath, if anything, is your own affair.'

Judith glanced up sharply, but she could no discern no salaciousness in the speaker's expression. In her aroused state after the canings, the idea of going naked under a cloak gave her a decided frisson and she made up her mind to do just that once she was clean. Sylviane went over to the door and paused on her way out.

'I shall return to take you to lunch. I trust you not to wander in the meantime. Then there is more business –' she stressed the word '– that has arisen from your manner of arrival. It will provide a useful demonstration of some of our principles.' With that she was gone and suddenly conscious of the state of her slept-in clothes Judith stripped quickly and went to turn on the taps.

An hour later she followed Sylviane along a corridor and up a flight of steps that gave on to a small dining room. It was a light and airy space though as with her

172

own cell the windows were high up and allowed no view of what was outside. As they walked, the housekeeper explained that the building had been designed for a reclusive sect who wanted to minimise their contact with the world beyond and in response to Judith's questions observed that its quality of being turned in upon itself was one that suited the present occupants' purposes very well. At that point her inquisitiveness had to be restrained for as they took their seats among a dozen or so figures Sylviane whispered that there was a rule of silence.

Lunch consisted of vegetable soup with crusty bread and water to drink. It was spartan fare but Judith ate hungrily, having shaken off all the effects of her uncomfortable and anxious night. Laying down her spoon she glanced up and down the long table at the others still eating. They were all women whose ages seemed to span the three decades that separated herself and the housekeeper and they all wore the purple cloak that she had first seen on Helen the day before. Her brown garment was more of a smock than a cloak and she sat with the coarse fibre of its cloth prickling her skin, wondering at the strangeness of being among these people whose lives were as yet a closed book and who seemed to pay her no heed at all. And there was to be 'business' next, some kind of 'demonstration', but what?

Then a woman in her thirties at the head of the table stood up and the rest of the company rose with her. As they filed slowly out of the door, Judith followed on, impatient for the afternoon's proceedings to begin. The housekeeper would say nothing but simply led the way into an adjoining small chamber that appeared to be an anteroom. There she told her young companion that again silence was required once they entered the judgement room through the door ahead.

'What you will witness, Judith,' she continued, 'is a central part of our régime here. It concerns the acceptance and purging of guilt through rigorous discipline

173

which gives us the name we know ourselves by: *Les Rigeuristes*. I must warn you that what you are to see is not for *une timorée* – how do you say? – one who is faint-hearted. And to be granted your wish to know more of us, you must play a part in the event yourself.' The speaker fixed her listener with an unblinking gaze. 'Are you ready for that?'

Judith thought, I've come this far; I have to trust these people or it's all for nothing. She swallowed hard and said, 'I hope so, er, I mean, yes, I'll try to be.' Her mouth was dry and she was only too aware of how she had failed to rise to the occasion in the past, but Sylviane seemed satisfied.

'*Bon. Entrez-nous.*'

At first glance it appeared to Judith that it was a small chapel of an entirely conventional kind. They stood in an aisle separated by spaced pillars from the nave which contained three rows of pews. To their right was a large stained-glass window that provided only subdued daylight, filtered as it was through the predominant reds and purples of the design. There was no altar, though there was a large wooden cross that stood upright in its place. She could make out straps that hung from its horizontal arms and for a fleeting second Judith thought stupidly of Mystery Plays she had seen where the Christ figure was tied in place. But it struck her almost at once that the shape before her had nothing to do with crucifixion, staged or symbolised: *this* thing was a whipping post. Then, as if cued by her realisation, a spotlight cut through the gloom to reveal the rough timbers swathed in leather bands at the level of ankle, knee, waist, elbow and wrist. Judith shuddered. While discipline was voluntarily sought by all those here – or so she understood – its rigours were plainly expected to go beyond what an victim could bear unsecured.

Also illuminated was a solid black table set to one side, with a high-backed chair behind it that was occupied by the woman who had presided over their

174

recent meal. Now, though, she wore a black tunic and as Judith watched a figure in a white shift was brought in and stood before her.

'Thetis, do you come before me freely today?' The voice had an authority beyond her apparent years and the woman called Thetis lifted her head to reply. The light caught her face, showing eyes swollen with weeping. It was Helen!

'I do.'

'And do you admit that through your actions an uninvited person was able to enter our premises?'

Judith squirmed. This was all about her following Helen in.

'I do.' Helen spoke clearly but there was an unsteadiness that betrayed her emotional state.

'Very well. Now, before I pass judgement, is there anything you want to say?'

'I – I had bad news from my mistress on the telephone. Well, she *was* my mistress. She appears not to want me to go back. I was preoccupied and didn't watch when I came through the passage. I'm – I'm sorry.' Helen tailed off and wrung her hands miserably.

'We regret your disappointment –' the tone was dispassionate '– but an offence must be corrected. Will you accept my sentence?' Judith watched, horrified. The girl was being asked to OK her punishment before she knew what it was. And of course she was going to be whipped, here and now in front of them. Why else was the post all lit up?

'Yes.' Helen's head was lowered again and her hands still twisted together in front of her.

'Very well. The minimum penalty for carelessness in security measures is a dozen lashes. As you should know by now, our rigorists' dozen is an actual count of thirteen. However, here we have two offences since access was gained through two locked doors. So, Thetis, I am obliged to decree two dozen strokes to expiate your

175

fault.' There was a rustling in the pews as the few who were gathered to watch registered the severity of the award.

'Silence!' The acting judge's face was set in disapproval. 'Alecto, strip the culprit and fasten her to the cross. Mark her well – back and buttocks. You know the rule: if I am not satisfied by your efforts I shall flog the girl again myself.'

A young blonde woman in a black leotard emerged into the light. She leaned forward to remove the penitential garment from the shrinking Helen and Judith noticed thongs bound into a handle that swung from her waist. Then she remembered that Alecto was the first out of three Furies, and recalled the occasion when Miss James had enthused about the brass-tipped scourge carried by their sister-nymph Nemesis. What she saw here seemed to have no metal embellishments but the tails looked weighty and their ends stiff. Judith shivered. A savage chastisement was to be enacted under the sanction of Greek myth.

Helen moved to the post and stood unresisting while she was fixed in position. Watching as the nimble fingers buckled straps into place, Judith saw with a start nails that gleamed blood-red in the harsh glare. It couldn't be, surely, could it? Then the woman's face caught the light and she was certain. While there was a mask surrounding the eyes, there was no mistaking the line of the chin, one that she had last seen when she was driven back from quitting the Meni. It was Melissa – Liss – and she was a long way from Bonn. Judith wondered how many other half-truths and downright lies she had been told in the two months since starting work at the Archive. But on reflection it made perfect sense that the tough Glaswegian from the Eumenides Corporation should be the one to play the lead role of its namesakes.

And now she was nearly done with the preliminaries to the flogging. The long hair of the victim, released from its customary clasp, was drawn forward over the shoulder and held in place by the ties of a leather mask

176

that that served as both gag and blindfold. There was the final touch of a thick pad secured between the victim's pelvis and the wood so that when the waistband, that also served to protect the victim's kidneys, was cinched tight and the knees drawn forward, the buttocks were thrust into obscene prominence. All was ready and the bringer of justice stepped back: Alecto was about to exact retribution from Thetis. The whole had taken on an air of unreality, thought Judith, but she remained aware that at the core of the staged ritual there was going to be all-too-real bodily pain.

On a command from the woman at the table, the cruel thongs hissed through the air and bit into the exposed white flesh of the penitent's back. Three strokes from the left followed three from the right and at each one the trussed body jerked, while muted sounds escaped through the wad of cloth in its mouth. Already dozens of dark streaks adorned the space between nape and waist, some curling to leave their imprint on the unprotected breasts. The chastiser turned her attention to the jutting rump and six more lashes were enough to paint its compact globes a fiery red.

Frozen where she stood, Judith felt dizzy and a little sick. Her senses refused to take in the sight before her and she fell into an abstracted state. Attending the formal caning of Sandra had induced a similar reaction and, God knows, this was ten times worse. It was as though her psyche had a defence mechanism against empathy, against the imagination even attempting to conceive the fearful pain that was being inflicted. So instead it drew back and numbed; all she perceived was the increasing discoloration of flesh and the muffled noises that greeted each blow. There was no blood, for which Judith was thankful; had there been she knew it would have caused her to faint.

There was a pause but she realised it was not over. Somehow a corner of her mind had kept count and there were two more strokes to come. The figure on the cross now hung limp in its bonds and the head sagged to one side. Then the flagellator moved to the left and, rising to tiptoe, slashed the whip down with full force. Its tongues curled round the flank to bury themselves in the dark furrow between the buttocks and the body came immediately to life. Spasms jerked its limbs violently against their fastenings and even the heavy upright of the post shuddered on its base while the strangled cry evoked was enough to raise the hairs on the scalp. A repetition from the right-hand side produced, if anything, even greater effects. Then the chastised body slumped once more and there was a shocked silence, at last broken by the sound of a chair being scraped back on the stone. The officiator of the proceedings came forward and made an examination of the victim's state.

'You did well, Alecto. I could scarcely have bettered this flogging myself.' She signalled towards the pews and two cloaked women came to the front. While they unfastened the drooping Helen from the cross, the dispenser of judgement turned to her agent and held out a hand. 'Now I shall take the scourge. You have not, I am sure, forgotten our rule that any flagellator requires, at intervals, a reminder of the pain they inflict. You will be provided with that service in my room at ten o'clock this evening.'

Freed from her fetters, the whipped girl's legs gave way and she was half-carried out of the chapel. There was a moment's hesitation as Melissa faced her superior, then she held out the instrument and bowed her head.

'Thank you. For now you may go.'

Judith was watching as if from far off but she came to herself as Liss headed in her direction. She saw the eyes fix her through the mask and felt a wave of hostility as the young woman pushed past her towards the door. Then she was brought fully down to Earth when the judge spoke again.

'There is a stranger here today who would be with us for a while. You will know that it is she who set in train the events for which Thetis has been disciplined, and it is my decision that she should tend to her. That ends the proceedings.' She clapped her hands and the remaining audience got to their feet and filed out.

Judith stood appalled at the thought she was to come directly in contact with the results of the flogging she had been unable to contemplate with full awareness. But she was given no time to demur.

'Come now. Hurry. You must get to work.' Judith obeyed and was led out into the corridor. Inside an adjoining chamber the housekeeper stood by a table that contained a bowl of water and an array of jars and bottles. 'Sylviane will show you what to do, but the task is yours.' She nodded in the direction of the figure that lay face down on a padded bench. 'Thetis is not aware of much at the moment – it is the mind's way of dealing with extreme pain – though she will come round as you work. You feel guilty, that is obvious. I should recommend you deal with it by easing as best you can the suffering you have indirectly caused.'

The instructions were simple: bathe the afflicted areas with cool water to reduce the burning, then apply – with the utmost gentleness – the soothing unguents provided. Though ungagged, Helen was still blindfolded and before she left, the housekeeper laid a hand on the girl's neck and spoke softly into her ear. '*Repose-toi, ma chérie*, and let your injuries be attended to. Allow your mind to drift and the discomfort will ease.' So saying, she left the room and Judith set to business with a succession of wet cloths. When she judged that no more could be done to reduce the inflammation, she paused for a few minutes for the skin to dry.

As yet her patient lay quiet, her stillness broken only by an occasional flinch when contact was made with a

179

patch of extreme tenderness. So far so good, thought Judith, but now she must use her hands to anoint this body that had been so harshly treated: the body of a young woman who had hated her even before she had caused her to be flogged. Praying silently that her fingers would not in some way betray her identity and that Helen would remain in her present soporific condition, Judith opened the blue bottle and dribbled a line of its semi-liquid salve across the shoulder blades.

After a few minutes Judith relaxed a little. The worst of the contusions were on the back (she clenched up inside at the thought of how those lashes must have felt) and they had been successfully negotiated. Helen had whimpered now and then but there was no indication of leaving her prone position. And while the glistening weals looked even more alarming than they had done before, Judith knew the ointment would be working its balm. Next she attended to the flanks, where the whip tails had bitten most fiercely, and she began to feel the body moving a little in response to the massage of her fingers. Emboldened, Judith took a rolled bath towel from the table and, lifting the slim, waist slid it beneath the belly.

The behind, thus raised up, glowed deep red and as she smoothed its hot surfaces there was a sharp stab in Judith's loins. Then the buttock cheeks started to twitch deliciously under her hands and she trickled some oil right into the cleft between them. The compact rounds of flesh hid nothing: Judith could see the swollen ring of the anus and the lips of the cunt itself blotched purple where the hard leather tips had found their way at the end. Unable to help herself, she delved with ever so light, exploring fingertips into these places that had been so cruelly treated and was rewarded by a quivering of the hips and the smallest of moans from the young woman's throat.

Gripped by an urgent need, Judith thrust her left hand under her robe and into her throbbing centre.

With the right she hooked a finger down between the spread legs on the bench and made contact with the hard wet nub. She noticed it was much more elongated than her own clit (after all, she was in a position to make a direct comparison), though plainly just as sensitive for the prone figure twisted round, gasping.

'Oh, no! No! You musn't – it's not allowed!' Helen cried out but it was too late: they were both past the point of no return. Before control left her, Judith pressed a knee down in the small of her patient's back and brought her quickly to a peak. While Helen writhed and shrieked, her own climax burst, channelling all the pent-up, warring emotions of the afternoon. There was a moment – an eternity – of oblivion then Judith came to, panting, and her blood froze. The blindfold was off and Helen was staring at her, wild-eyed, her face contorted.

'You. *You*. Get out!' The voice was hoarse, thick with venom then it turned into a scream. 'FUCKING GET OUT!' She stumbled to her feet and picked up a glass bottle. Judith stood open-mouthed, rooted to the spot. Then the missile smashed against the wall beside her head and she bolted for the door, slamming it behind her. With no idea of the way back to her cell, she stood dithering. From the left, there was someone coming, so in a panic she made a dash to the right. Ahead of her, where the passage took a turn, a door stood ajar. The room beyond was dark so Judith slipped inside and closed it, leaning back in relief, heart pounding. The footsteps passed by and died away so she took a deep breath and reached for the light switch. As she did so, a door opposite was flung back and a woman stood outlined in it. Her features could not be deciphered with the light behind her but the voice spoke with authority.

'This is not what I had planned. However, it is high time that we had a talk.'

10

Mistresses

The long velvet dress swept the floor as she crossed the room and pulled a cord to draw back heavy curtains. Light streamed through French windows that opened on to a walled garden. It was bathed in the golden sunlight of a late summer's afternoon and seemed a world apart from the display of sadism and hatred Judith had witnessed in the past hour.

'Take a seat, if you please.' An upright wooden chair was indicated, whose back curved forward into arms and Judith sank down thankfully. The speaker had white hair, close-cropped, and lined features which seemed to put her a decade or even more beyond the fifty years of *la gouvernante*. However, when she positioned a swivel chair to face Judith and sat down, the eyes that fixed her were anything but feeble with age.

'You came here as an uninvited visitor and by a pure chance you were able to gain entry. It was not what I would have preferred; I can assure you that 10 Rue des Vierges is not an automatic gateway to the Order. I understand that the more usual means of access to us – through the Archive or Eumenides – were through your own actions closed off. Most would have accepted these indications of their unsuitability; however, you decided to arrive and push your way in.' The English was almost perfect and the tone was far from friendly.

Judith shifted uneasily in her seat; she was clearly in the presence of Marie Bonnard herself. While she knew, of course, that the young woman who had written the manuscripts that so drew her would now be around sixty, she had not expected the austere, formal demeanour which now greeted her. And the founder of the Rigorists was clearly not impressed by what Judith had done.

'How you made your way in has already had repercussions in two canings and a serious flagellation. Worse still, when called upon to make some small recompense to Helen for the pain she suffered as Thetis, you transgressed a fundamental rule.'

Judith's heart sank at this reference: she had dared to hope that no one would find out if Helen – Thetis – didn't tell. And why should she?

'Yes, I know what you have been doing, but it is not what you might think. We use no surveillance cameras of any kind here.' For the first time her features softened a little and there was the ghost of a smile. 'Young lady, it would be enough to look at you to detect the aftermath of orgasm – though, were it not, I have a very keen nose for the sweet scent of a woman's arousal.'

Without thinking, Judith sniffed her fingers and indeed the smell of Helen's secretions alone was strong. She jerked her hand down in confusion and felt a hot flush rise to her face.

'So you give yourself away. And you reveal too that you do not know much about our ways here. The partner in your erotic episode will confess to Thérèse, whom you saw in today in the ritual persona of Tyche, *La Maîtresse Juge*. Indeed, she may have already done so. When she has healed, there will be further punishment, though I would suspect that yours was the greater fault. Am I right?'

Judith quailed: it seemed that her first taste of discipline was in the offing. But the criticism she had received made her stubbornly resolved to do better.

'Helen – er, Thetis – is not to blame. I got carried away and took advantage of her shocked state. She even tried to stop me but it was, um, too late.' Judith tailed off and blushed even more as the orgasmic scene came vividly back to mind.

'Very well. In that case I may be prepared to give you more of my time. But first I require a token of your good intentions.' She crossed to a corner cupboard and took out a yellowish cane some three feet long. 'In this case, I am prepared to administer summary justice outside the prescribed channels. I shall decide the full penalty before you leave but, for now, six of its strokes in advance will concentrate your mind for our discussion. If that is agreed, come and stand here –' she indicated the centre of the room '– turn your back to the window and place your legs apart. Good. Now lift up your gown, bend forwards and hold your ankles.'

Judith did not know whether it was her newly found determination or the precise commands the voice gave, but she found herself in position, quaking inside with the fearful vulnerability of one who presents her naked posterior for chastisement. Marie Bonnard took hold of the raised clothing and pressed it firmly into the small of Judith's back, then she tapped the length of rattan against its target.

She said, 'Take a firm grip. I am going to beat you hard, though not unbearably,' and with those words the caning began. It was a devilishly intense pain that seemed to burn through the assaulted flesh deep into her being, but after the second stroke Judith knew she could bear it. At the end there was a pause of several seconds before she was ordered to rise.

'Keep the robe up and resume your seat. While we talk, I want you to be conscious of your bare buttocks against the wood.' Momentarily Judith had to struggle to regain composure, then with a deep breath she lowered herself gingerly into the chair. The surface was

184

at first cool against the hot stripes, though she winced when her weight pressed its hardness into them. She felt upon her the steady appraising gaze of the Rigorist-in-chief.

'You have done better than I had expected. There has plainly been development in the time since I had reports of you.'

The expression was less unfriendly and the words gave Judith a flutter of exhilaration. She leaned forward and instantly regretted it.

Marie Bonnard laughed. 'My dear, you *are* a novice. The cane will leave you tender for some hours and, remember, there is more to come. But let us get down to business. You may call me *maîtresse* and now, Judith, I want you to give me your account of yourself and what it is you think we can do for you.'

Back in her cell, Judith stood in the shower cubicle, letting cool water run over the welted cheeks of her bottom. Twelve strokes in all and she had taken them! Somehow there had been no question of refusing punishment as she had done at the Archive, nor had she regressed into the spanked child of her last days at the Meni. It had hurt like hell but it had felt like her due and she had consented to it. She put her hands back and tentatively explored the throbbing corrugations; at once there was an answering throb from between her legs. 'Damn you, give it a rest!' she said angrily, frowning down at her all too responsive cunt. Then, suddenly self-conscious, Judith stepped out and grabbed at her towel. Fuck, if anyone could see her, talking to her own clit. All she had to do was keep her wandering hands off it and concentrate on the undertakings she'd given to her new *maîtresse*.

First of all she had agreed to work alongside Helen/ Thetis in the garden and orchard for a week. Although she had at first protested that the girl had disliked her

185

from the very start, Marie Bonnard said the principal cause of it was her insecurity and not a natural enmity between them. Samantha – she referred thus to the director of the Nemesis Archive – had always played on her fears of rejection as she was doing now by letting her believe she might not be taken back. It was reprehensible, thought *la maîtresse*, but that was not for her to say. However, it required Judith to make a special effort to overcome the hostility that resulted from that situation.

So be it. It was not as if she had anything against the girl. Hardly, given what she had done. Judith stood in front of the small mirror fixed above the washbasin and thought of her hand exploring between Helen's swollen bum-cheeks. She blushed at the temerity of it and tried to concentrate on towelling her hair dry, but the itch in her groin would not be stilled. The image in the mirror showed quite a pleasing face framed by the dark layered crop: the nose was straight and trim with quite fine cheekbones and a firm chin. Judith pouted at her reflection, accentuating the sensual fullness of the lips: it was not going to be easy to 'transcend' the sexual side of this discipline game. In any case, was that what she really wanted?

The meeting with Marie Bonnard had not resolved anything. In the presence of the actual woman – the story of whose youth had so encouraged Judith's own inclinations – she had been confused and inarticulate about the purpose of her impromptu visit to the retreat. Tongue-tied, she had been almost glad to cover her embarrassment in accepting the remainder of her punishment. It had been delivered with greater vigour than the first instalment and, curiously, the chastiser had seemed proportionately more cheerful in her work. Judith had still been gasping from the cumulative effect of six of the very best when her *maîtresse* had taken from the desk a folder and said, 'Understand that no one else has seen this. I had erased these events from my memory until six months ago. Take it with you and read it; we shall speak again in a week's time.'

Judith came out from the tiny bathroom and pulled a clean brown shift over her head. In the file she had been given were a number of pages clipped together. They took up the tale where the earlier manuscript had broken off – Judith could see in her mind's eye the harshly pencilled I CAN'T GO ON WITH THIS – but the present account had been written with a firm hand that was in striking contrast to the other's fevered scrawl. There was a separate sheet on top that was dated March 14th and contained the following paragraph.

For all these long years there has been a voice in my head saying: I am to blame, the whole thing was *my* fault. And that was all. I was guilty and therefore deserved not only my prison sentence but much, much more. The guilt could never be expiated and in the end I was driven to found *L'Ordre de la Rigueur*. But now – who knows why, it is as if, at last, unseen cogwheels have moved in my mind – now I can for the first time face up to what happened and tell the story of that night. I am beginning to believe that I no longer need the purgation of rigour; that I am able to go beyond transcendence itself, so to speak. The Order is in the capable hands of Thérèse and will remain open to those for whom it is necessary.

Marie Bonnard/Michelle Brown

The clock on the wall showed the best part of an hour to go before the evening meal, so Judith drew a chair up to the narrow desk and sat down with due care for her recently caned behind. In place after a little wincing (itself a cause for pride in her newly found disciplinary prowess) she took the first of the sheaf of neat pages and began to read.

I have told already of how I left my room to see how Jean was faring and found him face down on his bed, moaning that he was too sore to bear even the weight of covers. As I applied some cream to the afflicted parts, his complaints stopped and in a very short time he was erect. In my hand his cock grew hard and swollen to a degree I had never seen before (I have since observed other boys thus affected in the aftermath of a beating) and the rampant organ induced in me a kind of madness. Perhaps too I was motivated actually to do the thing for which I had been mistakenly whipped and so earn my punishment in retrospect. So I lay down on my back, opened my legs and guided the engorged ramrod into my wetness. I had never done this before and there was pain as he ruptured my virginity, but then there was a climax such as I have rarely known. I covered his mouth to silence him when he shuddered and spurted deep inside me, then in seconds it seemed he was hard again and riding me once more into ecstasy.

It was well after midnight when I crawled, shattered, into my bed, but despite bodily exhaustion sleep was slow to come. My mind was in turmoil and my senses still burned with the cut of my mistress's martinet, the taste of her secret parts and the savage male thrusts that brought about my climactic deflowering. In the end I must have slept for I remember coming awake with a start, my heart beating hard. Yet there was no sound I could detect in the still summer night and I lay back and began to doze again. Now I believe that I was woken by the sound of the car that had arrived well after dark and that would – disastrously for me – be gone before the full light of day.

Then there were sounds whose reality was beyond conjecture and they halted at once my drift into unconsciousness. A door slammed somewhere in the building, hard enough to be felt as a slight vibration and I held my breath, listening intently. There was some indistinct bumping followed almost at once by a harsh cry. At first I was at a loss as to its origin but in the bright moonlight that shone through the drawn curtains I noticed the corner door to my spiral staircase standing open. I must have left it so in my distracted state earlier and through it had come the alarming noises I had just heard.

In a flash I was out of bed and straining my ears at the foot of the stairs. There was a crash as of breaking china and a second cry, louder than the first, that was this time cut off. In my nightgown I crept up the narrow spiral and, steeling myself, turned the handle of the door at the top. It opened behind a Chinese screen and my entrance went undetected to the point that I was able to peer out into the room.

What I saw – that had been for so long denied to memory – seems now etched into it beyond removal. My mistress was on her back on the bed with the burly figure of Hortense, the maid, sprawled, pinning down her arms and covering her mouth. Her lower half was bare and the master held the legs wide. His trousers were open and he was in the process of forcing a sizeable erection into her unwilling body.

'*Attrape ça, garce!*' he barked at her, and now that I can recount the scene, the words seem to ring in my ears as if I had just heard them. 'Take that, bitch!' it might go in English and I was aware at the time that this was a calculated rape intended to punish a wife for having the temerity to indulge a sexual interest in women. But the wife in question was not submitting without a struggle and I watched frozen as she wrenched her head free from the maid's grasp and spat in her attacker's face. He reared up and dealt her a vicious blow with the back of his hand that knocked her back on the bed and, at last galvanised, I leaped forwards on to him, shouting, 'No! No! No!'

Though my memory has returned after its protracted absence, the scene became a turmoil difficult to describe. Monsieur tried to fling me off his back, jerking my body round to the side. Then I saw Hortense coming at me with a gleam of metal in her hand. My mistress thrust herself forward – I think she yelled, 'Stop!' – and in the scuffle my head thumped sickeningly against the heavy iron of the bedstead. Just for a moment it seemed that the figures froze into a silent tableau, then I disappeared into blank oblivion.

When I came round it was daylight and I was immediately alert. Through my splitting headache and blurred vision came the perception of a still figure beside me on the bed. It was cold to the touch and my hand came back sticky with blood. It was my mistress and there was a metal handle sticking out from her neck. When I removed it there was more blood and I lay back, stunned. All I could think was that she was dead and I lay, body clenched in distress, while my mind rebelled against what my senses told me.

Then feet pounded up the main stairs and there was a hammering on the door. I seemed to have lost the power of movement and it was mere seconds before the lock burst open and two *gendarmes* were in the room, followed by the maid. She created an enormous fuss with her wails and cries of, '*La pauvre maîtresse*', while the knife was taken from me and I was commanded to relate what had happened. I was cold with shock and grief and could say only one thing, over and over.

'*C'est moi. Je suis coupable, je suis coupable.*' It was taken of course as an admission of murder that I would not – could not – retract, but greater than that, it stayed with me as a guilt so ineradicable that I would be impelled to seek more and more extreme ways of purging it.

Hortense continued her act by blurting out a story of my insane jealousy. I must indeed have appeared unhinged to the officers who had tried to question me and they seemed most interested in her words. She claimed that the mistress had made advances to *her*, Hortense, of a doubly indecent kind (which, *naturellement*, she had rebuffed). Pressed to explain her meaning, she gave a convincing display of embarrassed confusion, muttering about the use of *la verge* in shameful circumstances. Hortense had indeed been birched in front of the household, giving us all a view of her plump behind, but whether my mistress had tried to investigate her anatomy in more intimate detail afterwards, I neither knew nor cared. However, according to the maid, she had been importuned again just the day before in my hearing and she had heard us quarrel violently late in the night.

So the whole thing was sealed: my mind was locked in self-blame and I was headed for many years in jail as a convicted murderess. Hortense's revelations gave the popular press an irresistible tale of lesbian sadomasochism which in turn served to brand me as a violent pervert whose guilt could not be doubted. For the first time, now, I understand the plot that was hastily cooked up between the maid and her master so that I would pay the price for a death *she* caused. He had employed her to spy and so knew there was something between me and my mistress. (Indeed, I was not the first: an English woman in the old farmhouse across the field I knew had been a lover.) Thus informed, it must have occurred immediately to the real culprits how they could exploit their knowledge.

As I write this down and relive that night with a proper awareness of its events and their antecedents, the guilt that has wracked me gives way, little by little, to anger at what was knowingly done to me. I do not mean that they intended to leave me damaged by inarticulate self-reproach – I expect they thought I would deny their fabrications yet lose in a legal contest – but their carelessness of my mistress's life *and* mine was beginning to make me, for the first time, *enraged*.

Judith put down the page and eased back in her chair. It was heady reading, this tale of rape and, and – well, she supposed it had to be *manslaughter*, since Hortense had apparently not intended to stab Madame Dauvignon but Marie herself. And she had possibly not intended to kill anybody, though surely a court must have judged her actions likely to cause death if they had only known the true facts of the case. As it was, the cover-up of the crime was successful and the innocent party duly convicted.

The sound of a bell echoed in the corridor outside her room and Judith got up. Unsure at first of the direction of the dining room, she was able to follow the other figures that came past and once again the housekeeper Sylviane made room for Judith to sit beside her. While she ate in the obligatory silence, her mind chewed over the implications of what she had read: that this place, this collection of individuals she was among, existed solely because of a tragic accident and ensuing miscarriage of justice. And now that the architect of the Rigorists had uncovered the true basis of her once overpowering guilt, was that going to undermine the order she had founded?

After the meal Sylviane took Judith's arm and asked if she would go with her to the laundry room.

'You remember, I hope, that you agreed to work alongside Thetis for a period of time.' She had indeed made that commitment but Judith's lack of enthusiasm must have been obvious for the older woman went on. 'We know that there is *la rancune* – how do you say? –

192

bad feeling between you and Helen, as you called her. But it important for this to be overcome since it has no real justification and we expect you to make your best efforts. You will come with me now, please, to collect the clothes you will wear for the garden. Breakfast will be at seven o'clock, after which you will begin, therefore, it is best that you go early to your bed tonight.'

The three days that were left to the week passed quickly: there were many rows of potatoes to be lifted and apples, berries and tomatoes to be picked. It was exhilarating to be outside in the sun and air all day, though it took until the Saturday before Judith's aching muscles began to adjust to the unaccustomed exercise. The huddle of connected buildings was dominated by the towering mass of the cathedral to the north and the original monastic seclusion completed by the high stone wall surrounding the area of adjoining land. However, despite the designers' intentions, the outside world was not shut out completely. Any person who climbed a tree in the orchard – a necessity if she were to pick apples – was rewarded with a stunning view down the steep southern hillside to the old harbour and, beyond it, to the shimmering blue of the estuary. And that was not all. Tools and gardening equipment were housed in a substantial outbuilding at the end of the converted monks' cells that formed part of the outer boundary. It had an upper floor that could be reached – just – by the rickety remains of a ladder and its single leaded window opened on to a western vista of rolling hills.

These were the delights to be snatched between bouts of hard work, though what had been emphasised to Judith as a principal goal of the exercise, was no nearer being achieved. In fact, the situation was worse than that. Helen was as surly and antagonistic as ever, doing whatever she could to avoid any contact with her supposed co-worker, while *she* was becoming distinctly turned on by the lithe young body continually before her eyes. Judith lay on her bed and cringed at the thought. It was Saturday night and she should be relaxing in pleasant anticipation of a day off, but all she could do was think lustfully about this girl who hated her. What a clown!

What had really done it was the day before – Friday – when they had been in the orchard hidden among the branches of the trees. They both wore T-shirts and shorts with stout boots and already Judith had found herself watching Helen's figure as she moved under the thin cotton. But now the girl stripped off her top and hung it on a branch while she carried on filling her basket. It had not seemed deliberately provocative – after all, Helen consistently behaved as if Judith were not there – but perhaps it was some kind of malicious game designed to arouse her enemy and leave her frustrated under the rules of the no-sex régime. Who knows? If that was the plan, it had certainly worked. Her groin kicked at once at the sight of those small perfect breasts standing out as Helen reached for the ripe fruit and at the still-vivid marks from Wednesday's whipping that disappeared down under the waistband of sweaty shorts. Judith could imagine only too well how the traces of the lashing would look that had curled into the buttock cleft now damp with the exertion of plucking apples from their branches. She had always thought Helen looked neat – that was the word she had used to describe her back in the Archive days – though she had never dreamed that she would be consumed with lust for the girl.

But that was exactly what she was, and in an Order where even masturbation was frowned upon. Judith sighed deeply and swung herself on to her feet. There was nothing for it: she would have to try to read Dr Brown's dauntingly abstruse theory of the masochistic impulse which had lain untouched in her travelling bag

194

since she had left for Brittany. Judith stared at the title page, struck with misgivings. The paper dated back some twenty years, so it must be possible, even likely, that its ideas might have the ground cut from beneath them by the new understanding its author had acquired of herself. Pursuing this line of thought, Judith wondered that if transcending sex in rigorous discipline was no longer necessary for *la maîtresse*, then maybe she didn't need to fight any more against her own bodily desires.

The conclusion was a tempting one, but it didn't take a profound thinker to spot the partiality of it. In any case, she had given an undertaking and must, for the present at least, try to stick to it. Judith sat at the narrow desk and opened the typescript at a marked paragraph that began: 'The internalisation of suffering is the very foundation of an inner space that we call the self.' Sighing again, she folded her arms to constrain the hands that itched to wander into forbidden territory and read determinedly on . . .

The following morning, Judith came wide awake with a start before she remembered that it was Sunday. Sinking back on to the pillows, she fell into a fitful doze; then her thoughts turned to the room by the old chapel on the occasion she had tended the whip marks that covered Helen's back and behind. The memory of those trim buttocks so hot and red was a potent one and Judith's sleepy fingers began to caress the silky flesh between her legs and slip into the moistening folds.

'No!' Judith spoke angrily to herself and put her feet firmly down on the floor, throwing back the covers. A shower was what was needed. In the bathroom she luxuriated in the flow of hot water over her head and shoulders and tried to think objectively about what she was actually doing at *L'Ordre de la Rigeur*. She had certainly started the summer with a problem: a strong interest in corporal punishment combined with guilt and shame that disabled attempts to do anything about it. But the position had changed – if unaccountably – and she seemed capable now of accepting quite a sharp dose of the cane without any bad psychological consequences. OK, that was just a single experience, but Judith felt reasonably confident that she could take it further with practice. But how much further did she want to go? The thought of being flogged like Helen–Thetis still made her feel quite sick and she was by no means convinced of the principle that purgative chastisement that was all pain and no sex was necessary to conquer guilt. A dozen of the best had set her cunt on fire as well as her arse and she wanted both.

Goddammit! This was where rational thought had taken her and now she was horny as fuck. Judith turned off the water and emerged, dripping, into the sparsely furnished room. For a long moment she went rigid with shock, for standing silently side by side in front of her were the two youngsters from the kitchen.

'Oh God, oh God,' said Judith. 'You two could give a girl a heart attack, doing that. But then you don't understand what I'm saying. Do you?' She looked from one to the other, holding the bath towel to her chest.

The boy pointed to himself and said, 'Carlo,' then to the girl, saying: 'Carla.'

'Carlo and Carla,' echoed Judith.

'We see – in orchard – so we come. We like – no T-shirt – understand?' He looked hopeful and the girl nodded vigorously beside him. Then she dropped her shorts and turned round, sticking out a bottom that was laced with fresh cane weals. 'You see,' Carlo went on, 'we got caught, watching. So swish, swish.' He did a little pantomime and Carla reciprocated, holding the marked cheeks she had displayed and turning down her mouth.

That did it. Judith simply melted inside and when the two took the towel from her hands to pat her dry, she acquiesced without a word. Nor did she resist at first when eager hands began to caress her nakedness and lips roved over her breasts and haunches. Then she stepped back, saying, 'Slow down, slow down.' Judith strove to subdue her raging passion and gain some control. There was no going back now, so if she was going to fall she wanted to wring the most out of her transgression.

First she had the brother and sister strip completely and lined them up side by side in front of her. The figures were so alike, fair, blue-eyed and fresh-faced, and their enthusiasm for the sexually perverse had an innocence that Judith found quite irresistible. Taking her time she circled round the pair, fondling a buttock here, a breast there, before cupping a hand under Carlo's cock. The size of it made her recall what Marie had written about her young lover's organ after his beating, and this one grew even more distended as she stroked it. He gasped almost as if in pain at her fondling of him but kept his place and Judith turned her attention to Carla's less conspicuous sexual parts. This time she knelt before the girl and gently parted the outer lips that nestled below the lightly haired pubic mound. Her fingers were at once covered with secretions and Carla gave two little sharp cries at the touch to her genitals. She was clearly just as aroused as her brother and, indeed, as Judith herself.

Perhaps more so, for she was the first to make a move to bring the encounter to a climax. 'Please,' she said, pushing Judith backwards to the bed, and again, 'Please,' as she guided her to sit down. Then she spread the legs to expose Judith's dripping orifice and dropped down before it. '*Viens*,' she said to her brother and put a finger to the anus revealed between her upthrust buttocks. So the three joined together: Carla fastened her mouth on Judith's cunt while Carlo eased his glistening cock into the opening in his sister's behind.

Judith watched the stiffness sink deeper and deeper in until his thighs pressed against the wealed curves, then she took his head in her hands and their mouths were filled with tongues as the convulsions started to rack all their bodies.

Then there was the sound of theatrical cough and a voice said, 'Is this a private party, or can anyone join in?'

Judith's eyes jerked open to see Melissa standing in the doorway with an ironic smile on her face. For a moment they all froze, heads screwed round in the direction of the speaker, then Carlo pulled out of Carla with a popping noise that very nearly brought Judith down with an attack of hysterical giggles. She struggled up from the bed, the adrenalin of orgasm still pumping in her veins while her two partners cast around on the floor for their discarded clothes.

'*Allez, allez!*' The intruder clicked her fingers at the youngsters, who promptly scuttled off, half-dressed, down the corridor. Judith pulled a robe over her head in an attempt to regain some dignity, but her visitor did not look impressed.

'Melissa.' Judith began to speak, then stopped and cleared her throat. She started again. 'Melissa, I know I've broken my word and I regret it. But I've been thinking since I made that promise and I really don't think what we just did was wrong. Does it have to go any further?'

'Hen, Liss would drop her knickers in a flash for that wee boy's big cock.' The Glaswegian accent was suddenly strong to the point of caricature. But not for long, and the rest of the speech was icily 'correct'. 'Problem is, Judith dear, you are dealing with Alecto, and she is made of sterner stuff. I am afraid the matter must come before *la maîtresse juge*. You have seen Tyche at work in sentencing Thetis to my lash; but I am also an expert with the penal cane. Perhaps I shall have a chance to

198

exercise that skill in the morning. The chapel, ten o'clock sharp. Lateness is *always* punished.'

The cold expression and the glint in the eyes brooked no argument. The demeanour befitted one of the Furies and, the figure who had assumed the identity of Alecto turned abruptly and left, closing the heavy door behind her with a thud. Judith sank back down on the bed in a turmoil. It seemed the disciplinary stakes had been unexpectedly raised. She was, of course, free to go at any time, free simply to walk out back to the railway station and back to the flat she had left behind in England. But that was unthinkable; whatever her punishment was to be. She would simply have to endure it. It's only pain, she said to herself in a feeble attempt at levity; it won't kill you. But the sense of foreboding that stayed with Judith for the rest of the day was not without an erotic charge. She was heading for an encounter with 'the real thing', descriptions of which held such a fascination for her, and dread at the prospect was tinged with excitement. That night she thought of Janina Čyprik's chastisement in the town square and fell into a fitful sleep disturbed by nightmarish images of powerful arms wielding disciplinary instruments of an impossible severity.

11

Pain and Passion

The atmosphere of the former chapel was as daunting as when she had seen Helen flogged. But now it seemed certain to be her turn to experience the disciplinary rigours in honour of which the Order had been named. Judith shivered and she could taste bile in her throat from the ill-digested breakfast of an hour before. She stood to one side with her fellow culprits and could not help thinking that their now solemn figures in penitential white looked scarcely capable of the sexual frolicking that had brought them to this place of judgement. As on the previous visit, bright lights illuminated the area at the front, though this time they were shining on *her*, and of those who were there to watch, she could make out only a few dark shapes. All too visible, however, was what occupied centre stage, replacing the cross-shaped whipping post. It was a block with a domed surface flanked by side pieces and its function was at once obvious. The victim's torso went across the top and her knees and elbows were strapped to the lower ledges, thus presenting the posterior for whatever treatment had been decreed. Judith recalled just such a device described in the first manuscript of Marie's as being in regular use at her convent school. Perhaps its design was peculiar to Brittany; perhaps, even, this was the very same piece of equipment over which the founder's teenage body had been frequently arrayed for punishment.

These speculations were interrupted by the opening of a door and the purposeful clack of heels on stone flags as Tyche came into the light accompanied by her agent of discipline who carried a long rectangular case. When last here, Judith's attention had been focussed on Helen and the mysterious masked figure with the scourge; now she studied with anxious interest the person of *la maîtresse* who would judge her. The woman wore a black shirt belted at the waist, under which leggings disappeared into shiny black boots. The hair was in a mannish cut, parted on the side and slicked flat to the head with gel, while the whiteness of the face was accentuated by the crimson gloss of the lips. She looked younger than Judith had thought before, maybe not even thirty, though the eyes gave the disconcerting impression of having seen much more than her years should allow.

Mistress Tyche took her seat and folded her arms on the table in a gesture that signalled she was ready to begin. It had been explained to Judith in her meeting with its head that the Order functioned at two interrelated levels. For each member there was an individually tailored programme of exercises for mind and body which, while always exacting, did not necessarily hinge on the experience of corporal punishment. However, along with these private tasks went the public displays that used the transgression of rules as an occasion to enact a form of retribution or purgation through physical chastisement of a severe kind. These events were regarded both as a test of the penitent's endurance and an opportunity for others to witness rigorous chastisement in action. That was what was about to happen and Judith thought wryly of how she had felt quite sick to watch Helen treated so. Now in the spotlight herself, she would have given a very great deal to be a mere observer, inconspicuous in the gloom.

La maîtresse juge cleared her throat. 'As you all know, the Rigorists' code prohibits sexual relations amongst inmates, except under very special circumstances. Yet misconduct of this kind is lamentably frequent –' the speaker pursed shiny red lips disapprovingly '– and I am here this morning to order corporal punishment appropriate to another breach. Judith, will you come forward, please?'

Two paces brought her in front of the substantial table and out into the full glare of the powerful lights overhead. Judith felt beads of sweat forming on her forehead and neck. Mistress Tyche continued, her pale composure seemingly imprevious to the heat.

'Judith, you are not a member of our group with her own training scheme, rather a visitor who, reluctantly in some quarters, has been allowed to participate on a casual basis. Therefore, I believe that to impose the full weight of rigour would in your case be excessive. You have been caned once with an English school instrument, I understand, so I propose a second such lesson.' She snapped her fingers and Alecto produced a crook-handled piece of rattan that looked identical to the one Maîtresse Marie had used on Judith. 'No restraint will be necessary, so you can take the punishment where you are standing. Do you accept my sentence?'

'I do.' It was said firmly. She was being asked to lift her garment and bend over for the kind of caning many a schoolgirl could have expected to receive in days gone by, albeit for a rather serious offence. Judith's main feeling was relief that it was not to be worse: she had come some distance since the day when fear and pride compounded to make her bridle at Miss James's tawse.

'*Bon. C'est decidé.* Now, however, I must deal with *nos employés de maison. Très mechant comme les enfants gâtés. Alecto, l'instrument pénale, si'l te plaît.*' It was clear that the 'spoiled children' were not to get off so lightly and the instrument was produced with a flourish.

For many years a feature of penal institutions, the name had stuck to the fearsome length of pale wood with one end of its four feet braided with leather for a hand grip.

'Carlo, Carla, *venez ici.*'

They stood beside Judith and she could feel their distress. To the left of them was the block hung with straps and before them was the penal rod; together they promised ferocious pain. The boy's colour had drained completely from his face and the girl began to whimper. Judith could not bear it, and found herself speaking.

'*Maîtresse, pardonnez-moi.* Please listen. They *are* like children and I cannot let my actions cause them to be punished as you propose. I led them on, I encouraged them. If I had said no, they would have run back to their quarters. It is I who am to blame for what happened.' As the words tumbled out, they came to acquire a formal cast befitting the surroundings and the plea was received with a grave consideration. In the silence before *la maîtresse Juge* made her response, she stared hard into Judith's eyes. Then she spoke to the youngsters.

'*Bien. Carlo et Carla, regardez-moi.* You will both come to me at ten o'clock – *à dix heures – pour la grande fessée.* I can promise that you will take two very sore bottoms to your beds tonight. Now go before I change my mind. *Allez, allez.*' She waved her arm and there was a moment's hesitation as if the twins could not believe their luck. Then they were away in a trice and the thud of the oak door behind them echoed the heavy beat of Judith's heart as she waited to learn her fate.

Again the black-garbed figure gazed hard at her, then she said, 'Very well, Judith, you leave me no choice. It will be a dozen with the ash plant that you see in front of you. That is the minimum judicial sentence. Do you accept it?'

'Yes.' It came out as a croak, for Judith's mouth had gone suddenly dry with the enormity of what she had done, of what she had consigned herself to by interceding on behalf of the youngsters. Yet despite her fear there was – incredibly – a prickle of arousal at the idea that she was to be ritually thrashed.

'Then remove your shift and place yourself on the block.' Judith stripped and the garment was taken from her. She was aware, of course, that behind the mask it was Melissa who wore the black leotard, but it was into the hands of Alecto that she consciously gave herself in order to be fastened down for punishment. It helped, strangely, to believe that what was to happen was not individually vengeful, but rather the work of a mere agent of impartial justice. Straps were tightened around forearms, knees and ankles before a waistband pulled her tight against the curved surface of the hard wood. She was not sharply bent to give the genital display many accounts at Nemesis had described. Instead, her body arched in a way that made Judith acutely conscious of the plump masses of her buttocks perfectly posed to absorb the full measure of each stroke. Finally a leather pad was fixed between her teeth, pushing the tongue back and providing something to bite on during the extremity to come. Its function seemed entirely benign and Judith felt almost tearfully grateful. The tension was becoming unendurable: please, please let it start!

She heard Mistress Tyche's voice once more. 'Now, Alecto, remember that force must be combined with accuracy. Should you break the skin, I shall have you hugging the block for a double dose from my own hand. Begin.'

Judith felt the cane patted against her bottom three times: it had a weight and suppleness that made her shrink with dread. Then, after a pause during which the blood pounded in her ears, there was a swoosh, a grunt and a jolt that knocked the breath out of her body. For a fraction of a second she registered only impact, then a line of fire seemed to cut her in two. It was impossible

that anything should hurt so much and yet its atrocious-
ness grew and grew as Judith writhed uncontrollably in
her bonds. For three more strokes she fought with fury
against the unyielding restraints: every pore screamed
with agony and escape was a blind imperative. Then, as
the caning went on – five, six, seven, in a slow-paced
progression – Judith's body surrendered to the inevi-
table. There was only pain, the whole universe was pain
and to survive it was going to require the total
concentration of her whole being. Struggle was a
distraction, a luxury she could no longer afford.

There were six more strokes to make the thirteen of a
Rigorist's dozen but Judith wasn't counting. She came
to herself gradually out of a haze, aware that the beating
had stopped. It couldn't have been very long ago for she
could hear Alecto breathing hard from her exertions.
She ached all over and the attempts to wrestle free had
chafed her arms; and as for her buttocks, they felt like
so much molten lead. But she had come through it into
a world where pain was no longer the be-all and end-all
of existence, and she was profoundly thankful for that
deliverance.

Later, in the recovery room, Judith felt a hand on her
neck and heard a voice say, 'I just found out this
morning that you took all the blame for last week, for
making me come after the whipping. Thanks, J. You
didn't have to do that.'

It was Helen and Judith made to lift her head.

'No, don't move. You're still in shock: that penal
cane is a total brute. Just lie quietly and let me massage
some of the tension out of your shoulders.'

It was easy to obey and in a short while she felt the
muscles that had seized in the trauma of the event
beginning to unknot. Now her mind was becoming
clearer, she realised there were only vague memories of
the immediate aftermath. Upon release, her legs had

given way and she knew it had taken two people to get her where she presently was, face down on a cushioned surface with an iced pad on her behind. Already the experience of the block was receding into the past: it was something – an excruciating, appalling thing – that had happened elsewhere and it was over. Judith felt a trickle of cold water run between her thighs and shivered.

'Here, I'll take that off. It won't do any more for the bruising and it's making a mess.' Helen busied herself mopping up then lifted Judith's belly enough to push a pillow underneath. 'I've got some really special oil I was saving and I think this is just the occasion for it.' So saying, she dried the chastised area, wielding a fluffy towel with such exquisite gentleness it seemed to have no more weight than a feather. Then with a touch that at first was barely perceptible she began to anoint the assaulted globes.

Judith lay basking in these expert ministrations, afraid almost to wonder at the change in Helen's attitude in case it should suddenly revert back. But before long there was something else on her mind. She was – astonishingly – being caressed by the hostile, disdainful girl that she had so lusted after out in the grounds, and her cunt had started up a throbbing that was soon going to insist on a share of the attention being given to her welted arse.

Helen's aftercare had reached the soft flesh at the undercurve of the buttocks that had received some of Alecto's most vicious strokes, and even the lightest hand was enough to make Judith wince and suck in breath. Yet the burning in her loins grew only more intense and she felt her thighs beginning to tremble.

'J, no one's watching, and I won't tell if you won't.' Helen's voice spoke quietly in her ear and then two oiled fingers slipped in between Judith's bottom-cheeks.

Oh God, oh God, oh God. The touch was like a jolt of electric current and, as if in a reflex action, Judith pushed her throbbing behind up into the probe. It flitted through her mind that perhaps Helen was not to be trusted, that she would, after all, betray them both. However, the idea of a second beating following hard on the first was so dreadful as to be quite literally unthinkable, and Judith gave herself up the urgency of her bodily need.

The climax came from deep inside her and it was like no other. There was a profound, tempestuous release that was simultaneously physical and psychological. Through extremes of suffering she had found heights of passion: it was her nature to do so and she saw it with complete clarity. In that instant Judith knew – whatever else happened in her life – she was destined to return and cleave in savage embrace to the block or the post. There had been unspeakable pain, now there was unspeakable pleasure; and the force of it carried her far far away into a realm beyond thought altogether.

From Tuesday to Saturday the two young women worked once again in the walled grounds. While there had been no change to the heat of the early September sun in the space of the weekend, the emotional climate was transformed. Desire thwarted by cold indifference had burst into flames of mutual lust. Judith was at first painfully stiff, and her deeply bruised behind provided a ready excuse to disappear into the privacy of the outside loft for twice-daily remedial treatment. For her part, Judith was fascinated with the fading pattern of purple lines left by Helen's whipping, and after passion was spent she would lie tracing their contours with a fingernail. It excited her beyond measure to think of the scourge tails printing their burning kisses on the tender skin of her lover's back and these examinations soon gave way to the more intimate inspection of Helen's surprisingly prominent clitoris with her tongue and teeth.

Their haven was no *boudoir*, perfumed and frilled, and in particular the discarded mattress they had requisitioned for their lovemaking would not have borne close scrutiny. But the eyes of each were on the other alone, except for the intervals when they lay sated to gaze through the open window across the green hills to the north-west.

It was on the Saturday, in just such a post-climactic lethargy, that their tryst was discovered.

'Down here, now!' The voice was a bark of displeasure. The shock of it induced a mad scramble for clothes, followed by a hurried descent of the rickety ladder that landed the pair in a dishevelled heap in front of *la grande maîtresse*.

'I am glad to see that you have overcome your differences. In fact, one might say from appearances that you have gone a little too far in the opposite direction.' They got to their feet, squirming under her sarcasm. 'It seems to me it is just as well that you were not caught by Mistress Tyche, or you could each expect a further appointment with Alecto in the chapel.' A wry smile had displaced the frown and Judith relaxed a little, managing to take hold of Helen's hand behind her back.

'I came to find both of you, for different reasons. First, Helen, you have been summoned back by Samantha to the Archive. You know her way: it was not a request but a command. I told her I was certain of your obedience.' Judith squeezed the hand in hers and it was squeezed back, hard. Helen's eyes had gone misty and she stood speechless, her mouth working.

'As for you, Judith, I think it is time for you to leave us. That is a request, though it is one I hope you will follow. Come to me tomorrow morning; I have an errand for you to run in England. You may prepare to travel next week. As this morning's episode confirms, you have – shall we say – a knack of creating sexual situations around you which is a disruptive influence to the efforts of our dedicated rigorists. Some have complained, and I must respect their opinions. Please do not be offended; at a late stage in my life I quite sympathise with your nature. In fact, I may tell both of you that I too shall depart next month and leave *la maîtresse juge* in sole charge, but you will please keep this information to yourselves for the present.'

Judith nodded solemnly. She was taken aback by what amounted to summary dismissal from the Order – it was hardly a request when she couldn't really refuse it – but she was more than pleased that Helen's anxiety had been ended. Now, though, Mistress Marie looked stern once more.

'There is one more thing. I said you were lucky that Thérèse did not happen upon your *amours*; however, I did not mean you are to go uncorrected. I may be quitting the Order but rules are still rules, while I am here.' There was a stout wooden chest inside the door and the speaker sat down firmly in the centre of it and rolled up the right sleeve of her cloak.

'I shall take Helen first. Lower your shorts and come across my lap.'

La maîtresse may have been sixty but it was clear her arm had lost none of its youthful strength. A sharp volley of full-blooded smacks had Helen's bottom the colour of the strawberries they had picked in the morning and, twice repeated, left her gasping. When Judith took up her position, Marie ran a hand over the marked cheeks. 'Oh, my dear,' she said softly, 'you were well caned,' and proceeded to deliver a series of stinging slaps to the backs of the thighs.

Ordered back to work, the miscreant couple made for the seclusion of the orchard. Seeing the other subjected to an intimate spanking – to say nothing of its direct effects on the recipient – had made each aroused to a degree that had to be addressed. Clutched together, their exploring hands brought mutual orgasm in a rush that left the two breathless and sweating. Afterwards, they perched on the rise in the corner of the boundary wall that looked down on the boats in the harbour below. There was silence for a while, then her lover moved a little apart from her and Judith knew before she spoke that the hot urgent sex they had just had was going to be the last.

'My mistress has claimed me now –' Helen stared fixedly ahead across the sunlit estuary '– so I must be faithful to her.' The declaration was like something from a tale of chivalry and sounded odd in the flat Essex speech. But Judith suppressed a smile, for the young woman was deadly serious. 'It doesn't apply to *her*, of course; she takes whoever she wants into her bed, *our* bed . . .' The sentence petered out and she was suddenly shaking with sobs. Judith risked an arm round a heaving shoulder and pulled the slender frame against her own body. Helen's head came down on Judith's breast and she felt the wet tears through her cotton top. In a while the flow diminished and Helen sat up and blew her nose on the bottom of her T-shirt, looking shamefaced.

'What an exhibition. It's just as well we're not going to be an item; you'd soon want shot of a girl who went on like that all the time.' She tried a smile and Judith hugged her again then took her arm away.

'J, you deserve a proper apology. I've been a right bitch ever since we first met and I'm really sorry.' Helen had adopted the initial for her name and Judith liked it. She took it as a sign their relationship would remain special.

'There's really no need, girl. I'd probably be the same if I were in your shoes.'

'But you wouldn't be. You'd tell my mistress where to get off. In fact, you already refused to bend over for her –'

'– and lost my job over it. And landed in a real mess in my head, so I'm no model.'

'Thing is, J, I can't bear to think of living without her, so I'm always afraid she's going to find someone to replace me with. That's what I thought *you* were going to be when you came to the Archive. And then you turn up here cool as a cucumber, and what do *I* do?' Judith grinned, pleased to see Helen's spirit returning as she spoke.

'I'm so bloody upset about *her* that I let you follow me in here and then, to cap it all, I get whipped for it! Are you surprised that I wasn't too friendly? But then I did feel sorry for screaming at you in the recovery room. You looked really *shocked*.'

They both laughed.

'Tell me one thing,' said Judith, 'you knew how much I was fancying you out here last week, didn't you? And you were just trying to make me really hot and bothered.'

'Yeah. With those sheeps' eyes you were making, how could I miss it? I was just being real *mean* and you should have smacked my bum. But we made up for all that this week, eh?' Helen dried her eyes on her sleeve and stood up. 'Hey, we'd better go and tidy up. It's got to be knocking-off time. Come on, J, race you to the tool shed.'

After lunch on Sunday Judith sat in her room lost in thought. *La grande maîtresse* had given her a small pile of books and the draft of what amounted to an autobiography to deliver to Samantha James at Nemesis. But why hadn't she given these things to Helen, who would be back at work there before Judith was even on the train? It was difficult to avoid the conclusion that she was being pointed in the direction of her old job in the Archive, which would necessitate a much delayed encounter with Miss James's leather strap. Judith turned down her mouth at this last prospect, though it wasn't the physical ordeal in store that daunted her. The tawse would surely be no worse than the founder's school cane (the penal variety was in a different league and she winced at the memory) which she knew she could bear with a degree of composure. No, it was the thought of going cap in hand to recant her refusal; that was too demeaning, too subservient. But the idea of plunging back into all those manuscripts was far more attractive than returning to study for her English degree and it appeared she had not yet been replaced. What was needed was some way of taking the initiative, yet at the same time submitting to a dose of corporal punishment . . .

A sharp tap at the door made Judith start. Outside was Melissa – Alecto – but the avenger's leotard had been replaced by a white penitent's shift. Judith's stomach clenched at the sight of the one who had inflicted on her so much pain but she steeled herself to invite the visitor in.

'I dare say I'm the last person you want to see, but I'm asking you to hear me out.' The tone was appeasing, quite different from Melissa's usual brash confidence. 'I wish I could make you understand that what happened in the chapel was nothing *personal*. There was a time I'd not have bothered one way or the other *what* you thought. After the carry-on at the Meni I had you down for a wuss meddling in things you could no handle at all. But after last Monday I ken you're serious; you were lined up for a wee schoolgirl caning and you jumped right into the big thing. That takes guts, girl. The point is, Judith, that out there I am Alecto, who is thrashing a ritual victim with all the force and precision she can muster. How I feel about who it actually is tied down is irrelevant. And, if it's any comfort, I have taken, myself, worse than I ever give. In fact, that's exactly what this costume is about. In an hour's time, I must go to Tyche's private punishment room. She keeps pieces of apparatus there you don't want to know about. Let's just say that I'm no likely to be fit to do duty in the chapel till the middle of the week.'

It was quite a speech and Judith was both attracted and repelled. There was a coldness, a detachment in Melissa she had observed before, and while it was no doubt essential for Alecto's role, Judith did not see herself becoming this woman's bosom pal. But she was gratified to have earned the professional chastiser's respect, so when Melissa stuck out her hand she shook it firmly.

'OK, no hard feelings. It just takes a bit of getting used to. I never dreamed I would get into anything so extreme and the sight of you just makes me panic a bit.'

'Well said, girl. Too many folk in this game come on all macho and deny they're scared of a flogging. I mean I'm shitting myself at what Tyche's going to do to me later and I admit it. But if you're into this stuff you have to face your fear as fear and then carry on.'

The idea of *la maîtresse juge* at work in what sounded horribly like a torture chamber gave Judith the shivers. Then Melissa laughed and said, 'This talk is getting too fucking gloomy. I cam here to give you a going-away present, if you'll accept it. And maybe a wee demonstration. Tell me if I'm jumping the gun here, but at a guess I'd say you've started to think about dishing out some of this discipline malarkey.'

Judith blushed at the accuracy of the observation. During the sessions with Helen in the loft she had indeed fantasised about how it would feel to lay some stripes across those beautiful little bottom-cheeks.

'So I'm right.' Melissa chuckled. 'OK, Judith, here it is.' From behind her back she produced with a flourish a straight length of light-coloured rod. It was warm to the touch where Liss had been holding it and felt, surprisingly, both dense and flexible. 'It's a wee bit

213

shorter than the usual – it'll fit nicely into your travelling bag – but it is very effective. Can I show you?'

For an awful moment Judith thought that she was being asked to offer her still-bruised rump for the purpose, but Melissa opened the door and blew a shrill whistle through two fingers down the corridor. After a few seconds a boy in his mid-teens came running and the summoner took him by the ear and drew him into the room. Dressed only in a workman's shirt and boots – the trousers had clearly been left behind – he had a shock of black hair and dark eyes that looked nervously at the cane in Judith's hand.

'He's the chief errand boy,' explained Melissa to Judith, 'and he made off with some groceries last week. Selling them on the side. He owned up and replaced them, so it's nothing that a good hiding won't put right. *Oui, Marcel, la baguette pour toi, sur les fesses!*' This last was directed to the boy who looked resigned. Such an event was clearly not uncommon in his life, for when Liss pointed at the small table that had served as a desk, he placed it at once in the centre of the room and, raising his shirt-tail, bent over its top to grip the far edge.

The sight he presented made Judith's loins prickle immediately. In the couple of weeks since her arrival in an environment where corporal punishment was routine, each display of buttocks bared to be chastised excited her more and more. She could not imagine that it would ever lose its appeal. In the present case, Marcel was a stocky youth whose behind was almost aggressively rounded, positively begging for the cane, she thought. Judith licked her lips in anticipation then caught Melissa's eye and blushed again at her tranparency.

'I think we have an eager pupil here,' said Liss. 'So, girl, shall we get on with it?'

Judith nodded and handed back the cane.

'OK. Basically it's all about *accuracy*; you can build up your force later. Now it's best always to start in the middle –' she leaned forward and drew a blood-red nail across the fullest part of the boy's globes '– then work outwards, both above and below. If it's to be a high count you can come back to the middle, which will take plenty of overlapping strokes without the skin breaking. You're unlikely to do that with this cane, anyway, but who knows what lethal weapon you might graduate to when you get a real taste for it.'

Judith noticed she said 'when' not 'if'; the enthusiasm was infectious and an image came to mind of herself swishing a penal rod viciously through the air. She cleared her throat and tried to concentrate on the specifics.

'The other important thing is where the tip of the cane lands. Full into the opposite cheek is fine but a wee bit beyond so it whips into the dimple, here –' she touched the pronounced hollow offered by Marcel's muscled figure '– and you can really make them jump. But too far over and you're on the hip, which can get nasty. Right, then. We'll do turn about in threes, OK? The boy will be expecting a dozen anyway, so we can take him to two, no bother. Just watch me and then see if you can do the same.'

Judith watched while three times the cane was a blur that thumped into the solid meat of the arse. Then she took the instrument in her left hand to follow suit.

'Ah, a southpaw. Excellent. Just stand opposite me and we can keep our positions.'

The cane tracks had come up most clearly on the buttock nearest her, so Judith aimed two strokes below them and one above, as instructed. Her efforts seemed feeble in comparison to the expert start of the punishment, but the feel of the instrument was exhilarating. On her second go she tried to copy Liss's use of the whole arm from the shoulder and was rewarded by

215

some much heartier thwacking sounds and vivid red marks. Flushed with success, she grew careless, and with her ninth (the boy's eighteenth) she caught him with a low one that curved down and round the muscle of the thigh. Up to that point the assault on his posterior had elicited no more than a series of grunts; now Marcel leapt up howling and clutched at the instant dark weal.

Melissa waited a second then pushed him gently but firmly back down. '*Pardon. C'était une erreur. Je le ferai un coup de moins.*' The boy nodded and true to her word Liss laid on only two then returned the rod to Judith. Determined to finish well, Judith placed three perfectly horizontal strokes close together that each evoked a yelp of pain. She was breathing hard, intoxicated by the whirr and smack of the instrument in her hand, and watched the marks coalesce into a purple band just below the line first indicated by the painted nail of her tutor.

'Well done, Judith. I think you're a natural.' It was high praise and she flushed awkwardly while Melissa put a hand on the boy's neck.

'*C'est fini, mais reste là pour un moment.*' She lifted the shirt-tail that had slipped down slightly so that the caned bottom was fully available for their inspection. Two dozen strokes (less the remitted one) had left it quite startlingly welted and Judith could not resist exploring the hot purple swellings with her fingers.

'It's quite a sight, eh?' Liss was smiling. 'But it looks more serious than it is. He's not going to want to sit down for a bit and he'll have some pretty bruises for a week, but there's no real harm done to a healthy lad like this one. *N'est-ce pas, Marcel? T'iras bien, hein?*'

He straightened up holding his bottom but managed a rueful nod. There was a pronounced bulge under the front of his shirt. 'In fact,' said Liss with a cackle, 'I think he's recovering rather quickly.' She lifted the material to reveal an impressive erection, at which the boy had the grace to look a little discomfited. Once again Judith was confronted by evidence of the erotic after-effects of a beating: it must make life very difficult for a dedicated rigorist, she thought.

'I can't touch this,' said Melissa. She looked serious and suddenly tired. 'But you're not one of us, really, and you're leaving, so if you wanted to indulge the boy, who's to worry? After all, he took his walloping like a trooper.' Judith wanted nothing more than to pull Marcel down on top of her and have him thrust into her wet cunt: she would come in two seconds flat. But she guessed it was a hand job that was being suggested and that was already way out of line, so she'd better not push it. In any case, it would give her a buzz to wank this lad whose bottom bore the marks of the cane – *her* cane, no less!

Judith reached for the stiff protuberance and looked into Marcel's eyes. '*Tu permets?*' She didn't know the young man, but '*vous*' seemed pretty silly when his cock was sticking out in such a vulgar display. The answer was a wicked grin and a thumbs-up sign, so she began to move the foreskin back and forth over the slippery head. His climax was not far off, by the way the boy had started to moan, so she slowed down to draw out his pleasure. Her own would have to wait until she was alone, though after all this she would have no compunction at a bit more rule breaking.

Melissa seemed preoccupied, almost as if she were trying not to watch. 'You know, they say it's great stuff for taking the sting out of your arse, after. The lads downstairs, that is, after the cane . . .' She tailed off. Judith could hardly believe her ears.

'You mean, when he comes, I'm supposed to rub the stuff over –'

'If you fancy. I'm supposed to be beyond all that here. And in a very few minutes I'm going to be beyond anything . . .' The last remark was a low aside that

217

Judith only just caught. Then the cock reared in her grasp and she cupped one hand underneath it to catch the hot spurts of milky fluid, feeling her cunt pulse in sympathetic response. Melissa lifted the shirt-tail and Marcel bent fowards obligingly while Judith spread the small pool in her palm around the swollen cheeks, risking a quick probe of his anus with a wet finger. Then Liss handed her a towel and dismissed the youth with a smart slap to the glistening rear cheeks.

'*Va-t-en. Vite!*' He made for the door and she giggled with an edge of hysteria, wiping her hand. 'Nasty, sticky stuff. Give me a woman's juice any time, not that I'm getting any here. I've got to go to my appointment.' She looked hard at Judith for a moment, her face pale and drawn. 'You'll be away before I'm ready for company. Take care.' She turned on her heel and was gone.

The room could not be locked so she would just have to trust she would be undisturbed. In a trice the brown robe was on the floor and Judith was under the shower with hot water coursing down her back between her buttocks. A finger to the clitoris gave her such a blast of raw sensation she nearly screamed. The convulsions started almost at once and she rode out the extraordinary pleasure-pain with clenched teeth. When the first craziness of lust was appeased she brought herself again to climax, slowly and deliberately, replaying in her head the feel of the cane biting into young male flesh.

Afterwards she thought of Melissa–Alecto, the strange hybrid of straight-talking Scot and aloof, ruthless disciplinarian who had thrashed her without mercy a week ago then delighted this afternoon in the aptitude she showed for her new present. The whole complex personality was infused with the kind of sexuality that made Judith imagine a dark secret that no one would ever be let near enough to uncover. She did not want to think of what was being done to the woman at that very moment that had made her look sick with dread and that would put her out of action for days.

To distract her attention from these grim thoughts, Judith picked up the books she was to take back with her. There were what seemed to be two first editions of posthumous works by Sade printed in Paris in 1929 and a three-volume treatise called *Sadism and Masochism* by Wilhelm Stekel that looked as impenetrable as the essay by 'Dr Brown' on the subject she still hadn't managed to finish. Then a book in an unmarked leather binding caught her eye. There was not even a title page, but its first paragraph declared it to contain a true record of discipline in the ladies' seminaries in Brandenburg in the second quarter of the eighteenth century. A casual search through its contents revealed one account after another of proud young women shamefully bared and whipped and Judith smiled to herself. It was a pretty blatant piece of pornography thinly disguised as fact, and it would do very nicely for a juicy bedtime read.

Her mind turned to how good it would be to be employed again on just such material when the idea hit her. The cane she had been given, *that* was it! She could donate it to Samantha James on her arrival and it would be the most obvious thing in the world to bend over on the spot to take her long-postponed correction. Being chastised with a gift she had, in effect, brought for the purpose would put her on a much more equal footing with her boss. And through any future occasions – and there were bound to be future occasions, she thought wryly – it would become the thing they shared uniquely. Judith pulled herself up from the reverie: it was time for supper and she was starving. She reminded herself firmly that she had yet to be offered her job back, but she could not wipe the grin completely from her face as she made her way through the corridors to the dining room.

12

Fucking Women

Judith stood in the hallway of the flat, gaping at the mess. It looked as if a thief, finding nothing of value in ransacked drawers of clothes, had strewn the contents about in his frustration. Except these things were dirty, and the trail of socks, knickers, trainers, shirts and jeans led rather obviously into Catherine's room. Then there was that smell ... It was coming from the kitchen where, next to an overflowing bin, a torn black liner sagged, spilling its collection of opened tins and left-overs on to the tiled floor. Judith gagged and rushed to throw open the window, then leaned out on the sill and gulped in some fresh air. OK, she knew that Cat wasn't the tidiest of flatmates, but what the fuck was all this?

Even her own bedroom was a tip but that was the result of her inability to settle on what to wear while away. At least the scattered garments that had been rejected were clean, though it was ironic that there had been no need to agonise over the choice. Between the cotton shift, coarse-spun gown and work shorts provided for her stay, she had needed to take only a supply of socks and the pants, jeans and sweatshirt for the journey that she was still wearing. She threw her bag down on the bed and consulted the mirror. Her short dark hair was getting wispy and it would need a trim before she made any approach to Nemesis; otherwise she looked surprisingly well on the two-week diet of stretching experiences. Judith got to her feet and rolled up her sleeves. There was only one thing for it and she marched into the kitchen where the fresh air blowing in had dispelled the worst of the stench. It wasn't just the foul refuse that had to be cleared; every surface was covered with used crockery. She shook her head in disbelief and made a determined start.

It took more than an hour to dispose of the rubbish downstairs in new bags and wash up the dirty dishes. Then she filled another bag with the discarded clothes, dumped it in the total chaos of Cat's bedroom and closed the door on it. Finally she took a mop to the kitchen floor and finding, miraculously, a bottle of beer in the otherwise empty fridge, sank down with it at the table. Now she was done the place was actually cleaner than usual and Judith felt a self-righteous glow as she drank.

The outside door banged and there were footsteps on the stairs followed by the sound of the flat door opening. There was a brief silence, then a head appeared in the kitchen doorway. Under the familiar curls and snub nose, the mouth looked worried.

'Oh, shit. Judith. When, er, when did you get back? I – I was going to clean up today, honest.'

'Seems I beat you to it.' Judith did her best to look cold and censorious but her pulse quickened. Suddenly she knew what she was going to do.

'I've been away since Sunday. You know what a slut I am.'

'I guess I do now.' The sardonic words made Catherine wring her hands.

'Jude, I'm so sorry. What a thing to come back to.'

'Sorry's all very well. Easy to say.' Judith had a flashback to her old teacher expressing just such laconic disapproval. Maybe it was only in rumour that she went

221

on to apply a strap to the offender's rear, but the tone was perfect for the present occasion. 'I wonder just how sorry you really are, Catherine. We could find out. Do you remember that old plimsoll?'

Cat went bright red. 'Oh, shit, you mean when I'd been reading that thing about the convent and asked you to –'

'That's it. I would say now might be just the time: you can think of it as your penance.' Judith made herself speak deliberately in spite of her rising excitement. 'Go and take off your jeans and bring it here.'

The item of footwear was duly handed over. Still sitting at the table, Judith demanded a sharp knife and when it was brought cut away the worn canvas until she was left with a thick rubber sole whose instep made an ideal handgrip. Cat stood in front of her in T-shirt, knickers and socks. She looked very young, though in the vulnerability Judith was sure she detected an arousal that matched her own. She got up and placed the chair she had been sitting on in the middle of the floor.

'Over there.' She pointed with the implement she had just fashioned. 'Now!'

Cat obeyed in a trice, bending across the back and holding on to the seat. Her top rode up to reveal wispy white pants stretched over a dark cleft. Each side of the vulval bulge between the legs sprouted a fuzz of blonde hairs. Judith patted the taut cheeks a few times experimentally then, without further ado, raised her arm in the air and for a while the only sounds were of lusty smacks interspersed with sharp little cries.

Judith paused and waited but the submissive figure gripping the chair made no move to halt the proceedings. She took the waistband of the knickers in her fingers and uncovered the pert little bottom which had already turned a rosy pink. Colour apart, the sight was identical to the one she had been presented with in the bathroom at the beginning of the summer. If only she could have done this then, thought Judith, but that was all the more reason to make up for lost time. An exploratory finger found Cat to be as wet as she was herself and Judith launched into a fresh series of whacks to the now bare flesh. When eventually she laid down the rubber sole, her flatmate stayed in place, though she was jiggling on the balls of her feet.

'Please, Jude . . . uuhh . . . in the top drawer . . .' She was breathing hard, clearly in the grip of intense sensations. Judith knew exactly what was needed – she had after all borrowed it herself when Cat was away once – and came straight back with the purple vibrator. She lubricated the thumb of one hand between the juiced labia, then pushed it into the tight brown hole above, after which she used the other hand to guide the dildo deep into the receptive cunt. A flick of the switch caused a dramatic response; for a second she hung on to the bucking, yelling body, then the chair went over and they both collapsed on the floor. In a few more seconds Cat's spasms eased and they found each other's mouths in a bout of hungry kissing. Then, taking her friend's hand, Judith pulled her through to her own room and, dumping her unpacked bag on to the floor, pushed Cat down on her back on the bed. She removed the tangle of pants from around the legs, then spread them wide and, cupping her hands under the girl's spanked bottom, buried her face in the pungent ooze of the exposed crotch.

It was 8.30 at night before the young women surfaced from their wrestlings in Judith's bed and she ran a bath while Catherine put the pizza she had brought with her into the oven. They took it in turns to soap each other in the large, old-fashioned tub and it was then that her lover spotted for the first time the long, deep marks that were still visible on Judith's behind.

'Puts my little bum-warming into perspective,' she said solemnly. 'Are you OK?'

It was Cat who had looked after her in the wake of the ill-advised escapade at the Eumenides Corporation and she was looking worried. Judith explained about the block and the penal cane, that she hadn't been lined up for severe treatment but had brought it on herself by protecting the twins.

'I thought I was going to die, and I still don't know how I got through it.' Judith shuddered. 'But it kind of changed everything. Makes refusing the strap from Miss James look pretty silly. And you may not believe this – I'm not sure I do myself – but I've got a feeling that I'll be back for more before this year's out.' Catherine looked suitably awed by this statement and Judith tactfully forbore to mention the colossal orgasm at Helen's hands after the thrashing. She felt a little scared herself now she had put the vague intention to revisit the Order into definite words.

Judith dug out a couple of large baggy T-shirts (her pal had the grace to be shamed at her own total lack of clean ones), so they put them on and sat in the kitchen to eat. Cat produced a bottle of red wine to wash it all down and they finished the day back in bed, entwined in drowsy amorousness. However, in the morning the idyll came to a dissonant end. Judith tried to say how great it had been to fuck but that she wasn't planning to be an item with anyone just yet, and Catherine huffily responded that while a dose of the plimsoll had been a real turn-on, she wasn't expecting to go steady, thank you very much, since she still had a thing for this guy. She was late and would not be back until Monday, though it was not made clear whether she would be occupied with work or boyfriend or both. Judith's peace offering of doing her washing while she was away was rejected and Cat hurried off, clutching a bag of it. Judith told herself it was only to be expected that their leap into frenetic intimacy would leave them both raw and prickly, but she felt, nonetheless, sadly deflated as she sat drinking the lukewarm remains of her coffee.

In the hairdresser's later that morning she was attended to by a woman she recognised as a member of the large band of Marsha's occasional fucks.

'You're Judith, aren't you? The one who went to Brittany?'

'Jude. Yeah, I did.' She studied the expression in the mirror but there were no clues to what this lady knew about the Order. 'Isn't it Alex?'

'Right first time. Now what can I do for you?'

'I'm trying to get it together to go basic. You know, number one all over. What do you think?'

Alex looked closely at the front and back of Judith's head, and at each profile in turn. Then she ran her hands over the skull rather in the manner of a phrenologist.

'I'd say go for it. Your hair's nearly black and the head shape is great. And with the straight nose and the full lips, well, let's just say you won't need to take *my* word for it. Plenty heads are gonna turn, Jude, and I don't just mean dykes.'

So it was done and as Judith watched the transformation in the mirror she was given an update on some of the latest gossip. Predictably there had been more skirmishes between a growing group of puritanical anti-porn feminists in the university and 'Marsha's Babes'– as they called them – based at The Phoenix. Of course the name had been intended as a put-down, said Alex, but they'd all thought it was cool and had taken it up. T-shirts were being printed. There was also something more personal.

'Marsha got into a fight with that black girl – you know, the real good-looker.'

'You mean Gwen?'

'Gwen, that's her. Well, she's been spreading a story about you and the outfit that's in St Mary's. I couldn't make out what she was saying but one night in the Cellar Marsha took *real* exception to it. They landed on the floor, glasses flying, the whole bit. Both ejected double-quick and we dragged Marsha away pronto before she got hurt. I mean, she's no youngster and that Gwen's a tough cookie. I heard she ended up in the cop shop just the other week for knocking a guy out cold.'

Alex was busy with the final tidying up of the crew cut, but Judith wasn't registering her new appearance. She was lost in dismay that the girl she had once taken such a shine to seemed now to be so hostile. And there was worse.

'The last time I saw her, she was saying you wouldn't last five minutes where you'd gone. Though, to be honest, Jude, I don't think Gwen knows fuck all –' she bent close to mouth the two words so as not to alarm an older woman in the next seat '– about that kind of stuff. I mean, it's Marsha who's the s/m lady. Anyway, that's all a bit heavy for me; I just hang out with the babes at the club, you know.' She laughed and held up a hand mirror for Judith to inspect the results.

'Phew.' She looked at her image with a gulp. 'It's, er, very neat.'

Again Alex laughed. 'Bit of a shock, eh? Just take a deep breath before you go out.' And when she counted out Judith's change at the cash desk, she added, 'Don't let Gwen's carry-on get to you. The way you're looking now, you'll be able to take your pick. You just wait and see.'

Nervous about appearing in front of the Friday night throng, Judith stayed in. She took out the screeds of draft autobiography and tried to get started on the events that followed the accusation of murder. She had promised herself that she would appear at Nemesis on Monday without fail to deliver it and the books, and it might perhaps help her cause if she could comment

226

intelligently on what Marie had to say. She would also, of course, hand over the cane that Liss had presented to her, though the scheme that had seemed so perfect from the distance of Vannes was making her nervous as the time to put it into practice approached. She had been the one at fault in refusing punishment when the possibility of it had been made quite clear from the outset and it began to look arrogant and wilful to roll up with a ready-made instrument and expect it to be used just like that. For a lowly trainee assistant that was pretty cheeky behaviour. But then it was quite in character for Miss James to be amused by just such a piece of presumption. There was only one way to find out and that would have to wait for Monday.

But it was not easy to settle down to her reading. In addition to the anxieties about getting her old job back – and the more she thought of it, the more she wanted it – the thing about Gwen was beginning to fester in Judith's mind. It wasn't just the new stuff Alex had told her; she could remember only too well coming upon Gwen and Marsha after they'd spent the night together, when Gwen wouldn't go all the way with her. That fucking hurt. And she'd said then, about the Meni débâcle, 'how *could* you?' as if it was a personal insult that Judith had somehow delivered by letting herself be treated like a naughty little girl. Clearly she was important to Gwen – way beyond the sex they'd nibbled at – otherwise how could she act as if she had been so let down?

These thoughts running obsessively in her mind, Judith put the manuscript aside. It was time for an early night and she reached for the book about the correction of Prussian schoolgirls. That would send her to sleep; at least, it would after her body had responded as it always did to a lurid tale of corporal discipline. She stood up and headed for the bedroom, resolving to put Gwen out of her mind. The girl was obviously on a collision course

227

with her which would, sooner or later, come to its crunch. And until it did there was no point dwelling on the subject.

As it turned out, it was sooner. At the back of two, the following day, Judith left the flat, intending to catch Marsha in her Saturday afternoon break from The Phoenix. Wanting reassurance about her cropped head before the first public appearance that night in drinking company, she felt too that Marsha deserved a report on the visit to Brittany, even though she had not quite forgiven the American woman's one-night stand with Gwen. So it was that Judith turned into the gate of the park and came face to face with her least best friend of the moment who, once again, was occupying her thoughts.

Gwen tossed her mane of glossy hair with a contemptuous look. 'So the wanderer returns from the mysterious Order. But leaves her hair behind. And did little Judy get her bottom smacked again?'

Judith flushed but kept a tight rein on her anger. This was like a playground taunt that masked a strong underlying attraction and she was certain Gwen felt its pull as much as she did herself. Besides, the black girl was devastatingly sexy when she sneered.

'You could say I did. Only this time it wasn't a mistake. And I got given some tips on how to deal with troublemakers.' Judith let her displeasure show and Gwen's eyebrows went up. She reached out and touched the cranial stubble in a gesture that recalled the easy intimacy they had known.

'Troublemakers.' She repeated the word gazing at the ground. 'You going to show me how you stop their nonsense?'

'Yeah,' said Judith. 'You want to come with me?' Their eyes met; then she turned back the way she had come with Gwen in tow. In the flat she went to her bedroom without a word and took the cane from her

228

bag. The dressing-table mirror showed a mean-looking skinhead all in black. Good. That was the persona she needed for the next bit. She stomped into the kitchen in her Doc Martens and laid the cane ostentatiously on the table, then the two women faced each other.

'I been a real bitch, ain't I, Jude? What with Marsha and all?' The black girl stooped and peeled down her yellow satin breeches. Judith looked at the thick black bush above the fig of the vulva her fingers had once explored.

'OK, where do you want me?'

Judith's reply was to pick up the cane and point to the table. Gwen leaned forward and gripped its two opposite edges. She was holding herself away from its surface and the angle of her body reminded Judith of how she had been positioned on the block in the chapel. Now it was Gwen's buttocks that were poised to be chastised, hanging succulent and full like a pair of exquisite fruit.

With all her might Judith lashed into their dark ripeness. There was no movement and no sound, though after the third stroke the bending girl said quietly, 'Fuck. Sister, that hurts.'

On the count of twelve there was sweat in beads on the victim's brow and her leg muscles had started up a tremor. 'Six. Another six. If you want to give me more you'll have to tie me down.' The voice was not quite steady but the force of her will kept the body exactly in place for the rest of the caning. Judith laid the strokes across the upper thighs and now each one elicited a jerk of the body and an answering, 'Oh!'

'That's it.' Judith spoke quietly but the response was immediate. Gwen shot upright and clutched the assaulted area with both hands. Hissing through her teeth, she writhed for a full minute before control was re-established. Then she drew Judith to her by the waistband of her leggings and pulled them clear of her crotch.

Without a word, Gwen knelt in front of her chastiser and put her lips to the brimming cunt she had uncovered. Not even a thong between us, thought Judith, her head spinning. What a pair of sluts.

She came almost at once, though the busy tongue worked to keep her on the heights for what seemed an age of delight. Then she lifted Gwen up and they hugged close for a long time. When they separated, Judith's pants were restored in a trice but it took a full minute's wincing to ease the tight breeches up over the black girl's swollen behind.

'I was always being told I deserved a fucking good hiding as a kid but I never got one. Not until now, that is.' She stuck out her palm just as she had done when they first met. 'OK, girl, can we call it quits?'

'Quits.' Judith grasped the offered hand and shook it.

Gwen walked out into the hall with a certain amount of care. Sticking her head back round the door she said, 'OK, see you around, sister. *After* I've cooled this arse off in a bucket of ice.' And with a chuckle she was gone.

It was Sunday before Judith made it to The Phoenix, just in time to find Marsha locking the doors after the lunchtime customers had been hustled out. After the bar manager had welcomed the new recruit to minimal hair – 'It's the only way, honey, shows you mean business' – they settled in at the bar for Judith's résumé of the trip to Vannes. After giving her impressions of the place, she went into some detail on Melissa's prowess as implacable agent of discipline.

'I'm not surprised,' said Marsha. 'She scared *me*.' Judith remembered Liss had been one of the many casual visitors to the American's bed. 'Not because of what she did – there was nothing too rough, as I recall – but because you felt this steel just under the skin. And I couldn't tell whether it was for giving or for taking. But from what you say – and I'm happy to skip the experience and just accept your word for what that penal cane feels like – she's opted for the "s" rather than the "m".'

Judith shook her head. 'Uh-uh. You were right first time. In between flogging the daylights out of us in public, she had appointments with Tyche where she was on the receiving end in private. Whatever went on was enough to make her scared –' Judith grimaced at the memory of Liss's white face '– yet it was obviously all part of the same deal. Like the proper s/m deal.'

Marsha opened another two bottles of Pils and put them on the counter. 'And what about Helen? Are you two getting on any better?'

In her mind Judith saw the naked body beside her in the loft and felt again the long clitoris slippery under her fingers; gulping some beer she spluttered, embarrassed.

'I'll take that as a yes.'

'Stop smirking. Me and Helen, we're –'

'– just good friends,' finished Marsha.

Judith stuck out her tongue. 'Well, it's all we can be, *here.*'

'I wouldn't be too sure about that, honey. I knew that girl would have the hots for you as soon as her boss wasn't a factor in –' She was cut off by the slamming of the outside door, then Gwen shouldered her way through the back entrance into the bar. 'Uh-oh,' said Marsha softly.

The young black woman walked right up to Judith and kissed her full on the lips. 'Thought I'd find you here.' She leaned back with an elbow on the counter and gave Judith a broad wink. 'You'll understand if I give the stool a miss for now, eh, girlfriend?'

Marsha stared, open-mouthed, from one to the other and Judith laughed. It took a lot to make her show surprise. Then Gwen spoke again.

'Give us a beer, will you, Marsha? I'm fucking parched and I left my purse at home.'

231

This time it was Judith's turn to goggle at the easy familiarity of the address. 'But – but – last I heard you two were doing fisticuffs. Now, wait a minute . . .' She glanced sharply at the pair, imagining that there had been a repetition of the one-night stand that had upset her before.

'Not what you're thinking, sugar.' Gwen put an arm round Judith's shoulder. 'Since yesterday, I only got eyes for you, baby.' Judith felt the colour flood to her cheeks and Marsha hooted behind the bar. 'No, the lady and me made it up without the pillow talk this time. After all, the fight was about you, girl, and I set my mind on putting *that* record straight. Though I didn't know what I'd be letting myself in for . . .' She let the unfinished sentence hang with a wicked grin at Marsha who was clearly itching to know more but reluctant to admit it. In the end curiosity won.

'OK, you girls have got me. Just what is it you've been up to that –' But she was interrupted for a second time by the sound of the door. 'Shit. This fucking place is supposed to be closed,' she said and they all turned their heads to see who was coming in. It was Catherine and she stopped dead at the sight of the linked bodies.

'Oh. I came back early and thought you might be here. But I'll just –' She made to turn but Judith sprang forwards. 'No. Don't go, Cat. Er, this is Gwen and we were just having a drink. Gwen, this is my flatmate, Catherine.' There was a moment's silence while blonde curls and black mane confronted each other.

'Flatmate? You didn't tell me about no fucking flatmate.' Gwen looked ferocious but Judith knew her enough to see – with some relief – it was mostly for effect. She pulled Cat by the hand to the unoccupied stool, put the bottle of Becks Marsha had quickly supplied into her hand, and began asking her about her weekend while Gwen questioned Marsha ostentatiously about some mutual acquaintance. Then, after a couple of awkward minutes, the bar manager acted.

'Jude, honey, will you come through behind the bar? There's something I want to show you.'

Having established that Cat wasn't going to run away, Judith jumped at the chance. 'Excuse us, won't you, ladies?'

Without giving the other two a chance to object, Marsha swept Judith with her through the small door to the side that opened on a storeroom. Once there, she put a finger to her lips and they stood listening.

'Right, flatmate Catherine.' Gwen's voice was unusually mollifying. 'What you say we make a truce? I got no quarrel with you.'

'I don't want to fight with you either. OK, I'll shake on that, er, Gwen.' Judith could imagine the familiar gesture of the outstretched hand.

'So, is it Cathy, or . . .?

'Yeah, why don't you call me Cathy?' The eavesdroppers raised their eyebrows at the new short form of Cat's name, but then the voices fell to a level where they could not easily decipher the conversation.

'Give them another five,' whispered Marsha, quietly closing the door, and they squatted on a bench beside the barrels to finish their beers.

Back in the bar they had one more drink and the talk circled round bringing Cat up to speed on the local gossip. When they all got up to leave, she said, 'D'you want to come round, Gwen? There'll be some food ready in a while.'

'Well, Cathy, if you're sure. That sounds great.'

Judith could hardly believe her ears. Catherine cook? She'd used every single plate in the place when Judith was away but the pots and pans had been untouched. And how were these two so amicable? They walked through the streets of the town in silence, but when they came into the park Cat and Gwen fell back deep in conversation. Judith might be walking in front but she was not leading the way and she sensed that events had somehow passed out of her control.

Once in the flat, her suspicions were confirmed in a dramatic way. The two women went straight to the cupboard in the hall and took out Cat's sea chest which they deposited in the middle of the kitchen floor. They fell on Judith before she had a chance to resist and dragged her face-down over its curved lid. In a trice Gwen straddled her body, miniskirt riding up, and inserted her hands under the waistband of her clinging shorts. Suddenly Judith felt her bottom bare and the damp prickle of cunt hairs pressed into the small of her back. Out of the corner of her eye she saw Cat coming back into the room, holding the rubber sole Judith had fashioned herself. She had taken off her blouse and was slapping the thing against her palm as if she meant business.

'No! You can't do this . . .' Her speech faltered as she realised that they very well *could* and indeed were actually *going to* do it.

'You dished it out, girl, to both of us,' said Gwen, 'and now when you're the one in the wrong you are going to take it. You got a problem with that?' She put on her best growl and Judith capitulated with a meek, 'No'.

So the spanking began and quickly gathered momentum. Gwen pointed with her finger to indicate which part of the exposed behind sprouting from between her legs needed attention next. Cat laid on with a will and Judith could feel in each smack the resentment that was being worked out. It wasn't long before the whole was aglow with stinging heat and she was juicing uncontrollably.

'My, oh, my,' said Gwen putting a hand to the swollen wet vulva, 'I reckon this young lady needs some tougher treatment.' She got up and went to her bag while Judith lay waiting. Restraint was no longer necessary, for while she was nervous about what tougher might mean the craving for stimulation would not be gainsaid. Then there was the smell of new leather as Gwen dangled a shiny black tawse in front of her. 'I been shopping, sister. The plan was for it to keep me in line but now I think – *we* think, Cathy and me – a dose will do you the world of good.'

She moved to the back and Cat took hold of Judith's shoulders in a surprisingly tight grip. There was a moment's suspense, then a supple thwack landed full across her sore bottom. With stroke after stroke the pain escalated rapidly, but so did the furious genital throb and Judith realised, shockingly, that she was going to come. And soon. Tears streaming and mouth agape, she buried her face between the blonde girl's breasts and stuck her arse out for the black girl's strap, and as the swishing tongues curled low into the buttock-cleft, the first ripples of the climax began to shake her body . . .

When Judith came down from the clouds, Gwen was fondling Catherine's breasts, with one hand down the front of her unzipped jeans. Tentative kisses turned urgent and, without even a glance at her flatmate still draped over the chest, Cat steered them towards her bedroom. They vanished from view and there was the sound of a door being firmly closed. Judith got to her feet and stretched the lycra back over her behind with a shake of the head. Well, it had to be better they were fucking than fighting, but she did feel a bit left out.

On the counter by the sink were two bottles of wine beside a large crusty loaf and there was something in the oven that smelt mouth-watering. It was a large casserole, and a quick taste confirmed that the meat was cooked. Suddenly Judith was ravenous: this newly found domesticity would have to be encouraged. She went to the bathroom and washed her face then opened a bottle and set the table. Outside Cat's room she listened; the passionate noises of the last while seemed to have died away so she gave a stage cough and called, 'Dinner is served, lovebirds.' In two minutes Catherine appeared with Gwen behind her, each wearing one of the old T-shirts that served her as a dressing gown. Cat came up to the table and kissed Judith on the cheek.

'Sorry about that, Jude. I'm anyone's if they go for my nipples. Oh. Sorry, Gwen, I don't mean you're *any*body . . .

'Time to eat,' said Judith sternly, pouring out the wine, 'or *I'll* have to go and fetch my cane.'

It was late the following morning when Judith woke alone and looked at her bedside clock. Just over two hours to go before she was due at Nemesis and she had no idea how she would be received. The appointment – for Monday two o'clock sharp – had been made on her behalf while she was still in Brittany and it wouldn't do to be late. It was, after all, an earlier case of lateness she was going to expiate if all went well, one which had taken her on the long detour from which she was at last coming home.

The flat was quiet and surprisingly tidy when Judith went through to run a bath. The afternoon's beer and the evening's wine had left only hazy memories, but one that stood out was of the black strap-on that Gwen produced from the depths of her bag. While the details were lost in an alcoholic mist, Judith had a nasty feeling she'd insisted that it penetrate all available orifices in turn before the night was done. And from the ache in her ring of anal muscle, she had not escaped quite vigorous buggering. Another first, thought Judith, feeling a thrill of indecency, though she was glad not to be facing her fellow orgiasts in the cold light of day.

Bathed and glowing, she selected what she would wear. First came a plain white blouse with a tailored waist that sat snug just above the hips. The high collar set off the black-stubbled head rather well, Judith considered, consulting her reflection. Then came the satin thong that she had been persuaded into for her interview and over that a pair of black trousers. The shiny elasticated material moulded itself to hips and thighs, and tight into the crotch raised and separated the buttocks in a most satisfactory way. The lady has to jump at the chance to cane these beauties, Judith said to herself in a fit of nascissism, turning this way and that in front of the mirror.

It was only when she took out the instrument to wrap it that she came down to Earth. Here she was, acting like a young girl putting on a new frock when it was no party she was dressing for but what was likely to be a painful beating. Sobered by the thought, she sat and zipped on her clunky boots. There was just time for a cup of coffee.

Judith was at the entrance to the Archive at 1.50 and, as hoped, she spotted Helen returning from lunch across the quad. As she came up she said: 'Hi, J. I heard you were coming,' and Judith took a deep breath.

'Look, Helen, I've been worrying about what you might think. I *promise* you I'm not going to poach on your territory if I come back here. Even if –' she broke off, surprised. Not only was the secretary not scowling, her rather severe ponytail had been replaced by orange tints of hair closely permed to the head.

'Relax, relax.' Helen was grinning broadly. 'I moved into my own place as soon as I got back. Maybe what we did in Vannes gave me a bit of confidence. Now that the boss lady can only fuck me by invitation, she's stopped treating me like dirt. I mean, I need a good arse licking now and then – don't we all? – but I can do without the betrayals.' She giggled. 'Hey, don't look so shocked, J. You'd better go on up; she's expecting you. I've got to get some stuff from the store down here. By the way, the haircut's really ace.'

Judith rode up in the lift prickling with desire. Helen looked terrific. Reaching the empty office she was trying to compose her mind when the inner door opened and Samantha James was there. All thought of Helen were banished at once and Judith felt like a naughty school-girl quaking in her boots. She fumbled with packages, trying to separate the materials for the Archive from her own present.

'Miss James, I was asked to bring you these from the Order.'

'Ah. Thank you, Judith.' The face was an impassive mask. 'Will you come into my office?' Inside she stood behind her broad table in silence. It was plain Judith was to get no help in what she had to do. There was nothing for it but to plunge in.

'I brought you a gift of my own, too. I hope you will accept it.' She handed over the offering and waited while it was unwrapped. The director crumpled the brown paper and dropped it into her waste basket, then bent the cane into an arc between her hands, appraisingly.

'This is, I believe, a length of original Malay rattan, noted for its effectiveness in shorter instruments of this kind.' One eyebrow was raised as if awaiting the answer to an unstated question.

Suddenly Judith found the words she needed. 'Miss James, on the last day I worked here I apologised for being late but I refused to submit to your discipline. I've come back to make amends, if you will allow me.'

'Very well. I'll have you over the front of the desk. Just as you are, to begin with.'

Judith needed no further instructions. She moved the tall piece of old schoolroom furniture out from the wall then, rising on to the balls of her feet, stretched forwards across it. Her belly against the slope of the lid and her breasts hanging over the far edge, Judith gripped as far down the back legs as she could reach. Acutely aware of her prominently presented posterior,

238

she tried to prepare herself mentally for what was to come.

She was expecting something like the caning received from Maîtresse Bonnard but the first stroke made her gasp in disbelief. The earlier punishment had been an ordeal but it had not really pushed to the limit. Whether the difference was in the instrument or the chastiser, Judith could not tell (she suspected both), but now each cut suspended time while she struggled against the urge to leap up and knead the atrocious smart out of her buttocks. It was not, of course, as severe as what had been done to her in the chapel, but there she had been bound. Here she had to fight both for self-control and the pure, basic survival of intense pain.

After six there was a pause and Judith held on until the edge of the hurt had dulled a fraction. She knew, sickeningly, what was expected of her at this point. Releasing her cramped grip from the wood she straightened slowly and with trembling hands peeled the close-fitting garment down clear of her flaming rear cheeks. Then she returned to the original position, observing idly that her left forefinger had been bloodied by a splinter. In her head a voice said, again and again: 'Let this be over. Please, let this be over.'

In the end, of course, it was. If anything, the delivery of the second half-dozen was even more forceful than the first and the effect on her bare bottom was indescribable. Afterwards there was a long silence in which Judith heard the cane being placed on the table, but she did not rise until she could be sure of keeping her hands at her sides. Eventually she rolled the black garment, little by little, back up over buttocks that felt twice the size they had been a quarter of an hour before. There was one more thing to be done and Judith summoned what was left of her dignity.

'Thank you for your correction, Miss James. I'm afraid it was long overdue.'

The tall, raven-haired woman beamed. 'It was a pleasure, my dear, a real pleasure. And thank you for your fine gift. I think that its merits have been amply demonstrated, wouldn't you say?' Judith's discomfort was too great for any repartee and she was glad when the director sat down and opened her diary in a business-like manner. 'You are now reinstated, Judith. I take it that is what you wish. Very good. In that case I expect you to report to me at nine o'clock tomorrow. We shall take up where we left off two months ago. There is work to be done.' She stood up and saw Judith to the door with a smile.

In the outer office Helen had a high colour that suggested she had overheard the physical part of the encounter, if nothing else. Judith felt free for the first time to rub and squirm, though by then the worst of the beating's effects were beginning to abate. Helen got out of her chair and came over, speaking in a whisper.

'You should go and bathe your bum. I can't touch you here, but if you can keep your hands off *this* –' she cupped her fingers into Judith's crotch '– till five o'clock, then I'll kiss *this* better –' she gave the trousered seat a light pat '– round at my new place. Deal?'

With a spasm of pure lust Judith said, 'Deal.'

Helen scribbled an address on an envelope, dropped in a key and handed it over. The flat was just round the corner from Nemesis and in five minutes Judith was inside squatting over a bath of cold water. As she sponged the throbbing welts that covered her behind, she did her best to keep well away from the slick lips between her legs. Almost two hours to wait. It was going to be difficult, but it would be worth it.

NEXUS NEW BOOKS

To be published in July

PENNY PIECES
Penny Birch
£5.99

Penny Pieces is a collection of Penny Birch's tales of corporal punishment, public humiliation and perverted pleasures from nettling to knicker-wetting. But this time Penny lets her characters do the talking. Here she brings you *their* stories: there's Naomi, for instance, the all-girl wrestler; or Paulette, the pretty make-up artist who's angling for a spanking. Not least, of course, there's Penny herself. Whether finding novel uses for a climbing harness, stuck in a pillory, or sploshing around in mud, Penny's still the cheekiest minx of them all.

ISBN 0 352 33631 5

PLEASURE TOY
Aishling Morgan
£5.99

Set in an alternate world of gothic eroticism, *Pleasure Toy* follows the fortunes of the city state of Suza, led by the flagellant but fair Lord Comus and his Ladyship, the beautiful Tian-Sha. When a slaver, Savarin, appears in their midst, Comus and his ursine retainer, Arsag, force him to flee, leaving behind the collection of bizarre beasts he had captured. Their integration into Suzan life creates new and exciting possibilities for such a pleasure-loving society. But Suza has not heard the last of the slaver, and its inhabitants soon find that Savarin's kiss is more punishing than they had thought.

ISBN 0 352 33634 X

LETTERS TO CHLOE
Stefan Gerrard
£5.99

The letters were found in a locked briefcase in a London mansion. Shocking and explicit, they are all addressed to the same mysterious woman: Chloe. It is clear that the relationship between the writer and Chloe is no ordinary one. The letters describe a liaison governed by power; a liaison which transforms an innocent young woman into a powerful sexual enigma. Each letter pushes Chloe a little nearer to the limits of sexual role-play, testing her obedience, her willingness to explore ever more extreme taboos until, as events reach their climax, the question must be asked: who is really in control? A Nexus Classic.

ISBN 0 352 33632 3

To be published in August

THE LAST STRAW
Christina Shelley
£5.99

When Denis Mann loses his job, his life hits a hiatus of junk food and daytime TV, much to the consternation of his wife Helen and her wealthy mother Samantha. Soon, the women realise that he would be more use to them as a feminised sissy maid, and set about enforcing their will with the aid of the mysterious Last Straw Society. It seems the women have found the way to mine the seams of Denis's dark perversity forever. Will his contempt for the aims of the Society prove a match for the waves of masochistic desire its members have awakened in him?

ISBN 0 352 33643 9

THE MASTER OF CASTLELEIGH
Jacqueline Bellevois
£5.99

When Richard Buxton is forced to leave the delights of nineteenth-century London, marry, and run a country estate, he assumes that the pleasures of the whip are no longer his to be had. Both the estate and his new wife Clarissa, however, provide unexpectedly perverse opportunities, and he is diligent in making the most imaginative use of them.

ISBN 0 352 33644 7

PARADISE BAY
Maria del Rey
£5.99

Paradise Bay is an idyllic resort on a remote and beautiful island, where sex and desire are taken to extremes. It is the place where Alice, secretary to the beautiful and powerful Joanne, comes to terms with her inner feelings of submission. It is the place where icy journalist Amanda Trevelyan discovers the shocking erotic secrets of the famous and temperamental artist Jean-Pierre Giradot. A Nexus Classic.

ISBN 0 352 33645 5

If you would like more information about Nexus titles, please visit our website at www.nexus-books.co.uk, or send a stamped addressed envelope to:
  Nexus, Thames Wharf Studios,
  Rainville Road, London W6 9HA

BLACK LACE NEW BOOKS

To be published in July

SYMPHONY X
Jasmine Stone
£5.99

Katie is a viola player running away from her cheating husband and humdrum life. The tour of Symphony Xevertes not only takes her to Europe but also to the realm of deep sexual satisfaction. She is joined by a dominatrix diva and a bass singer whose voice is so low he's known as the Human Vibrator. After distractions like these, how will Katie be able to maintain her wild life and allow herself to fall in love again?

ISBN 0 352 33629 3

OPENING ACTS
Suki Cunningham
£5.99

When London actress Holly Parker arrives in a remote Cornish village to begin rehearsing a new play, everyone there – from her landlord to her theatre director – seems to have an earthier attitude towards sex. Brought to a state of constant sexual arousal and confusion, Holly seeks guidance in the form of local therapist, Joshua Delaney. He is the one man who can't touch her – but he is the only one she truly desires. Will she be able to use her new-found sense of sexual adventure to seduce him?

ISBN 0 352 33630 7

THE SEVEN-YEAR LIST
Zoe le Verdier
£5.99

Julia is an ambitious young photographer. In two week's time she is due to marry her trustworthy but dull fiancé. Then an invitation to a college reunion arrives. Julia remembers that seven years ago herself and her classmates made a list of their goals and ambitions. Old rivalries, jealousies and flirtations are picked up where they were left off and sexual tensions run high. Soon Julia finds herself caught between two men but neither of them are her fiancé. How will she explain herself to her friends? And what decisions will she make? A Black Lace Special Reprint.

ISBN 0 352 33254 9

FULL STEAM AHEAD
Megan Blythe
£5.99

Sophie wants money, big money. After twelve years working as a croupier on the Caribbean cruise ships, she has devised a scheme that is her ticket to Freedomsville. But she can't do it alone; she has to encourage her colleagues to help her, and some of them are a little reluctant. Persuasion turns to seduction, which turns to blackmail. Then there are prying passengers, tropical storms and an angry, jealous girlfriend to contend with. And what happens when the lascivious Captain decides to stick his oar in, too?

ISBN 0 352 33637 4

MINX
Megan Blythe
£5.99

Miss Amy Pringle is pert, spoilt and spirited when she arrives at Lancaster Hall to pursue her engagement to Lord Fitzroy, eldest son of the Earl and heir to a fortune. The Earl is not impressed, and sets out to break her spirit. But the trouble for him is that she enjoys every one of his 'punishments' and creates havoc at the Hall, provoking the stuffy Earl at every opportunity. The young Lord remains aloof, however, and, in order to win his affections, Amy sets about seducing his well endowed but dim brother Bubb. When she is discovered in bed with Bubb and a servant girl, how will father and son react?

ISBN 0 352 33638 2

A SECRET PLACE
Ella Broussard
£5.99

Maddie is a busy girl with a dream job: location scout for a film company. When she's double-booked to work on two features at once, she needs to manage her time very carefully. Both films are to be made in the English countryside during a long hot summer. Luckily, there's no shortage of fit young men, in both film crews, who are willing to help. She also makes friends with the locals, including a horny young farmer and a particularly handy mechanic. The only person she's not getting on with is Hugh, the director of one of the movies. Is that because sexual tension between them has reached breaking point?

ISBN 0 352 33307 3

NEXUS BACKLIST

This information is correct at time of printing. For up-to-date information, please visit our website at www.nexus-books.co.uk

All books are priced at £5.99 unless another price is given.

Nexus books with a contemporary setting

ACCIDENTS WILL HAPPEN	Lucy Golden ISBN 0 352 33596 3	☐
ANGEL	Lindsay Gordon ISBN 0 352 33590 4	☐
THE BLACK MASQUE	Lisette Ashton ISBN 0 352 33372 3	☐
THE BLACK WIDOW	Lisette Ashton ISBN 0 352 33338 3	☐
THE BOND	Lindsay Gordon ISBN 0 352 33480 0	☐
BROUGHT TO HEEL	Arabella Knight ISBN 0 352 33508 4	☐
CANDY IN CAPTIVITY	Arabella Knight ISBN 0 352 33495 9	☐
CAPTIVES OF THE PRIVATE HOUSE	Esme Ombreux ISBN 0 352 33619 6	☐
DANCE OF SUBMISSION	Lisette Ashton ISBN 0 352 33450 9	☐
DARK DELIGHTS	Maria del Rey ISBN 0 352 33276 X	☐
DARK DESIRES	Maria del Rey ISBN 0 352 33072 4	☐
DISCIPLES OF SHAME	Stephanie Calvin ISBN 0 352 33343 X	☐
DISCIPLINE OF THE PRIVATE HOUSE	Esme Ombreux ISBN 0 352 33459 2	☐

MAIDEN	Aishling Morgan	☐
	ISBN 0 352 33466 5	
NYMPHS OF DIONYSUS	Susan Tinoff	☐
£4.99	ISBN 0 352 33150 X	
THE SLAVE OF LIDIR	Aran Ashe	☐
	ISBN 0 352 33504 1	
TIGER, TIGER	Aishling Morgan	☐
	ISBN 0 352 33455 X	
THE WARRIOR QUEEN	Kendal Grahame	☐
	ISBN 0 352 33294 8	

Edwardian, Victorian and older erotica

BEATRICE	Anonymous	☐
	ISBN 0 352 31326 9	
CONFESSION OF AN ENGLISH SLAVE	Yolanda Celbridge	☐
	ISBN 0 352 33433 9	
DEVON CREAM	Aishling Morgan	☐
	ISBN 0 352 33488 6	
THE GOVERNESS AT ST AGATHA'S	Yolanda Celbridge	☐
	ISBN 0 352 32986 6	
PURITY	Aishling Morgan	☐
	ISBN 0 352 33510 6	
THE TRAINING OF AN ENGLISH GENTLEMAN	Yolanda Celbridge	☐
	ISBN 0 352 33348 0	

Samplers and collections

NEW EROTICA 4	Various	☐
	ISBN 0 352 33290 5	
NEW EROTICA 5	Various	☐
	ISBN 0 352 33540 8	
EROTICON 1	Various	☐
	ISBN 0 352 33593 9	
EROTICON 2	Various	☐
	ISBN 0 352 33594 7	
EROTICON 3	Various	☐
	ISBN 0 352 33597 1	
EROTICON 4	Various	☐
	ISBN 0 352 33602 1	

Nexus Classics

A new imprint dedicated to putting the finest works of erotic fiction back in print.